SPE(...)E

****

Andy Rivers

Byker Books

Published by:

Byker Books
Banbury
Oxon
OX16 0DJ
www.bykerbooks.co.uk

ISBN 978-0-9569052-3-9

Printed in Great Britain by Lightning Source, Milton Keynes

Andy Rivers is a Geordie author (*Maxwell's Silver Hammer*, *I'm Rivelino*, *The Spy Who Bluffed Me*) and the driving force behind upstart indie publisher, Byker Books.

He grew up reading stuff like *The Famous Five* and wondered how come he didn't know anyone who had picnics or spoke 'BBC' English. This, indirectly, led him to start writing about foul-mouthed, council estate tearaways and the shenanigans they got up to.

He now loves to read things by the type of people like him; who never got encouraged to use a pen for anything else than stabbing their siblings with and will shout long and loud about Newcastle upon Tyne and how great it is, if you're stupid enough to give him the opportunity.

You can find him at ***www.andyrivers.co.uk***

To my nephews

You can achieve anything you want,
don't ever let anyone tell you different.

CONTENTS

SUNDAY

A fucking Professional

Colly eased open the window and shone his torch into the gloom beyond. This job would be a piece of piss; the tip he'd had from Falcus had been a good one: five hundred thousand square foot of lights and lamps, all made especially for the retail market and all very, *very* saleable. Heaving his considerable bulk through the frame he tried to drop onto the floor below, knowing it was only a couple of feet and that the alarm system and CCTV were dummies. Sweating with the effort, he finally got his legs clear of the sill, put his torch in his mouth and tried to push himself off the window.

"For fuck's sake," he whispered in exasperation. "I'm stuck on the bastard thing now."

He tugged at the stubborn pocket of his jeans that had caught on a nail in the window and left him hanging in mid air.

"Supposed to be a *fucking professional*," he growled at no one in particular, "and this shit's happening. I'd look a right twat in court if this was read out."

He'd had a few mishaps in his twenty-year burgling career, but none as potentially embarrassing as this. The thought of being discovered in this position dominated his mind and concentrated his efforts to free himself. He vigorously tugged at the offending pocket with renewed urgency.

'Falcus'll go mad if I fuck this up,' he thought, *'and I still owe him for the last one as well. I'd best crack on; he said there was a transit out the back I could use.'*

1

Rrrriiiiiipppp...
> *Thump.*

> *'That's got the bastard. Right, game on.'*

Picking himself and his torch slowly up from the floor, Colly flashed his beam around the warehouse to locate the goods. Spotting a couple of BHS flashes on the boxes, he headed towards them, pausing only to pull a half-eaten Mars bar from his jacket pocket and shove it into his mouth, *'Waste not want not and all that.'* Then he set to work.

Outside the warehouse, in the bushes surrounding the building, a figure crouched motionless. He was comfortable in the dark. In fact, he positively welcomed being enveloped by blackness, and he could see the transit from his position. The fat burglar was going nowhere without his permission. He'd waited a long time for this and tonight was just the start; the planning, training and preparation... would all be worthwhile. The results would be there for all to see and the benefits would be tangible, he was sure of that. Checking his watch, and then pulling on his balaclava, he leaned back onto his heels and breathed slowly.

> *'Not long now,'* he thought.

Psycho-ology

THUD

    THUD

        THUD

The three darts lashed into the dartboard as if thrown by Fatima Whitbread and the audience cheered at the accuracy of the shots as the thrower announced, "Next round's on me."

Shouts of, "Nice one, Axe" and, "Cheers, Axel" resounded around the bar and the barmaids started filling glasses with an intensity normally only reserved for their bits on the side after closing. The small, smoky bar was full of happy punters and the cheerful atmosphere was lighting up the drabness of the nicotine stained walls.

Mind you, not all of the punters were happy.

"Crowbar... untie that daft twat," the man known as Axel shouted across the room to a lumbering hulk of tattooed muscle and sinew who duly started to oblige, growling at the man still attached to the dartboard.

As Alexander Falcus, aka Axel F, approached the bleeding man he reached for his back pocket, observing how the man shrank back and whimpered at the movement of his arm.

'Psychology,' he thought to himself, *'beats the fuckers every time.'* He whipped his hand from his pocket and flashed it in front of the man's face in one swift movement. The captive's discomfort was made evident by the growing damp patch on his trousers and the whimpering from between his burst lips and broken teeth. Falcus ran the comb he'd taken from his pocket through

3

his long, greying and thinning hair then repositioned his head to within an inch of the beaten man's. He stared hard into his eyes.

"Now Jimmy, if you *ever* try and fuck me over again you know what'll happen... don't you?"

Jimmy couldn't speak; a combination of fear and pain rendering him temporarily mute. He stuck to just nodding furiously.

"So," continued Falcus. "Your next payment's due in a week's time. You'll make sure you've got the money, won't you?"

Jimmy's nodding was threatening to break his neck before Crowbar got the chance to, he just wanted out of there. More than anything else in the world at that moment he just wanted to be on the settee, watching programs he didn't like, with a wife who didn't love him and kids who couldn't stand him. He'd have said anything Falcus wanted him to just to get out of that bar.

Falcus broke eye contact to nod over to Crowbar, but leaned back into Jimmy's face instantly.

"You know why I'm nicknamed Axel F, Jimmy? It's to do with my weapon of choice and how often I use it on people who don't pay their debts. Next time it won't be a couple of clouts and a couple of darts. Bear it in mind, bonny lad."

Only then did he nod at his giant minder who took that as permission to give Jimmy his own spiel.

"Aye, son... and I'm called Crowbar cos I get stuck into anything me and divvent you forget it."

Falcus glared at Crowbar for his amateurish interjection. In the silence, Jimmy took a deep breath, gathered himself up and headed for the door as swiftly as the situation allowed. Once outside he ran as fast as his bruised and bloodied body could cope with and then, a safe distance away and sure he wasn't being followed, he stopped, dropped to his knees and vomited, all the while silently weeping in frustration and anger.

The Vegetable

Two hours later and Colly was well satisfied. The transit was loaded to the brim with hundreds of fifty quid lights and Falcus would be happy; there'd be enough to pay his debt as well as a decent drink for him. Being out of debt to Axel Falcus was something to aspire to on this estate and much better for your health than owing him. It had definitely been a good night's work. Fiddling with the ignition barrel he noticed something move out of the corner of his eye next to the driver's door. He looked round, seeing nothing but blackness.

'I must be getting old and jumpy,' he thought, laughing at himself as he bent back down to the barrel and pulled the wires out. *'Probably a fucking fox or something. You'd think I'd welcome the dark in my line of wo—'*

The driver's door opened. Colly was startled and stared at the space where the door had been; a figure stood, all tooled up and wearing a balaclava. Obviously another firm. The figure wasn't moving or speaking, so Colly thought he'd best clear this up before things got silly.

"This is a job for Falcus, mate. You'll know who he is; don't interfere and keep out of it. If you want it then there's plenty more back in there for you."

The figure still didn't reply; just stared back at him. Colly could only see the eyes glaring through the slits in the balaclava; he was probably annoyed that he couldn't hijack this job. Mind you, Falcus's name had that effect on people round here – *nobody* fucked with him in Byker. Still, Colly was a fair man; he only needed what he had already loaded into the van, so this numpty could have the rest if he wanted it.

He was getting a little fucked off by his silence though, and knew he couldn't afford to hang around for too long.

He leaned forward a little towards the man's face, "Listen, mute boy. I'll say this one more time. I work for Falcus, this is his gear now and if you want to stay attached to your bollocks you'll shut that door and get out of my face. Understand, charva?"

By way of reply the mystery man smacked him in the face and started dragging him out of the van. Colly wasn't a fighter, his big belly saw to that. His mates called him Large Colly for a laugh and the irony of not eating vegetables wasn't lost on him as his obviously much fitter adversary started beating him to the ground.

Colly was bleeding heavily and was in pain; he couldn't catch his breath properly and was just covering up on the ground as best he could. He knew this wasn't a local firm, as the name of Falcus would have stopped this before it started; the bloke was booting into his ribs now and still not saying anything. *What the fuck was going on?* The silent, controlled beating was bad enough, but the fact that the man obviously had no fear of Falcus or his gang was the real scary part.

Colly was slipping into unconsciousness and everything was becoming quieter as blood filled his ears and blocked out the singing of the early birds. His last thought was, *'If I survive this then I'll be nicked and I'll still owe that twat the money.'*

Changes

Falcus, happy that he'd taught someone a public lesson and confident that everyone would know about it well before last orders, leant back against the bar and scanned The Tyneside Chronicle. To the casual observer he was simply interested in what was going on in his part of the world, however, someone privy to the workings of the Falcus criminal empire, such as it was, would have known exactly what story he was looking at with such diligence.

STUN GUNS DISGUISED AS TORCHES
By Robert Docherty

A naïve tourist took an underworld backhander to transport a haul of outlawed stun guns from the Costa Del Crime.

Barry Patterson was recruited whilst on holiday in Spain to take delivery of a package home. Newcastle Crown Court heard he was never told what kind of goods it would contain and he found himself jailed when investigators discovered the parcel was packed with fifty potentially lethal stun guns.

The high voltage weapons – sold for a few pounds as personal security devices in Madrid – were disguised to look like harmless torches but police warned the guns could cause almost immediate collapse and even death to someone with a heart condition.

On jailing Patterson for 10 months, Judge Paul McCulloch said: "They could only have a criminal purpose."

Judge McCulloch also said he accepted the 34 year-old from Charlotte Street, Wallsend, had never known what would be in the package but added:"You were persuaded by someone who must be part of the criminal underworld to receive a parcel from Spain for money.

"Your address was to be used as a safe house until the parcel was collected and the extent of your knowledge was that it contained some illegal contraband, the precise nature of which was unknown to you. I conclude you took a risk. It could have been anything and you didn't care."

7

Patterson admitted possessing the prohibited weapons at an earlier hearing. He was arrested in June last year after the package was intercepted and a police officer posed as a postman to make the delivery. He was now "appalled" by what he had become involved in and the long wait since his arrest had taken a heavy toll on him, said Karl Robson, defending.

"He has been duped and used as a fool," Mr Robson told the court.

After the haul was seized, Detective Constable Darrell Irvine said:"These weapons are potentially dangerous. If held against someone for as little as two seconds they could cause the victim to collapse."

Falcus turned the page. Again, to the casual observer, he simply sniffed as he did so... but the trained, and informed, eye would have seen him mouth, "for fuck's sake" under his breath as he contemplated the loss of a few thousand pounds worth of trade. Not only had he put money into this scheme, conceived and executed by a criminal family much higher up the food chain than him, but also he now had no chance of getting it back and couldn't exactly threaten the people concerned.

'Still,' he thought, *'at least I'm not in the frame for it. That's one good thing.'* And then smiling to himself, *'Mind you, I can't do nowt about getting me money back now, but in a few months' time well... maybe I won't be nationwide league in this town anymore. Once I've squared off the Manchester connection and ticked all the boxes where security's concerned, then we'll be ready to rock 'n' roll.'*

Looking over to the pool table, he saw Crowbar lurch against it drunkenly; disturbing the balls in the process, the pints and chasers he held, spilling their contents onto the cloth. The two players smiling at him indulgently not prepared to scold Falcus's right hand man in any way.

'Big daft bastard. He's handy for the physical stuff but, if I'm ever gonna move up the rankings, I need more than a hard case as me right hand man. Aye, Crowbar doesn't need to know what's going on just yet, but if the Manc boy comes through like he says he can, then things'll change round here.'

* * *

The man in the balaclava stood motionless in the car park of Walker Lighting; the light drizzle reflecting crystal-like on his mask, then he looked down at the prone figure of the fat burglar and smiled. Reaching into his pocket he removed a card, it simply read:

V
'IT'S TIME TO
CLEAN UP THE STREETS'

Placing it onto the forehead of fatty, he pulled a staple gun from another pocket and expertly stapled it to the burglar's head. The scum in this town would learn; go straight or go down... and if they didn't learn, well, he was just the man to teach them. As his dad, God rest his soul, had said: "It only takes good men standing idle to allow evil to prosper," and he was one good man that wasn't standing idle anymore.

MONDAY

What women Want

Vicki Hughes had known she was going to like the job almost as soon as she'd arrived. Even though it was her first day, everyone had treated her like an old friend and she'd been sat down and given a cup of coffee before she'd even got her coat off. Her new boss, Mr Edmonds, had explained that they'd been short-handed for weeks and Vicki was seen by them all as the cavalry arriving.

Her first few hours had been quite pleasant as well; she'd been learning to use the checkouts, check stock in and replenish shelves meaning there was a bit of brainpower involved, which she liked. Having been quite an intelligent girl at school she'd naively fallen prey to teenage lust and lost her cherry to the mean and moody Dave Marsh from sixth form. After this, studying and grades had become unimportant and she'd fallen like a stone through the sets until she'd ended up in the misfits class with the radgies that no one cared about. So, when she'd skipped school day after day nobody was really that bothered and she hadn't even turned up for her exams, reasoning that Dave would look after her forever... he'd said as much *hadn't he*?

He'd told her that he'd been to raves and everything when he was younger, acid house parties and that. She was well impressed and had dropped her knickers willingly and often, all of her mates had warned her against him, saying he'd just hump and dump her but she wouldn't have it. They were in love and she knew it. Even when the pregnancy test had proven positive she'd known he would stick by her and, to her mates' surprise, he did... for about seven months.

Special

Unfortunately, two months before she'd had young Nicky, Dave, the love of her teenage life, had left her for a younger, prettier, and most crucially, un-knocked up model. Presumably he impressed her with his tales of dodgy dealing and his tattoos and recreational drug habit. The judge at his trial a year later however, was less than impressed and Dave had got three years for receiving stolen goods, leaving Vicki a single mother supported by the state.

'*Still*', she thought closing her eyes and leaning back in her plastic canteen chair, '*it could have been worse; the twat might have got off with it and come back to me.*'

The cackling in the staff dinner room that had been going on for about fifteen minutes now snapped her back from her reminiscing. Her two dinner companions were Gladys and Vi, fifty something, saucy and proud of it. She'd made the mistake of mentioning that she'd started seeing a lad from the warehouse on the industrial estate at the back of the shop and that had got them started.

"Eeehh... does he work in a whorehouse, pet? Did you hear that, Vi? The lass's new boyfriend works in a whorehouse. Ha-hah-ha-ha."

"Well, Gladys. You know me, live and let live. Does he have to strip as well, Vicki? Have you got any pictures? Ha-ha-ha-ha-ha."

"No, it's a *warehouse*. They do washing machines and that. You know, freezers and fridges?" Smiling at them, Vicki hoped she'd never become a nutter.

"Frigid! You mean he's not giving you anything? Oh, you need to finish him, Vicki. Doesn't she, Gladys? If she's not getting nowt?"

"Ah, aye, Vi, a woman cannit live on battery power alone! Ha-hah-ha-ha."

Vi joined in again tears of laughter streaming down her face: "Do they do batteries there as well then, pet? Is that why you stay with him? Hah-hahah-aha."

Fighting a losing battle to keep a straight face, Vicki felt herself smiling and then thought, *'fuck it, this is what I've missed for the last fifteen years; adult banter. Too much Thomas the Tank Engine dulls your brain.'*

"No, I stay with him cos I misheard him in The Raby the night we met," she replied, pulling a little frown at them both, these happy go lucky sisters.

"Eh, what do you mean?" asks Vi, all straight-faced and worried that she might have offended the new girl on her first day.

"Aye, errrr... we divvent mean nowt, Vicki. We're just having a laugh. What did he say, like?"

"Well," Vicki continued, all pokerfaced. "I bumped into him at last orders and asked him what the time was, just cos I was wondering where my taxi was, like."

"Aye," they replied in unison. "And what did he say?"

"He said come back to his cos he had a big cock!" she blurts out at them as they look shocked. All bark and no bite these two, she can tell.

"He never did," said Vi, gasping.

"Did he?" asked Gladys, "Have a big cock, I mean? Ha-hah-ah-ha-ha."

"Well," Vicki replied coolly. "I got back to his and got into the passage and he says to me all proud and that, 'there you go, pet. It's half eleven,' and points at the wall."

They're both looking confused now.

"Eh?" Gladys said. "Why did he point at the wall?"

"Cos," she went on, starting to laugh. "That's where his grandfather clock was and he wasn't kidding, it was fucking massive."

They're in fits now, Gladys's bent over the kettle struggling for breath and Vi's holding her sides and gasping out.

"I bet that takes loads of batteries, pet. HA-HA-HA-HAH-AHA-HA-HA!"

Vicky knew she was going to like it here.

An Englishman in Newcastle

Deep within the bowels of Clifford Street Police Station in Byker, Barney Netherstone was also starting a new job. His wasn't going as smoothly though; the bollocking he had just received for leaving the secure door open in reception as he came back from the baker's saw to that.

'This can't be the reason I studied for so long,' he thought to himself as he closed his boss's door. *'All that time at university, in the best private school Oxfordshire had to offer, all those exam passes with top marks and I end up here in Byker; the land that time forgot. I don't even know where that bloody grove is either.'*

Stomping back along the corridor to his new office, Barney caught the eye of the young WPC assigned to help him find his feet while he got to grips with his new role.

"Susan, have you got anything for me yet?" he shouted across to her, a little louder than he would have liked; still he had to assert himself.

"No," she replied coolly, defensive stance and ice blue eyes looking through him, her casual reply and obvious refusal to be cowed by this newcomer, educated or not, threw him off balance a little.

"Right," he mumbled, head down. "I'll be in my office."

Once in, he threw himself into his big leather chair, logged back into his computer and started playing solitaire, wondering how he'd ended up in the wrong side of this rough, cold and loud city. He'd been employed as Northumberland Police Force's first Regional Criminalist, it had been described to him as a plum job in an up-and-coming city and he had been chuffed to get it in the face of some fierce competition. Darren Lake, his main rival from

13

university had, for instance, been forced to accept a position as a Mortuary Assistant with Thames Valley Police in Oxfordshire and was going to spend the next five years covered in urine, excrement and blood while Barney would be at the sharp end. He'd be using new techniques and creating new thought processes to solve baffling crimes committed by criminal masterminds, or at least that's what he'd thought. The reality seemed slightly different to the brochure.

Barney had expected a plush office in a contemporary, modern police service, somewhere that was more corporate and where targets and goals were what mattered and dominated conversations. Here, in Byker, the talk was of who was seeing whose wife, how many people could a particular bouncer 'do' at any one time in a fight, the best way to help a prisoner 'fall' down the stairs and, most importantly it seemed, how to get on match day duty at Newcastle United so that you were facing the pitch. Plush, modern, contemporary and corporate were all alien to Byker.

Barney's father had been particularly proud that his son could contribute something to the police force, as he had himself for so many years, and really make a difference to society. He'd told him that Newcastle was a hard city where men were men and had to be able to look after themselves, but Barney had seen on the news and arts programmes that Newcastle was fast changing, more akin to Paris was how one commentator had described it. Numerous galleries springing up, fine architecture rivalled only by Bath and London itself, a thriving literary scene with many poetry readings and, of course, the Geordie love of the big, iconic statement; The Angel of the North, The Millennium Bridge and the Baltic Gallery were examples of this. Barney had debated this with his father and had been genuinely excited about relocating; even the thought of having to learn that strange local dialect had not dampened his enthusiasm.

Special

His mother worried that he'd be so far away and that he'd find it hard. Barney, not wanting to appear girly in front of his dad, had brushed off her fears with a simple, "I'll be alright, Mum. I'm a big boy now."

Now that he was here though, away from his friends and family in a city where everyone is in your face, he had to admit she was right. He was finding it hard. He needed to make friends and to adjust himself as fast as he could. His flat was in the city centre but Byker itself was a few miles out on the East side, meaning Barney had to drive to work as he didn't trust himself not to get lost on the metro system.

He needed to get stuck into a meaty job and develop a relationship with the team but there was nothing happening on that front yet either. The ironic thing was, that even in a police station that was based in a crime-ridden estate like this, there was no bloody work that required his special talents.

Staring at the phone and willing it to ring wasn't working, so he decided to acquaint himself with the local area; he'd only been the hundred yards to the baker's so far and thought he should at least hit the high street. Walking out of the station and back past the baker's and the cluster of charity shops he looked over at the Metro Station. Shabby-looking and dull, it could have been in any town in the world. The big BYKER sign and the graffiti covering the walls of the station suggested to him that it was a different place at night. Standing here now in the sunshine at eleven in the morning it was easily ignored but when darkness fell he imagined the sickly yellow lights from within the station throwing shadows in the bushes outside giving it a gothic, almost *Hammer House of Horror* feel to it.

Feeling a little shiver run down his spine he decided to move swiftly onto Shields Road; the main artery into the city from the East End. Apparently this had once been a thriving, profitable business area with shops and pubs making money hand over fist, but the general consensus round here was that the advent of Thatcherism had put paid to that, he'd best keep his political affiliations to himself. Be nice if these northerners took responsibility for their own problems once in a while though.

Someone bumped into him as he passed the pub on the corner of the street that linked with Clifford Street and he immediately mumbled, "Sorry." The man just glared at him, tattooed neck and ponytail, suggesting to Barney that discretion was the better part of valour. Moving swiftly on, he was just considering whether to go up or down the road when there was a shout behind him.

"NORTHUMBERLAND POLICE... STOP!"

Spinning round he saw Susan, his appointed guide, slamming ponytail man against the wall and telling him to, "DROP IT."

Barney, heart thumping, ran over to help but Susan was already cuffing the man and reading him his rights. As he got there, she simply proffered her left hand to him saying, "This yours, Mr Netherstone?"

She was holding his wallet; the tattooed thug was a pickpocket. Barney couldn't believe it.

"Y-y-yes, th-that's mine, Susan. Thank you very much."

As Ponytail was bundled into the newly-arrived backup van, Susan stepped over to Barney and pushed him further along his real life learning curve.

"Mr Netherstone, I don't know what the area you come from is like, or even what kind of schools you went to... but up here you have to be aware of what's going on around you. Next time he could have a knife."

"You're right, Susan. I can see I'll have to become a bit more... ehm... *street wise* if I'm to survive in Geordieland. Thank you again... and please... call me Barney," he said.

"That's okay, Barney, and please... call me Suzie," she said flashing the first smile he'd seen that day and beckoning back towards Clifford Street. "Now, you need to come back to the station and make a statement."

As he turned to head back to the station, he heard two older women on the other side of the street talking about the incident.

"Eeh, it's criminal that, Vi. Letting them out on their own like that."

"Aye, Gladys. Especially well-spoken ones like him. They're just a target for the scum. I've never agreed with this care in the community anyway, me."

Blushing deeply and hoping Suzie hadn't heard, Barney buried his chin in his chest and dawdled back to the station; this place was going to be a bloody nightmare.

A Company Man (1)

Matt heard the crash from the other end of the warehouse and, looking up the walkway, he could see a stack of washing machines had collapsed. He'd told Latimer about this hundreds of times, *you were only meant to stack them four high* it said so on the box, but the company, German Wizard, over-stacked them in order to sublet the saved space to a stationery firm.

'False economy... that's what it is,' he thought. *'They spend more on damages and bloody accident claims than they rake in off the other firm. Still not my problem is it, I'm only a pleb, I'd best tell Latimer and make him even more miserable.'*

Knock

    Knock

"WHAT?"

"Mr Latimer, there's a stack of Zanussi's gone over in chamber three."

"AGAIN? Jesus Christ, who was driving?"

"I dunno, I just heard it and thought I should tell you."

This wasn't strictly true as Matt had in fact, got the driver and fork truck out of the way before having a quick word with his mate in security about wiping the tape before approaching John Latimer, the miserable supervisor. Matt knew he'd go loopy, overreact and want the culprit sacking when in reality there wasn't enough room to turn properly in there, the bloke in question had only been here a month and, in typical German Wizard fashion, had been thrown straight in at the deep end.

Matt really couldn't be arsed with this shite either; his head was fucking thumping from last night's shenanigans and he was still coming down from the stuff he'd decided it would be a good idea to take at chucking out time. The new bird, Vicki, she was a bit anti-drugs so he'd had one last wrap for old time's sake before sacking all that off and he was fucking regretting it now.

'Maybe she's got the right idea, I feel fucking awful, I'm too old for this nonsense.'

Luckily, Latimer was off up the walkway in chamber three now, shouting and stamping up there instead of in Matt's personal space.

'He's got a real temper problem that twat. God knows how he got to be a special copper,' he thought. *'Anyway, it's not my problem now, I've done my bit and saved the lad's job so while PC Pissed Off is out of the way I can get on with something else.'* Turning towards the second chamber that held the stationery, he strode off.

John Latimer hated Mondays. He also hated his job; hated it with an absolute sodding passion, particularly times like this when he was being bollocked by his incompetent, brown-nosing and much younger boss.

Special

"It's not good enough, John. I want the culprit sacked."

"I don't know who the culprit is, Dave," Latimer replied, trying to sound matey. "Security have inadvertently wiped the tape and I don't know who was driving the forklift."

"John, you're a copper for fuck's sake. Surely you can find out who was driving a forklift from a team of ten operatives."

"That's not the real problem anyway though, Dave, is it?"

Depot Manager David Atkinson stopped him with a wave of his hand, his nostrils flaring and his ginger fringe in danger of self combustion.

"I don't want to hear that shit about space again, Mr Latimer. It's safe and it's adequate. Sort your staff out and take the necessary action because if I have to do it myself then I might just decide I don't need a shift supervisor. Now get on with it."

'Bloody idiot,' thought Latimer as the door slammed behind him. *'Useless ginger get spends all day drinking tea with the customer service girls and playing on the bloody internet then expects me to run the sodding depot for him. The prat shouldn't even be in the job.'*

The anger and bitterness at being overlooked for promotion yet again still ran deep in Latimer and it rankled even more that the man they brought in was younger than him. He had less experience than him and apparently looked like a bloke off that Bo Selecta programme. What did the staff say he was called again? Avid Merrion, that was it. He really hated that, all the lads on the shop floor called him it behind his back so John had let it slip one day and he'd went ape, exposing a serious chink in his armour, silly boy. If there was one thing John Latimer was good at it was taking chinks in armour and turning them into rather big holes.

Heading swiftly to the staff toilets, John dived in a cubicle and locked the door; taking out his big, black marker pen he composed his latest ditty to his boss:

Andy Rivers

There once was a gaffer named Avid
Ginger and usually livid
He licked arse to get up the ladder
When he failed it just made him madder
Then he foamed at the mouth and turned rabid!

'Smashing,' thought Latimer. *'Just enough bad language and poor form to be from one of the peasants on the shop floor but true enough to rile him immensely when I report it to him later on.'*
Then just for added effect he wrote underneath:

DAVID ATKINSON COULDN'T RUN A BATH.

Latimer smiled at his handiwork. It cheered him up a bit. He'd been in a mood all morning. It had actually started last night when Reg and he had come third in the pub quiz, which was enough to wind him up; bloody students shouldn't be allowed to enter. Then, rather than drink as much as possible in the time left as he usually would, Reg had skedaddled citing a job to do at home as an excuse. This had left Latimer with the choice of drinking on his own for an hour in a pub full of students or of going home early to face the start of the week. Understandably, he had chosen the latter but it had left him disgruntled, feeling as though he'd been robbed of precious free time.

Looking back at his poem he smirked again and then a thought struck him. He jumped up and left the cubicle, heading for the staff canteen. As he passed Atkinson's office he started whistling; his day had just brightened up.

Cleaning up the Streets

Barney was happy to have something to do at last, even if it wasn't exactly real crime fighting. A body had been found at the scene of a burglary this morning outside the warehouse of a light and lamp firm down under Byker Bridge. He'd had a severe beating and had a business card stapled to his head:

V
'IT'S TIME TO
CLEAN UP THE STREETS'

As the station's only criminalist, Barney had taken charge and, though he was a bit rusty through inaction, he'd collected swabs and samples from everything and everyone. He could already tell the man in question was the burglar just from his torn jeans pocket and the flap of denim hanging from the open window above his head.

The real question was why was he beaten? Another firm? A grudge? Maybe he'd been seeing someone else's wife or girlfriend? Leaving the photographer as he happily snapped away at the pool of blood from different angles, Barney caught Suzie's early morning stare; she'd obviously been out last night judging by the state of her eyes.

"Good Morning, Suzie. How are you today?" he called cheerfully.

"Fine," she mumbled. She clearly was anything but fine.

"Heavy night?" he enquired chuckling. "Looks like it."

"Thanks," she glared. "You look lovely as well."

"Oh I wasn't being..."

"A *twat*? It doesn't matter," snapped Suzie. "Let's do some

21

work shall we? The victim is Francis Collins, career burglar, general villain and all round scrote."

"Right," said Barney eager to put his little faux pas behind them. "Anyone likely to have a grudge against him?"

"Lots of people," she replied, self-consciously removing her cap and running her hand through her hair. "He usually owes money to a local hard case named Falcus, whose son coincidentally was the man who picked your pocket yesterday."

Barney thought on this, drumming his fingers against his stomach nervously. "This Falcus character, how much of a hard case is he then?"

Suzie smiled back at him, enjoying his obvious discomfort but inwardly chastising herself for being mean.

"The nasty kind of hard case. He rules most of the estate but is nothing in the grand scheme of things. This leads him to keep his grip on things tight to keep people in line."

"Oh, will there be any chance of me getting trouble then?" Barney asked as casually as he could.

"I don't think even *he* would be stupid enough to try and intimidate a copper, but if he does you just let me know Barney." She chuckled back punching his arm lightly.

"Right," said Barney walking back to a squad car. "I'll see you back at the station."

As he got in the car Barney glanced back at Suzie to give her a smile but she'd already turned away to interview the members of the early shift at the warehouse. *This place was getting more interesting by the day,*' he thought looking at her backside, '*much more interesting.*'

A Company Man (2)

Matt loved dinnertime; he loved reading his paper, not having to listen to any bollocks about *fucking white goods* and he especially, above all else, loved eating his sandwiches. Processed ham in white bread with loads of butter and topped off with crisps... the food of the gods... *magic*. He knew it was unhealthy and that he should have salad or some sort of pasta bollocks, but he didn't care. His last bird had tried to turn him into some sort of vegan freak so she'd got the bullet.

"Why are you finishing with me, Matt? I'm only trying to help you. It's because I love you and I'm concerned at your eating habits. Even if you don't take any notice of me you should listen to Jamie Oliver. You're harming yourself eating that rubbish."

"Listen, pet," he'd said grabbing his coat. "I love food more than I love you. In fact I love Sunderland more than I love you, so don't bother ringing me anymore. Oh, and next time you see Jamie Oliver, tell him he's a cockney twat from me."

And that was it, Matt was single again, not that he'd been bothered anyway, Janine had only been a shag and a bit of a diversion when his mates were busy. Love wasn't something that entered Matt's vocabulary, not then anyway. In his opinion it was a concept invented *by* women *for* women, in order to sell books. Mind you the new bird, Vicki, she was nice and didn't harass him all the time. She just let him be and gave him a bit of space, fit as well. The only cloud on the horizon with her was that she had a son. He'd never been keen on kids, but reckoned if things went well he could consider it... *but* only when the time came like, there was plenty of getting to know each other to do first and that was definitely his favourite bit.

Chuckling to himself, he had a quick glance around at his

workmates; thick as mince the lot of them – not a thinker like him – he was unique in this warehouse but then he always had been. Even at school he'd just floated through, doing the bare minimum to keep the teachers off his back. He knew he was a bit of a one-off even then so he hadn't bothered his arse, thinking that something would turn up. He was still waiting, mind. Perhaps being an intellectual wasn't all it was cut out to be after all.

'*Fuck it, thinking too much again.*'

Then, just as he was turning back to the music reviews, a shadow had cut across his paper and darkness entered his world. '*Fucking Latimer,*' he thought. '*What does that twat want now?*'

Latimer could sense the rage and hate being silently directed towards him from the ten seated employees in the canteen; not only had he interrupted their dinner break but he was giving them bad news on top of it – bloody marvellous, that'll teach them.

"It gives me no pleasure to do this," he lied. "But you all know what happened today in the chamber and you all know it's not the first time. The company cannot afford to keep writing off damaged products due to employee incompetence and as such disciplinary action will have to be taken."

'*Oh lovely,*' he thought as he scanned their faces, '*Blake's about to pipe up. Come on, Blakey.*'

"How can you discipline anyone when you don't know who it was, Mr Latimer? You haven't any evidence and nobody saw anything. That would be unfair, I think," he smiled.

Latimer had never particularly liked Blake; he'd always thought of himself as a bit too clever for this job and had tried to organise the staff into a militant unit a number of times. When that had failed due to apathy and fear of unemployment he had settled back into a routine of sniping and undermining while doing just enough to keep his job. The man seemed to think he was special.

'*Well, junior Scargill,*' thought Latimer, '*here's a bit of public payback.*'

"That is correct, Mr Blake. None of you claim to have seen anything and the CCTV tape is mysteriously blank at the time of impact. Although how you are aware of this fact is something I may investigate further in the coming days."

Pausing to look around at their faces Latimer stared into each man's eyes coming to Blake last.

"Unfortunately for you all, what is on the tape shows that one minute before the incident you were all in the vicinity of the falling washing machines and would logically, therefore, all know who the driver was. This means that you are withholding evidence in a serious internal investigation into an incident which could have caused injury and death."

Pausing to look round again to see if they were getting the gist of this, Latimer was pleased to see they were all still smiling and thought they had him by the balls, all that is except Blake; his face had fallen as the information hit his brain. Latimer knew that he had guessed what was coming next and the taste of defeat looked like it was bitter on his tongue.

"Now, if you read through the company handbook – I'm sure you've a copy that you can lend to everyone, Mr Blake," he nodded pointedly at Blake as he knew he was the orchestrator of this ring of silence and as such the one the men would blame. "This withholding of evidence in a serious health and safety matter makes you all guilty of gross misconduct... which means that I can sack you."

The smiles left their faces as soon as they heard that; everyone, from the lowest paid cleaner on a minimum wage to the highest paid executive knows that when you have a disciplinary hearing regarding gross misconduct, then you're out the door.

"Gentlemen, you have until the end of the day to get your statements to me detailing exactly what happened and, just in case any of you are still feeling brave, I have already arranged for ten agency staff on standby from tomorrow. The ball is now in your court."

With that Latimer left the canteen, pausing only to sneer at

Blake, who was already the recipient of several accusing stares and hard looks that had turned to an angry babble of voices before he'd even got to the door.

'*Ah yes,*' he thought whilst contemplating a celebratory pub lunch. '*The old rulebook shuffle works again.*'

Barney, Sue and John too

Barney wrinkled his face and grimaced as the last of the coffee hit the back of his throat. '*Bloody cheap shit,*' he thought. '*I'm definitely getting a percolator and some good Italian stuff in here before long,*' then, putting down his police issue mug he turned back to the witness statement from the warehouse.

STATEMENT OF EVENTS – Dean Wood – 18/09 –
Francis Collins assault case

I came to work at me normal time and I just saw this body on the ground; I didn't kna if he was dead or not like. I didn't want nowt to do with it and I had to clock in cos the boss docks the money if we're late. Then once I'd clocked in I thought I better have a look so I went over there like, and I could hear him breathing and sort of moaning but he looked in a bad way so I rang an ambulance and I rang youse.

I want to state though, that I do not know the man involved and do not know who done it or who might have done it or even who the man might owe money to for them to do it. Definitely, I don't know who done it.

Special

Barney sighed and gently banged his head off his desk; all of the witness statements were virtually identical and concerned only with keeping the witnesses out of the firing line, which made them useless at helping to solve the crime.

All of the samples taken were at the lab and the results wouldn't be available for a couple of days; the only one he held out any hope of was the calling card. It looked like a very professional beating so you would assume that the assailant had been as professional about his DNA and fingerprints, which only left the chemical makeup of the card itself. There could only be so many places where card was made round here so Barney was hoping to track down where it came from and go from there.

He had the feeling that he'd probably have a few more scenes of crime to attend before this one was solved.

WPC Suzie Holmes had hung around the offices for as long as she could reasonably make excuses for after her shift ended and now she was contemplating going home. Barney had either cleared off or he was otherwise engaged in the bowels of the building. Either way, she wasn't waiting any longer to ask him if he fancied a drink, it's not like he was going anywhere soon so she had plenty of time anyway.

The decision was made easier for her by the arrival of Special Constable Latimer, it wasn't something immediately apparent about him or even anything obvious he said or did but there was definitely something she didn't like. There were times when he spoke to her that his eyes seemed to be boring through her clothes and his speech always seemed to be laced with double entendres

27

that she found a little sleazy, she shivered involuntarily as he approached, smiling.

"Evening, Suzie, my little cherub. Are you off, then?"

"Yes, John. See you later."

"You sure you don't want to hang round with me, then? See if anything comes up? Ha-ha!"

"No, thanks. I've got to go."

"Okay, then. See you later, Susan." He gave her a wink and then he was off down to see the custody sergeant, leaving Suzie in need of a shower and fighting an overwhelming feeling to go for a drink anyway.

'You could have her easily, John,' he thought, looking back at her disappearing backside as he approached the custody desk. *'She's fucking gagging for it off you that one is. Remember though, you've got standards and she's been round the block a bit, I can tell. Why don't you just tease her a bit, keep her hot in case of emergencies. She's definitely a no-go in the girlfriend stakes anyway; we don't do slags, you know that.'*

Still smiling at the thought of it, he approached the desk and asked the sergeant about a prisoner that had caught his attention 2909; Falcus.

"Alright, Bob. Who's this fellow, then?" he pointed at the name on the record.

"It's Falcus's son, John," Bob replied. "Caught him dipping the new criminalist."

"Falcus? You mean we've finally got one of them for something? The dad'll be furious, won't he?"

"Aye, John. He will – it's great, isn't it?"

"It certainly is, Bob. It certainly is. See you later."

Latimer stepped away whistling; that was a right result getting in the son of the mighty Falcus. With a bit of luck they could help him fall down the stairs later and *really* upset the bastard.

Special

'I tell you what,' Latimer pondered as he got his uniform from his locker, *'I've certainly had worse days than this.'*

It might be a Girl

Ellie Mackenzie was standing opposite the cheap clothes shop halfway up Shields Road when she noticed the coppers coming her way; she pressed the send button on the mobile in her pocket and felt it vibrate to tell her the message was sent. She smiled at the coppers as they walked past, the special was staring at her; she recognised him as the sleazy one the other girls all talked about.

Ellie was fourteen and not a complete virgin. In fact, she'd had a couple of lads and had done most things with them, usually after necking Breezers and cider at parties, but she always felt dirty after the special had looked her up and down, like he'd raped her or something. He had that unnerving way about him, just from a look, that could make you feel violated.

Anyway, the dick was gone now so she glanced back into the store and gave Beany and Pike the nod; they acknowledged her with a smile and started filling their bags again while the shop assistant was busy getting ready to close. It was always the same on these late night openings, not enough staff to cope and the ones who were there were all anxious to get finished as soon as possible, so they took no notice of you. Easy pickings.

Beany had taught her that, he'd taught her how to keep watch and to let them know when there was trouble coming without giving herself away, he'd also taught her how to give a blow job and how to sniff glue; she loved Beany.

Ellie felt excited just thinking about him, once they'd got the gear from here and stashed it back in the car they would have their celebration shag up in the underground car park while Pike kept watch. The car park was their place and it was special to Ellie as it was where she'd first done it properly with Beany and become a woman.

Her mam and dad didn't care what she did or what time she came in, so she stopped letting them know what she got up to a long time ago; her dad had been on the dole most of her life and her mam sold cigarettes round the bars to make a living. Ellie didn't want that, she wanted love, excitement and real money. She got all that with Beany, he was seventeen and knew loads of stuff, sometimes he would make a hundred quid from the gear he sold and he would always share the glue and the tac with her.

"ELLIE... NASH! IT'S ON TOP."

Ellie looked up from her daydream and saw Beany and Pike running from the shop pursued by the two coppers from earlier.

'Shit,' she thought. Fear freezing her to the floor as the shop assistant grabbed her, 'I can't be nicked; I don't want to go to prison.'

She lashed out at the assistant: "I'VE GOT A KNIFE. FUCK OFF OR YA DEAD. I KNOW WHERE YOU LIVE, YOU BITCH."

Fists and arms flailing she managed to beat off the assistant, who at five pound an hour wasn't that interested in getting stabbed to save company profits, and head for the back lanes that ran off the road. Racing towards the car park Ellie saw that Pike had been captured and was sitting in the back of a police car and there was more coppers milling about. Remembering what Beany had told her she stopped, stepped into a side street and reversed her jacket, changing the colour from red to blue, then she messed up her hair to look like a goth, put some earphones in her ears, took a deep breath and stepped back out on to the main street.

Special

Strolling confidently down the street towards their car park, Ellie was amused to see the coppers looking around but ignoring her; almost invisible she made it to the car park and slipped inside. There was Beany putting the bags in the boot, her heart was bursting, she really hoped he would still want to celebrate with her in their cubbyhole.

* * *

Barney was still hungry, his microwave chicken dinner for one hadn't really done the trick and there was nothing in the cupboards, so he'd rang for pizza and was now absent-mindedly going over his case notes.

It was obvious that every potential witness at the warehouse was in fear of someone as they were all saying as little as possible but had intimated that Collins owed somebody money. Suzie had surmised that the somebody in question would be the famous Falcus, who apparently everyone in Byker owed money to and, as far as she was concerned, it was an open and shut case.

'How can that be, though,' he thought checking the clock. *'If someone's doing a job, even a criminal job, that will make them money that they can then give to you... you wouldn't stop them from doing it because you wouldn't get paid.'*

Barney moved to the window and looked down. Below him was the famous Newcastle city centre, magnet for partygoers all over the world; renowned for cool clubs, jumping pubs and up-for-it girls. It looked quite busy now, even on a school night. Monday was student special apparently, where everything was cheap – even if you weren't a student – and everyone got lashed and got off with each other.

Sighing, he stepped back from the bright lights and the bustle and looked at the bare walls and minimal furnishings of his new flat. He picked up his phone: NO NEW MESSAGES screamed out at him, mocking and mean. Looking back at the table covered in statements and reports Barney sighed louder, reasoning that no one was here to call him a drama queen so he might as well be one. Drifting back towards it and the checking and re-checking of statements that he knew would inevitably go on until the early hours, he caught sight of the clock on the kitchen wall and his spirits lifted.

He was in a win-win situation, if the pizza wasn't here in five minutes then he didn't have to pay for it and if it was then he got to eat it quite soon. Tremendous! Hardly daring to believe it in case it wasn't true, Barney approached the fridge, he thought he remembered a stray can of bitter in there. *'Fantastic,'* he was elated to see his memory wasn't playing tricks. *'See how things can turn round Netherstone,'* he chided himself. *'Now all I need is the bloody pizza.'*

The buzzer on the entry phone rang just as Barney double-checked the clock again... two minutes left. Smiling he got a tenner out of his wallet and went to the door. *'You never know, it might be a girl.'*

Community Spirit

"All the powers of law enforcement will be brought to bear on this individual once caught."

"But, Chief Superintendent, has the law not already failed the community if, as is alleged, the 'Ghostboy' is already subject to ASBOs and banning orders? Has the criminal justice system simply given up on protecting society from this young thief?"

"I cannot comment on who this individual may or may not be. Nor on whatever punishments have been previously meted out—"

Special

CLICK

Vicki switched off the television. Her previously light mood evaporating rapidly as she contemplated that Ghostboy wanker getting away with his crimes forever. He'd been caught loads of times; she knew he had, and he was constantly getting ASBOd and slapped on the wrist. They'd even sent him to a fucking holiday camp once at the taxpayers' expense; all that meant was he had some new contacts around the country when he came back.

The bastard had robbed old Mrs Wilkins down the road, took her pension money and the cash she'd saved up for her bills, the money had even been in envelopes marked up Electricity and Gas and he still took it. The poor old cow was a widow and had fuck all; she'd been in bits about it and had worried herself sick. Luckily they'd had a whip-round in the pub and covered her heating but it still left her eating beans on toast for a month.

The best of it was everyone on the estate knew who the little twat was, but he couldn't be touched, nobody employed by Falcus could be touched and he knew it, the little shit. It made her laugh, really. This estate was full of tough men who all said what they'd do if they caught a burglar in their house and how they wouldn't ring the law but just do him in. In reality, they were all cowards, as they all knew who this twat was and they did nowt about it. He was stealing from his own for fuck's sake, it's not like he even went out of the area to places with money; he robbed the people who could least afford it and most of it went straight to Falcus. Yet everyone cosied up to him in the pub, tried to keep on his good side and lapped it up when he got the drinks in. They couldn't see he was using THEIR money to fucking do it, either that or they were too petrified of what would happen if they said anything. Probably that, really.

Falcus was nicknamed Axel F for what he claimed was his habit of using an axe on people who pissed him off. Vicki reckoned she knew different though; she didn't know anyone who'd ever actually seen him use an axe, but knew that his dad had been known to get handy with one in the sixties when he was making a name for himself on the estate. His dad had been banged up in the early seventies for torture and kidnap over a debt and was due to get out in the early eighties when he'd taken part in a prison riot. A screw had been found dead with axe wounds to the head and Falcus senior was chief suspect, nothing was ever proved but he'd done it by all accounts and the authorities knew it as well . The sentence he got on top of his original one for taking part in the riot was way above what anyone else got and he wasn't released until the mid nineties by which time he was an old man. Her ex had told her all of this one time, he was fucking star-struck by the bloke; he was typical of them dicks who read all the true crime books and assume the 'celebrity' gangsters are telling the truth. Falcus's dad had come to live back on the estate and lorded it up terrifying the locals, backed up by his son who'd risen up the gangster ladder, until one day he'd been struck by a car and killed on Shields Road. An accident apparently as he was getting on a bus but the driver had sped off when he'd realised who he'd hit, the car turned out to be stolen – fucking joyriders probably – and that was that. Falcus had threatened terrible revenge on the culprits if he ever found out who done it and he smacked a few of the local tearaways about for information but no one was ever caught. Her ex had asked around loads about it in a desperate attempt to get in with Falcus and his gang but nobody was saying nowt. If it was anyone from round here then they'd kept the secret well.

Anyway, fuck them idiots, she was home and warm and safe.

"Nick, do you fancy a cup of tea?" *'Probably on the PlayStation again.'*

"Aye, Mam," her son appeared on the landing. "Here, let me

make them, though. You can put your feet up and tell us about your new job, eh?"

As she watched him disappear into the kitchen Vicki marvelled at just how different her son was to his father.

'All of the sacrifices were definitely worth it. I might even bring up Matt while we're talking, see how he reacts.'

And then a thought struck her: *'He's very, very different to his dad. He's thoughtful, kind, considerate and never brings the police to the door.'*

"Nick, pet," she said, looking at the kitchen and laughing. "You're not gay, are you?"

Putting the cups on the table and grinning he gave his mam the V sign and said "Nar, Mam. Just happy!"

Glue Romance

"Did the bizzies get Pike, then?"

"Aye, pet. They did. Never mind though, eh? He's a big lad now and he knows the score. Now get your arse over here cos I've got a hard on that needs sorting out sharpish."

Ellie, giggling, scampered over to the love of her young life and grabbed his crotch as he pushed her roughly against the wall. Feeling his hand up her skirt and pulling at her knickers sent waves of excitement through her that she couldn't begin to explain in words. As he lifted her off her feet and pinned her to the car park wall she started biting his ear in anticipation of what was to come; her low moans disturbing the silence of the car park when he started pumping into her with all of the finesse you would expect from a seventeen-year-old professional shoplifter.

He was getting there. Ellie could tell as his legs started to buckle and the look on his face changed, she was close herself she reckoned but no matter... that would happen one day when they were married and could do it proper – indoors and on a bed – but as long as Beany was happy, then so was she. She loved him and he loved her, she just knew it.

Her dreamy reverie of their future together was rudely interrupted by the realisation that a figure dressed in black and wearing an SAS-style balaclava was watching them from across the car park.

"BEANY, *BEANY*, some pervert's watching us."

"What, *what*? aah a cannit stop... nooo, man. Ellie."

"But Beany he's got a baseball bat and he's coming over. BEANY, MAN."

BANG

Beany hadn't had time to turn around or even pull up his trousers before he was felled with a single blow to the head. He lay in a crumpled heap on the concrete floor, trousers round his ankles and a pool of blood rapidly encircling his head. Ellie stared down at him frozen with fear, she couldn't scream or run or even think. Her young heart was beating its way out of her chest and the only conscious thought she could muster was that she must put her knickers back on.

Still staring at her prostrate future husband she took her Top Shop G-string out of her pocket and slowly bent to cover her modesty. She didn't get as far as getting one trainered foot into it before the feel of the bat pressed against her chin caused her to stop. Numb with fear and confusion, she looked up into the eyes of their attacker; they stared straight through her with no emotion at all and she stepped back against the wall as the man looked her up and down. Casually pushing the bat between her legs he raised her skirt and then pushed the bat gently against her crotch, tilting his head as if asking a question. Ellie's throat was dry and she wanted to cry but wouldn't in front of this pervert, she knew what she had to do to stay alive, taking all of her courage she cleared her throat.

"I'll... I'll do anything you want if you promise not to hurt us."

The eyes just blazed back at her, the bat rubbing against her. She had to get out of this alive, if only to get an ambulance for Beany.

"I mean it. I'll do anything just don't hurt us."

She looked pleadingly at him, all pretence of hard case gone and the little girl she really was back in evidence; he removed the bat and showed her a business card that read:

V
'IT'S TIME TO
CLEAN UP THE STREETS'

She looked back at him, confused.

"Well, what do you want, then? I don't understand."

The man just reached down and took the car keys from Beany's pocket, walked over to the car and removed the stolen clothes.

Ellie tried to protest.

"It's only shoplifting, man. Nobody gets hurt and it's not like robbing people's houses, is it? Howay, man. Don't take them..."

BANG

As Ellie joined her lover on the floor, their blood mingling together in a bizarre parody of the Romeo and Juliet characters she thought them to be, the masked man took her G-string from her hand and shoved it into his pocket before silently dropping his business card onto their prone bodies.

Family Business

The bar was mainly quiet with it being a Monday. Crowbar had the night off and Falcus was happy enough to have his son with him for protection, not that any was needed though, after fifteen years of terrorising people there wasn't one person on this estate who would dare challenge him now.

Looking round the bar Falcus reflected that he knew everyone in this place, knew where they lived and who their family was. He could reel off their wives, girlfriends, children's names and descriptions to them and they knew it. No, there would never be any bother to him on this estate and, as long as he kept himself to Byker, then the big boys in town left him alone. That might not last much longer though, not after he made his move, so he'd enjoy the peace while it lasted. Leaning back against the bar he noticed a face he recognised on the telly and smiling to himself upped the volume a little with the remote:

"All the powers of law enforcement will be brought to bear on this individual once caught."

"But, Chief Superintendent, has the law not already failed the community if, as is alleged, the 'Ghostboy' is already subject to ASBOs and banning orders? Has the criminal justice system simply given up on protecting society from this young thief?"

"I cannot comment on who this individual may or may not be. Nor on whatever punishments have been previously meted out."

Keeping his poker face fixed in a neutral expression, Falcus turned back towards the bar and ordered a couple of more pints for him and Terry. Just as he was handing the money over, Terry, obviously perplexed as he'd been quiet for a couple of minutes now, piped up.

Special

"Dad, why do we let that little twat get away with robbing on our estate? He should be too scared to graft here unless we let him. Do you want me to find out who he is and have a word with the cheeky bastard?"

Sighing, Falcus turned to his son, a mirror image of himself, six foot two of ponytailed, tattooed charva.

"Terry, use your fucking loaf for once in your life. The little shit's already working for me and I'm getting seventy five percent of his takings every time. The fucker's making me a fortune, now stop broadcasting it, you fucking doylum."

His son was a worry to him, he'd been nicked the other day for dipping a fucking pig... a *pig* for fuck's sake. And now Falcus would have to sort it out. He'd been hoping to hand the business over to Terry in a few years' time but he'd need some intensive training before he was ready for that.

"You know, Son, I didn't build this empire up from me dad's little business just so *you* could fuck it all up. Try thinking now and then before you speak... now shut up, here's your mother and the lasses.

"Anne, what you having, pet?"

'Look at her; she's a fucking mess. Fourteen stone of foul-mouthed fishwife. I only married her cos she was pregnant with Tanya and she's turned out exactly like her mother as well; a shell suit wearing, alcoholic, pain in the arse.'

"Mwah, Mwah, and what about you, Tanya, pet? You're looking lovely tonight. Have you had ya highlights done?"

'Mind you, Lindsey's no fucking better. At least she doesn't look like her mother and is a bit fit; shagging everyone when she was younger though, so it was no surprise I was a granddad at a young age. Two more of the little bastards she's spawned since then. Three different dads as well, I'm sick of having people done in for her. Mind, that lad she's knocking round with now is thick as fuck, ideal for her. I know she's shagging a couple of other

39

blokes as well, but he hasn't a clue, just glad to be associated with the Falcus family cos it keeps him from getting hit. He's handy for shit jobs as well.'

"Usual for you Lindsey, pet?"

'Look at them, my fucking family: a bloated embarrassment for a wife, an identikit eldest kid, a pigshit-thick and useless son and a slag of a youngest daughter. The Falcus brand that is could sell millions with the right PR man, I reckon. Not that Max Clifford nonce, though. I wonder if David Beckham ever gets bored with having a perfect family and would fancy a swap? He'd love all the bling these twats wear.

'Vibration in the pocket, get the phone out so everyone hears the Beverley Hills Cop tune. Never hurts to promote the image a bit.'

"Keep the change pal, excuse me ladies, business calls."

'I'll have a wander outside and have a tab while I'm doing this, I think.'

"Hello, Pike?"

"Alright Mr Falcus."

"Axel, son Axel. You know me better than that. Have you got the gear?"

"Well no, Axel, I got nicked and..."

"WHAT DO YOU MEAN FUCKING NO? AND IT'S MR FALCUS TO YOU, GOBSHITE. WHAT THE FUCK HAPPENED?"

"I-I got nicked Mr Falcus and, well... I wasn't there but one of the coppers told me that Beany and Ellie have been battered."

"What by, the bizzies?"

"Nah, Mr Falcus. Apparently some bloke with a bat has done them both and cracked their skulls. Left some kind of calling card on them. They're in a bad way... Mr Fal—"

Click

Special

'Hmm that's two of them now; Colly and them two scrotes all smashed up and, more importantly, all the profit diverted from my pocket. Might be another firm. I'll have to keep an eye on this.'

WEDNESDAY

Employment

"Break time, Matty lad. I'm getting the drinks in. Tea or coffee?"

"Not for me, Jase. I've gotta make a couple of phone calls mate. I'll see yiz back on the trailer after break."

"Aah, ringing your lass to tell her you're missing her, eh? Love's young dream, Matty. You and your new bird. Hoo Tonka, Anth listen to this... young Matty's in love."

"Aah, Matty, I weally weally wuv you, Ha-ha."

"Fuck off, Tonka. I'm not even ringing her..."

"Ooh, Matty. You hang up first. No, Vicki, you hang up. No, you hang up. Ha-ha."

'Bastards, bastards! Don't go red, don't react or it'll get worse. Look at Anth pursing his lips. If he keeps that up I'm gonna fucking burst them. No, don't react. Just play along and it'll soon be over.'

"Listen lads, yiz know me better than that by now. It's just sex and she's very fucking good at it. Her nickname's not Sticky Vicki for nowt, you kna? Now yiz are wasting your break time here, but don't let me stop you taking the piss, I didn't want a cup of tea anyway."

'That's shut the fuckers up; they're flapping now about their precious fifteen minutes' grace from the mind-numbing boredom of this place. Aye, off yiz go.'

"Aye, Matt, ya reet. We'll see you in a bit."

'Fucking lost five minutes there, but I should still have time to do what I had planned to before I was so rudely interrupted.'

Deep down, Matt was still fuming about big Ecka getting the sack yesterday. In the end, the bloke had done the decent thing and went to Latimer himself and owned up that he'd been driving the forklift, saving the lads any internal conflict about grassing someone up to save their own jobs. Even so, it left a nasty taste in the mouth knowing that they all would have dropped Ecka in the shite to keep their wage packet. The worst of it was that Matt knew, deep down, if it came down to being on the dole again then he would have done the same.

'A man without money or means of support is nothing in this day and age,' he thought. 'And these bastards know it. You can't beat the system or the company. They hold your future, your mortgage, your children's education – your very well-being in their hands – and they'll squeeze every last drop of self-respect out of you if they have to, just to make sure you know your place.'

Heading towards the paper store he mused on how hard it must be to be a family man up North these days and working for a shit company like this.

'Oh, sure there's good firms about... your Proctors and your Flanagans, the type of places that give you a hamper at Christmas and have fun days and all that, but everyone wants to work for them and, as an unskilled man, I've got no chance. That means I end up here; in fucking Logistics, lucky to get Christmas off at all, never mind a hamper. And what do they say? "If you don't like it then fuck off, we'll just get another bloke in. There's a queue of people wanting jobs, so screw your loaf or get your coat." I mean, I'm not actually a family man or anything like that, not yet anyway, we'll have to see how it goes with Vicki I reckon, early days and that yet. I wish I hadn't mentioned our sex life to them fuckers though.

'The job situation is getting worse now as well, not only have we got the thousands of local lads wanting work but there's a load of eastern Europeans here now finding out that maybe Britain

43

isn't that great after all. Holed up in their council flats on the sink estates, they can't get work cos there isn't any, they all end up pimping their families out and robbing people down dark alleys just to fucking eat. The problem with that though, apart from the moral aspect obviously, is that the local gangsters aren't too happy with them muscling in, so they have to be on their toes all the time in case they get to go back home in a box.

'*Aye,*' he thought, '*it's best to play the game and keep your job these days. Go through the motions and score small victories when you can, that's the way to do it. Anything to let yourself feel that you're getting back at the bastards and to keep you smiling while they try to grind you down.*'

Smiling to himself and cheering up a bit, Matt quickly opened the dodgy padlock on the six-foot fence around the card and paper store and slipped unnoticed through the gate.

* * *

John Latimer was having another good day today. Recent events cheering him up no end, topped off by his boss, the incompetent David Atkinson, grudgingly admitting how well he'd done in tidying up the damaged washing machine incident. The sacrificial lamb in this case had come to him and confessed his guilt after they'd been told they were all getting the push as accomplices to gross misconduct. He'd only been there three months, so it was easy to get rid and cement his own position with the operations director as a ruthless, efficient operator. Atkinson ought to be careful as John knew that he was well thought of by the top men in this firm and he could cause trouble for him if he wanted to.

Inspecting the toilets, Latimer noticed a bit more graffiti about the ginger one and was pleased to realise it was by someone other than him. Smashing... it was starting to catch on now and soon there would be vitriolic jibes about him everywhere. He couldn't hide his fury whenever John reported these things to him. '*Oh, he tries to alright, but an old hand like me can see through the pursed lips and furrowed brow to the rage within.*

'No problem at all,' he thought. 'Keep pushing him gently and eventually he'll fall right over the edge, and that will be fun to see.'

Chuckling to himself Latimer checked his watch as he headed towards the paper store. 'Tea break; they'll all be in the canteen now. I've just got time.'

Matt had just loaded the last of the card and paper into his holdall when he heard a noise from about thirty yards away. It sounded like clicking shoes against the cold concrete floor of the chamber. Quickly, he stashed the bag in the middle of a pallet of paper and threw some reams on top of it, making the pallet look solidly stacked rather than layered, then he dropped down behind it.

The footsteps were coming closer as he pulled his legs into his chest and tried to soften his breathing.

'Fucking hell,' he thought, 'no bastard ever comes in here at break time. Not for the last six months at least.' Then another thought struck him. 'Oh god please don't let it be Latimer, I can't afford to lose this job, I couldn't stand being on the dole again.'

The memories of beans on toast for his Sunday dinner and the embarrassment of giving Christmas presents to his family consisting of a communal tin of Quality Street helped him shrink even further into the base of the pallet. He could barely breathe for the wood sticking into his stomach and ribs and a long, thick wooden spelk had pierced his arm and maybe even drawn blood, but had to bite his lip and try to keep his breathing as silent as possible. The footsteps had paused close by, so close now that he couldn't gauge the distance and had just closed his eyes and hoped for the best.

There was the noise of paper or card being moved and Matt's throat went dry and the sweat poured from him as he realised it was right above him.

'Fuckinhell, fuckinhell,' he thought. 'The prick's obviously *found my bag. Does it identify me? What's in there? Shit, I can't remember.'*

Then, almost abruptly, the click of the shoes started up again in the opposite direction as whoever it was headed out of the chamber. Matt cautiously opened his eyes and twisted his neck to look up but could only see the ceiling. Listening intently, he heard the footsteps fade away and realised he was alone again.

'Thank you God, thank you,' he thought, as images of big turkeys and expensive gifts flooded his mind again. Slowly and warily getting to his feet he decided to check the bag. To his amazement, the hiding place had not been disturbed and the bag, and its contents, were intact.

Deciding against removing it now that everyone was back downstairs, he started to creep out of the chamber, dodging in and out of rows of pallets stacked high. It was dark in between the columns and Matt felt safe. There was no CCTV in this chamber and you couldn't be seen from the entrance if you took this route out. He could feel his confidence returning. The lights flickered off and on which could be spooky but, in the circumstances, was the best thing for staying hidden. Still breathing softly and treading on tiptoes, he made it to the entrance.

A quick check revealed that the corridor was clear and, rather than fuck about with the lock and risk someone appearing in the corridor, Matt decided to vault the fence. Placing both hands on the top he pushed with his arms and sprang with his legs. He felt the whoosh of air past his ears as he cleared the top of the fence followed by the downward motion of his body.

Jumping back up painfully, Matt tried to look casual and affected his usual bored expression while his body screamed 'don't ever fucking do that again you stupid bastard, you could have killed us.' Then, congratulating himself on a successful extrapolation from a sticky situation, Matt was surreptitiously dusting himself down when a movement grabbed his attention out the corner of his eye. He looked to the door next to the chamber entrance and saw the Human Resources woman and, nightmare of nightmares, fucking Latimer stood behind it and watching everything he'd just done through the glass panel. As the bastard came through the door, smug smile all over his face, Matt felt his heart sink down into his boots; he knew that they knew even before Latimer opened his mouth. It didn't stop him though.

"I think we need to have a word in my office, Mr Blake."

Healthy Body, Healthy Mind

Latimer pressed start on the microwave and watched silently for a moment as the chicken pasta dinner he'd cooked and frozen earlier in the week spun round on the plate. Staring blankly at it, he mused on the day's events and decided he was going to buy a lottery ticket.

'Normally I wouldn't bother as the chances of winning are next to nothing but after catching Matt Blake in the act of trespass, I'm prepared to pay the stupidity tax as I really can't fail.'

Moving round his small, spotless kitchen he caught his dad's eye and winked at him. "They always get their comeuppance Dad. You taught me well."

The photograph didn't respond, however. His dad just stared back at him, unsmiling, while Mum clung to his arm grinning inanely, like a fifties Cherie Blair. Their wedding photo was the most recent picture he had of his mum. She'd died giving birth to him and his dad had brought him up alone. Dad had been determined not to let him go the way of some of the louts where they lived though and had kept a tight rein on him, almost *too* tight at times.

'Wouldn't be allowed these days,' he thought. *'A good spanking or belting when you've done wrong wouldn't hurt some of these little bastards though. I mean, it never did you any harm Johnny Boy, did it?'*

Slicing some uncut, wholemeal bread his thoughts drifted back to his childhood.

'The bully on the street got a shock that day we went round to his house,' he chuckled at the thought of it. *'I remember he'd attacked me on the way home from school and tried to steal my new shoes and I'd managed to push him off and run home. When I went into the kitchen Dad took one look at my torn shirt and bloody nose and went very quiet.'*

Pouring some of his favourite carrot and pomegranate juice into a tumbler and setting a place at the table for himself, he stared back at the photo of his dad.

"It was brilliant, Dad. Quite spectacular. Remember how you marched me round to the bully's house? You were on nights that week you had your truncheon with you and were in full uniform. I remember you banging on the door and telling me not to be scared when the shadow approached it and as the door opened it was the bully's dad and he seemed huge. He looked at you and then at me and just grunted, 'What?' and then you pointed out my torn shirt and bloody nose to him, but he just didn't care and said something about, 'Being a snitch just like his dad.'"

The tears were running down Latimer's cheeks as he removed his pasta dish from the microwave and put the revolving plate from the oven straight into the sink, already full of piping hot water. Then, placing the plate on the mat on the table, he looked at the photo again.

"You weren't scared of him like everyone else was, Dad. And you didn't hesitate, just banged him straight in the nose with your truncheon and then kept hitting him. He went down shouting and his son, the bully, came running out. You stopped and looked at me. I knew what you wanted me to do and even though I was scared I didn't flinch, I took heart from you and I flew at the bully with fists and feet and he ran. We won and he never troubled me again, I owe it all to you, Dad."

Raising his juice, Latimer saluted his dad. "Healthy body, healthy mind, Dad. Like you said."

* * *

Superintendent Pascoe took his seat on the stage at the community centre next to Reginald Runcorn, the Byker Residents Action Group leader, and prepared for the onslaught of triviality that he endured every three months. His local community beat officer had cried off, so he had to face the angry mob alone and listen to their tales of broken wing mirrors, graffiti and youths jumping into hedges. All crimes in their own right of course, but less serious than anything important he could be doing now rather than wasting his time here. There was a focus meeting on the new government ASBO initiative he could be attending for instance or chairing a meeting of his own pet project, the Committee for Raising Absconder Profiling, but no, he had to be here to be seen as having an interest in all of his area and not just the affluent side.

'Still,' he thought looking at the meagre attendance of about ten to fifteen people who'd ventured out on this wet and windy night, 'this shouldn't take long.'

Reginald was fiddling with his tie waiting for him to start things off; he was far too polite to dream of pre-empting such an eminent and well-respected senior policeman and would wait patiently until such time as Pascoe deemed it prudent to start proceedings.

"Shall we kick off then, Reginald?" Pascoe asked. He always called him that; his demeanour just seemed to demand it: always immaculately turned out in a suit and tie, his beard trimmed to within an inch of its life and his shoes so shiny you could see your face in them he seemed wasted in a shithole like this, he should have been a local councillor or politician. It took a special kind of person to put the commitment into these community groups and Reginald never let anyone down.

'Actually, forget going into local politics, he should just be sectioned. The bloody nutter.'

"Okay, then," Reginald raised his voice to carry to the first row of seats, pointless shouting as there was no one beyond them. "The first item on the agenda is the gang of youths who hang round the sports field at the bottom of Spires Lane at night. I believe you wish to say something about this, Mrs Kennedy."

Pascoe visibly shrank back into his seat as he contemplated ten minutes of whining from the obviously soft-in-the-head Mrs Kennedy. As he remembered from previous meetings, her house bordered the aforementioned field and she bore the brunt of any noise or disorder that occurred there.

"I don't think it's worth me while bringing these things to the attention of the police anymore as nothing is ever done about it."

Pascoe sat upright in his chair, slightly perturbed that someone as dramatic and self-obsessed as Mrs Kennedy had given up.

"That's not true, Mrs Kennedy..." but she cut him short.

"It *is* true, Mr Pascoe. But it doesn't matter anymore as it seems to me that someone else may well be taking responsibility for the safety of this community now that the police have given up."

"The police never give up on any crime, Mrs Kennedy. Sometimes we have to prioritise but we never relinquish control of our communities. Who is this person that you suggest will be taking over from us?"

"Oh, no one I know, Mr Pascoe, just what I've gathered over the last couple of days from reading the papers and talking in the street. I reckon criminals in Byker had better keep their heads down or have them taken off, that's all."

Special

"You'll have to enlighten me, Mrs Kennedy. I have no idea what you're talking about."

Pascoe was staring at Mrs Kennedy with an intensity he only reserved for sound bites outside the station when *News at Ten* were in attendance. Out of his line of vision another figure stood up to speak.

"She's talking about the vigilante, Superintendent. *Everyone's* talking about him. So far he's done a warehouse burglar and two shoplifters; properly done them as well, none of this slap on the wrist and a 'please don't do it again' malarkey. He's hospitalised the lot of them and I for one hope he gets hold of the mob on the field and does the same to them. He's better than your whole force put together."

The others were joining in now; a big burly man spoke up.

"Yeah, Plod. The little bastards have broken my wing mirrors off three times now. I can't afford to keep replacing them and the last time I reported it to Clifford Street Station the bird on the other end sniggered as she gave me the crime number. Have a look on the field, it's all gas cans, glue bags and empty WKD bottles, I hope he gets them all and *you* never catch him."

Pascoe stood up, spreading his arms before him in an effort to calm down the rapidly excitable group. "You must all be aware that what this man is supposedly doing is also a crime and, if caught, he will be dealt with in the appropriate manner."

"I hope he breaks their fucking legs," the burly man interjected again. "In fact, if you don't do something soon I'll do it my-fucking-self." He pointed at Pascoe, his eyes blazing, "That mugger that you can't seem to ever catch and that fucking teenage burglar that just does what he wants, I hope he does those pricks in as well. I mean, do you lot ever arrest anyone who commits a crime in Byker or are you not bothered as long as it's kept away from 'the party city' that's always in the tabloids?"

Pascoe wasn't sure what they were going on about. He'd have to check with Reg about the people mentioned after this. He'd know about them, he always did, but he wasn't just accepting criticism like that.

"I think you'll find we recently put away a person from this estate for gun-running. Obviously, I can't name names but it was reported in the local media that we'd caught someone bringing weapons into the city, so we do prosecute *all* crimes, no matter where committed."

"What, Donny bloody Patterson bringing a few stun guns back from Thailand? *Big deal.* What would he have used them for, the next BSE cull?"

Pascoe was lost for words at this attack, but luckily Reginald stood up. Polishing his glasses on his tie he held out one hand, "R-r-right, now that we've spoken about that can we move on to issue number two, tax discs."

Relieved that this little exchange had finished, Pascoe sat back down and caught his breath. The mood of the community had surprised him, as had the news that there was a vigilante on the loose. Planting his political smile on his face and pretending to glance at the cheap-looking paper newsletter that Reg provided, he privately resolved to nip this in the bud as soon as possible.

FRIDAY

Parklife

'There they are, the little shits. Must be about ten of them, a couple of girls in that number though, I think.'

CRACK

'Bloody loose twigs in this park... a couple of them nearly noticed me there. That's it, edge forward nice and slow and see what they're up to.'

"Hey, Bev... get a mouthful of this, man. It's *proper* belter this lager."

"LOOK AT ME, MAN. I'M OFF ME NUT!!"

"HA-HA, get off the swings, man, Dobba. You'll break ya neck ye daft bastard. HA-HA."

'Drinking in the park's definitely against the law, I can see one of them with a spray can as well writing his name on the slide. What do they call it – tagging? Looks like there's about to be a bit of underage sex going on by the picnic tables any minute now. I'll give them a bit longer and see what occurs; these little scumbags will soon do something really stupid.'

"Look, it's that daft owld bat again at her windows. I'll give her something to look at... Hoo, pet. Can you dee owt with this."

"Eeh, Stimp, man. Put ya cock away, there's ladies here."

"Where, Bev. I cannit see any, just you and Kaz. Can either of you two dee owt with this?"

"Eeeh, ya mortal man, Stimp. You wouldn't be able to get it up anyway. Like last time Kaz, eh? Ha-Ha."

'Right, one of them's flashing at Mrs Henderson's house now. We've got underage drinking and vandalism, causing a disturbance and generally acting like loud and noisy hooligans. Time to act.'

"Nick, what you doing up there, man. I can't skin up if you're up a tree with the gear, can I?"

'Marvellous, they've got drugs as well here we go...'

"POLICE. STAY WHERE YOU ARE. I SAID, *STAY WHERE YOU ARE.*"

"SCATTER! IT'S ON TOP. NASH, MAN. *NASH.*"

Latimer only had a Community Support Officer for assistance, but had already decided on his course of action: he was getting the delinquent in the tree that had the drugs. The idiot had made the mistake of trying to climb down and run instead of staying up there and swallowing his stash. This made him easy to catch as they were nearly on him before he reached the ground.

"GET OFF US, MAN. YA HURTING ME ARM."

The boy was shouting and struggling and trying to get free, still too stupid to get rid of the evidence which lay on the floor next to him. He looked aghast at it before resuming his struggle for freedom.

Latimer, realising he was stronger than the boy, held the advantage and sent the CSO on a fruitless chase for any stragglers. He then leaned in close to the boy's ear, relishing his frightened look and the racing heart he could feel almost bursting out of his back.

"If you keep struggling, son, I'll hurt more than your bloody arm," he whispered softly. "It's called resisting arrest and I can hurt you badly for that, little boy. So give it up now or you'll know all about pain."

Latimer was pleased to see the boy stop struggling and even more pleased to see the fear on his face and the tears forming in his eyes.

"Not such a hard man now, eh little boy? You don't think it's such a laugh to frighten pensioners anymore, do you? Incidentally, when we get to the station you'd better be giving up a few of your mates' names or you'll be taking the rap for everybody. There's been a lot of car wing mirrors damaged in the streets coming off this park lately and at this moment in time they've all got your name on. Think on that as well as the fact we'll be doing you for possession of a considerable amount of a banned substance, son."

"I'm saying nowt about nobody. I'm not a grass and I know I'll not go down for a little bit of smoke. It's been de-criminalised for fuck's sake."

The lad was trying to appear not bothered and hard like this was nothing new to him, but the wet patch on his trousers and the tears on his cheek were giving him away, so Latimer decided to press home his advantage.

"Well, one thing you should know, son... at the minute we've got someone else in the cells at Clifford Street, he should be in Durham nick by rights but their beast wing's full up and he can't be put in the general prison population for his own safety, mainly due to the horrific nature of the crimes he's committed. Obviously, I can't talk about them – data protection act and all that – but if I was to tell you his nickname was 'the dungeon master' well, you'd probably guess at what he'd done, wouldn't you? Unfortunately for you, I've got a feeling that you might have to share a cell with him for a couple of hours as we're having some work done down there at the minute and space is at a premium. Obviously, if you co-operate fully then I might try hard to keep you out of his cell but if you mess me about... well, then I've got no reason to bother helping you, have I?"

Latimer was mightily cheered by the sheer terror that enveloped the boy's face and which he made no pretence of hiding anymore. As the CSO came back empty-handed and they waited for the van, he reflected on what a good night's work it had been so far. Then his eyes alighted on the abandoned spray can that had been discarded in the haste to escape and a thin smile spread across his face. As the others were occupied with the prisoner, Latimer made a pretence of making a final sweep of the area and pocketed the spray can thinking it might come in handy at some point in the future. If not Reg could have it; he used all kinds of stationery on the Residents' Committee.

Put the Hours In

Anyone looking hard down Raby Street at that moment might just, out of the corner of their eye, have noticed a large shadow moving back and forth at the entrance to one of the numerous bush-lined cut throughs that populated the street. Initially put there to give the place a sense of community and an air of Bohemia they had quickly found their niche as boltholes for a large plethora of East End criminal types. So anyone suitably interested in investigating the aforementioned shadow would have come face to face with Lozzo and the fucking big knife he was carrying.

Special

Lozzo, or as the police and his mother knew him, Lawrence O'Brien, particularly liked Fridays due to the large number of younger punters making their way out of Byker with a week's wages to go to town. These 'clients' as he liked to refer to them would normally be half-pissed or stoned already, due to home consumption of special offer supermarket alcopops in order to save their pockets a bit once they were paying 'toon prices'. Oh, yes... Lozzo liked the Friday shift; he was already about five hundred quid up and he'd only done half the estate so far, he felt good tonight though and decided he'd carry on and push for the grand. By the time he'd paid Falcus his cut, he's still be left with about six hundred for himself and he could leave it for a week and move somewhere else until the heat died down again.

'Mind,' he thought, grinning to himself, *'that last one nearly went tits up. The little wanker fancied his chances until I cut his face then his lass was offering sucks and fucks just to save him. I reckon she fancied me like, the way she was smiling at me while he was holding his face. Shame I had to be professional, really. I should have got her number.'*

Still smiling to himself, Lozzo's well-trained mugger's ears caught footsteps echoing on the wind and he stepped back into the shadow of the bushes.

'Sounds like an expensive shoe that; you never know I could hit the jackpot and finish for the night after this one and gan for a couple of pints. I might even bump into that lass. She was definitely up for it, like.'

As the footsteps got louder, Lozzo took a second to rub his groin and then pulled his balaclava down over his face, crouched back unseen against the wall and waited.

*   *   *

Having just finished his late shift, Jimmy paused at his boss's door where the brass plate proudly proclaimed his title. They'd had to get a brass one because Jimmy himself had defaced the wooden one once too often and there's only so many times your boss can cope with being called The Fat Controller. He knocked and waited for the grunt that signalled he could enter.

'There was a time I would have just went in, kicked off about whatever it was I wanted to see him about, stormed out without waiting for an answer and then went for a pint. How times have changed.'

"Jimmy. Long time no see, what can I do for you?"

Jimmy gulped, feeling his pride sliding down the back of his throat.

"I'd like to put myself forward for as much overtime as possible, boss. Any shift, any route."

The fat controller smiled, feigning shock. The whole depot knew that Jimmy was into Axel Falcus for a hefty amount, so it wasn't really that surprising that he wanted overtime. But Fatty liked to play the game with anyone. Jimmy knew what was coming next, Fatty would pretend there wasn't much on in order to make him beg and then he'd suddenly remember a spare trip that needed a driver.

"Well, Jim. To be honest, we're pretty much covered for drivers at the minute and you know we've got all these Polish lads now; good boys they are, do anything for you."

"Aye boss, I just need as much as I can get me hands on like. A few personal problems, you know."

The fat shit loved this. "Weeellll... I shouldn't really because of the agreement we have with the Polish drivers' agency; they're cheaper than you lot, you see. But... you have been here a long time and you obviously won't let me down will you, Jim?"

Without waiting for an answer he ploughed on, producing a run sheet from the pile on his desk.

Special

"Your day off is on Wednesday next week, isn't it? You can do the 21 route from tea time. How's that?"

That was fucking shite, Jimmy knew it and Fatty knew it. The worst route on the schedule; he'd be picking up pissheads and nutters from ten bells onwards as they finished their darts and pool matches in the various shiteholes they inhabited.

"That's great, boss. Thanks for that."

"No problem, Jim. Always happy to help out one of the old school."

Jimmy gave the smiling, triumphant, fat fucker a nod and headed for the door. He hated himself for doing that, but he needed the cash. A wave of sadness overtook him as he thought of the home life he was trying to save.

There was a time me and her loved each other. Not now like, but we could still at least be friends. The kids as well, they used to respect me and look up to me when they were young. Then they got used to their dad being in the pub all the time and he didn't seem that important anymore. Fucking ironic really, they don't really know me cos I was always out of the house drinking with the lads and now, in the time of my life when I should be bonding with them properly and maybe taking them out a bit, I'll never be in the house cos I'll be working to pay off my drinking debts.'

Sighing, he headed to his locker, maybe a couple of pints in the bus drivers' club before home.

The Weapons of Mass Seduction

Latimer was pleased. The boy called Nick was breaking down in the interview room and was about to give up all of his friends for the crimes in the park, he could just tell. He tried to act tough at first, but every time he glanced up from the table to the door where Latimer stood guard the copper had first made a throat cutting motion with his fingers and as the boy had started to waver he'd then made the oral sex sign with his right hand and pointed to the boy with his left. The interviewing officer had his back to Latimer and was unaware of this so as the boy had broken down he'd been of the opinion that it was his skill as an interrogator that had prevailed.

Latimer knew different. *'Another glory hunter,'* he thought, *'just like that ginger biscuit at work, getting rich on my efforts.'* But it still couldn't stop the warm feeling inside at the thought of a job well done.

'These buggers in charge have got no idea,' he mused. *'It's the little things that matter to ordinary people, things like vandalism and criminal damage and just being able to live in peace in your own home. They're so busy chasing motorists and so-called hate crimes to appease the PC brigade as well as trying to get on the telly and advance their careers that they forget about the real people out there, the silent majority that they're actually employed to protect.'*

The interviewing officer, a young full-timer fresh out of Hendon training college came over to him.

"The boy's mother is in reception. We'd best have a word with her as well, I think."

"Bloody right," replied Latimer. "I bet there's no father; I can read these estate families like a book. He probably gets in from school and puts some Micro Chips on or goes to Burger King then runs wild for hours while she's in the pub."

The full-timer – Gibbon or something like that – gave him a look as if to say, 'out of order mate, that's not politically correct' but Latimer didn't care a jot, his shift was ending and the night was his, but in the time he'd been in he'd had a major impact on a local problem. Latimer knew that once these little buggers got a taste of youth court a lot of them would calm down and try not to go there again. Obviously, there'd be one or two who had a lifetime behind bars mapped out already but a short sharp shock now would do the majority of them a world of good. Who knows, some of them might even become taxpayers... stranger things have happened.

As Vicki entered the room at the station she sensed real animosity from the older copper and a bit of warmth from the younger one, not being one to look a gift horse in the mouth she immediately went to work on the younger one.

"I'm really, *really* sorry for all of this. He's normally such a quiet boy." She said, giving PC Young-and-Dumb her best sad face.

The older, less naïve one was having none of it though. "Miss," he almost spat the word out, "Hughes, my name is Special Constable Latimer and this is my colleague Police Constable Gibbon and we need to talk to you about the activities of your s—"

Vicki clocked a look of pure evil from the young one to the older one as he said, "Gibson, Miss Hughes. Police Constable Gibson."

She had also definitely heard the older one refer to himself as a Special, not a proper copper like young Gibbo here. That meant that Gibson was in charge and she was sure he fancied her. She didn't really want to play this game with them but the safe removal of Nick from the police station was imperative. He was a sensitive lad and she didn't want him mixing with the head cases that would be in here later. As well as that, she was going out with Matt in a bit and didn't want to hang round here all night making statements so, blanking the Special, she turned to PC Gibson in full charm mode.

"PC Gibson, can I just say that Nick will be severely punished when I get him home, I promise you that." She touched him lightly on the arm and let her hand rest there just a second too long then, looking as frightened as she could, she continued, "That's if I can take him home, I've never been in a police station before and I'm not sure what I have to do, really."

Then, adding a little more emotion to her voice and lowering her head she went on. "I'm not one of those mothers who doesn't care and lets their kids run wild. He'll be grounded for quite some time and his PlayStation taken away, I can assure you of that."

Looking up she could see he was smiling sympathetically back at her and running his hand through his hair. *'Bingo,'* she thought.

"Well," he said at her smiling, "I can see you're not typical of the parents we get in here usually and I can also tell that Nick isn't typical of the some of the young louts we pull in."

Sensing an advantage Vicki jumped in. "Oh yes, PC Gibson. And if you check with the school they'll tell you he's never been in trouble and is doing well in all of his lessons." She touched his arm again and tried to look like Princess Di in that Martin Bashir interview, all doe eyed and vulnerable.

He paused for a minute and cleared his throat, and then smiling at her he motioned the other copper to the door.

"Would you get young Nick please, John," he said, subconsciously letting both her and miserable John the Special know who was in charge. "I think a caution would be in order on this occasion."

"A caution?" the older man challenged. "*A bloody caution?!* What about all of the criminal damage, the drugs he had and the stress poor old Mrs Henderson has suffered? He's about to give up the names of the rest of his delinquent friends as well."

Vicki was a bit perturbed at the word drugs and made a mental note to quiz Nick thoroughly until she got to the bottom of that particular piece of evidence and she resolved to find out who Mrs Henderson was as well. If he was terrorising old ladies then he was really in the shit. All of this would have to wait until tomorrow; for now she just wanted him home and safe so she could get ready and go out with Matt knowing he was okay.

Special

With this in mind she leaned forward to PC Gibson, providing him with a good clear view down her cleavage and said in her huskiest voice, "I'm really, *really* grateful Constable Gibson."

That swung it; with one last goggle-eyed look at her tits and the bulge in his pants growing by the second, Gibson turned to Latimer and almost screamed at him.

"I'm in charge, John. Get the boy. We're cautioning him and sending him home."

Latimer's fury was as transparent as Gibson's excitement as he stormed out of the room slamming the door so hard that the handle rattled. Vicki just surreptitiously checked her watch and mentally counted down the minutes to her date. She'd quite enjoyed role playing and reckoned Matt might appreciate this newfound talent too.

McJobs

Matt was glad him and Vicki were going out tonight; he was still suspended from work and the boredom was doing his head in. Not only that but the thought that he was probably going to be sacked wasn't helping either; he'd been round a couple of agencies already in preparation but hadn't got anywhere. He knew why as well: for one he wasn't from Eastern Europe and therefore not prepared to work for four pounds an hour and secondly there weren't any fucking jobs anyway, well not if you discounted working in a call centre. They were like fucking battery farms them things, never mind humane conditions for cows and fucking pigs and that, what about the poor bastards who spent eight to ten hours a day with them stupid headphones on saying things like, "Welcome to Liars insurance services, your call is very important to us," or, "Blame, claim and no shame, how can I help you?"

Then being shouted at by some illiterate radgy and having to call him Sir while he tells you what a useless twat you are.

'No way,' thought Matt, shivering at the vision of himself in a shirt and tie and sat in an endless line of open plan office spaces attached to computers like the human bodies in *The Matrix. 'It's just this generation's version of working at fucking McDonalds. Bollocks to that, man.'*

He checked his watch again; she was nearly ready anyway, just bollocking her lad for being nicked earlier. To be fair to Nick it didn't sound like he'd been up to much, just drinking in the park and a bit of a smoke, nothing he hadn't done as a kid but he didn't want to get involved as he wasn't really part of the furniture just yet and Vicki seemed well annoyed about it.

CREAK

He looked up as Vicki and Nick came down the stairs, Vicki in front looking all stern but smiling at Matt when she thought Nick wasn't looking and Nick looking all shamefaced but also smiling at Matt when he thought his mother wasn't looking. Matt played his part and looked as neutral as possible while Vicki was in the living room with them both, but as soon as she went for her tabs and her coat, he turned to Nick and smiled.

"You daft bastard," he chuckled at him and gave him a playful clout on the head

Nick laughed back, shaking his head in mock horror at his own stupidity. "I know man, Matt. But I wasn't really doing owt that bad, she's just worried I'll go down the same path as me dad but I'm not that stupid."

Matt knew all about Nick's dad, he was an arse of the first order.

Special

He'd been out of prison quite a few years now and hadn't bothered at all with his son even though he only lived five or six miles away. Matt hadn't fathered any kids yet or even really thought about it much, but he was sure that if he ever did then he wouldn't just be able to abandon them. He didn't think it could do the kid much good either; in fact, it would probably lead to him being nicked for hiding up a tree with a tenner's worth of hash at some point in his life.

Smiling back at him, Matt just whispered, "If I get the chance I'll have a word with her... but quick, look sad again... she's coming."

"Alright, pet. You ready?" She looked as fit as fuck.

"Aye, Matt. I could do with a drink... after the day I've had!" she said, pointedly looking at Nick.

"Aye well, pet," Matt put his arm round her and steered her to the door, "let me show you a good time to put it out your head." Giving Nick a sly wink behind her back he patted her bottom as she closed the door and Matt wondered whether she'd ever had sex outdoors and, more to the point, whether she'd consider a quickie on the way to Shields Road.

* * *

Lozzo had checked his wad and was ready to call it a night.

'I'll get down The Hare, see Falcus and pay him off then catch the lads in The Raby. Maybe get some pills and gan clubbing.'

Happy at his night's work, he stuffed the money in his trainer and prepared for the off before noticing the faint sound of clinking bottles over the car alarm that had been going off for an hour or so. Smiling to himself, he pulled the balaclava over his head again and unsheathed the blade.

'Someone bringing a carryout home. They must have been out all day if they're coming back now, shouldn't take long at all and it'll be a nice little bonus I won't tell Falcus about.'

Andy Rivers

A Chip off the Old Block

"What did he look like then, this plainclothes copper?"

Terry Falcus paused for a minute, pint halfway between bar and mouth, as his brain fought a mental battle with his body over what to do with it. As ever, his body won and the beer went down his throat leaving his dad's question unanswered for the moment. Falcus senior used this pause to evaluate his offspring; dirty hands rubbing the spittle off his mouth, un-ironed shirt hanging round his arse and about three days of reddish stubble growing unchecked around his constantly gawping mouth.

'The cunt can't be mine. No way. That fat slag must have had an affair at some point, she must have.'

"He was a biggish lad, a bit of a fat fucker though. Looked a bit gormless like, kna what a mean, Dad?"

'Oh, aye. Gormless, yeah... I know exactly what you mean.'

"Aye, Son," he nodded encouragement, "owt else?"

"Well," Terry scratched his arse, "you know that programme you like, it's a quiz but it's a bit shit cos it's not *Millionaire* or owt like that?"

"Give us a clue then, Son," Falcus sighed inwardly, this could take a while.

"Well, people laugh at it and that and you say it's funny, but it's not really."

"I like lots of programmes and I particularly like quizzes, it could be anything, man. There must be something else you can tell us about it."

"Ehm, they show you pictures of politicians sometimes and the people on it have to make up titles for what they're doing."

"Who's on it?" Falcus growled at his son.

"That bloke that used to play for Arsenal," Terry suddenly brightened up, pleased with himself.

Special

"What Ian Wright, you mean? *They Think it's all Over*, the sports quiz? Does he look like one of them?"

"Nah, it's not that. What was his name? Merson, Paul Merson," Terry exclaimed, well chuffed with himself.

"He's not on any quiz I watch," Falcus said. He was befuddled and he'd only had four pints.

"He is, man. It's about the news and that, there's a little posh gadgy on the other team who pretends he knas nowt aboot football every week and everyone laughs."

A little light went on in Falcus's head and he looked towards his boneheaded son and asked gently, "Do you mean Paul Merton, Son? The comedian on *Have I got News for You*?"

"Aye," said Terry. "That's the one... used to play for Arsenal."

"He didn't, he's a... Oh, fuck it. Never mind. What about it?"

"Well there's a bloke been on there sometimes when I've watched it with you, I don't think its funny at all me like, and he's the spitting dabs of the copper twat."

"And who's that then?"

"He's an MP, sort of gingerish blonde, can't speak properly and he sounds like a right toff."

"Right," said Falcus. "Well, now we're getting somewhere."

"He was in the papers for having an affair as well," said Terry helpfully.

"Aye, Son. Well that would narrow it down, that; an MP that's had an affair... there can only be two or three million of them to the square foot."

Then Falcus had a brainwave

"Has he got a stupid name?"

"Aye, I think he did."

"Boris Johnson?"

"Aye, that's it, Dad, I think he was in the Frankenstein films or something. Anyway, he looked like him."

'Thank fuck for that,' thought Falcus. *'Now we've got*

something to work with, I can give Crowbar an idea of who we're looking for and we can try to keep numbnuts here out of jail. Mind you,' he thought, looking back at his son as he bumped into tables and scattered drinkers on his way to the toilet, *'maybe I'd be better off letting the twat go down for a while just to give my head a rest.'*

Sex on Tap

Vicki giggled as she pushed Matt backwards into the cut through, ramming her lips onto his as she fumbled at his crotch she thought how well her life was going at the minute.

'New job, more money in the house, new boyfriend, sex on tap... and good sex at that.'

Even the episode with Nick couldn't dampen her spirits as he'd gotten away with a caution but, and it was a big but, Matt didn't seem to be sharing her passion. In fact, he wasn't responding at all. She opened her eyes and looked into his but he wasn't facing her anymore and was pushing her behind him while he re-fastened his belt.

Vicki looked past him as he squared up and saw a balaclaved man standing over an obviously unconscious man. The man with the balaclava had a knife and was staring straight at them both. Vicki whipped her mobile from her bag and quickly called the police as Matt took a step forward.

The attacker just stared at Vicki, she could see his eyes boring into her through the slits in the balaclava, it was like he didn't consider Matt a threat at all, then he looked briefly at him and his eyes changed like he was smiling under the mask.

Matt stepped toward the fallen man and his assailant again, he really didn't want fuck all to do with this but couldn't run away in front of Vicki; she was relying on him to protect her. The bloke on the floor looked in a bad way; he was covered in blood and there looked like sick or something in his mouth, looked like he'd tried to hide his money in his shoes as well cos he could see some notes sticking out like he'd tried to grab them.

There was a mugger worked these streets sometimes but he hadn't been here for a while and Matt thought that maybe he'd fucked off for good. But now it looked like he was back; the bloke on the floor had obviously tried to take precautions against losing his money.

Matt took another step forward, noticing as he did that the sick in the knocked out bloke's mouth actually looked brilliant white rather than chunky and yellow. *'Fucking hell,'* he thought. *'I hope there's nowt pervy going on here.'* He looked back at the mugger; there was about ten yards between them now.

"I don't want any bother, mate."

He was shitting himself but he couldn't leave Vicki to this bastard. "He's had enough and the bizzies are on their way, so why don't you take the money and go? It's not like we can give a description or anything, is it?"

The mugger just shook his head slowly like Matt was slow in some way and then dropped the knife, blade first, onto the other blokes face leaving a nasty cut. The bloke started to groan and try to get up but the mugger booted him hard in the nose, bursting it again and completely sparking him out.

Matt's breathing was getting harder now as the fear was starting to overtake him, he knew he was going to have to move soon or he'd be frozen here forever, his own adrenalin would leave him fucked and an easy target for matey boy. He considered a grab for the knife but there was still a good distance between him and the mugger; the boy on the floor looked a big lad as well, so that meant the other bloke had to be quite handy.

Matt himself was no fighter so decided he would step back so the mugger could see he wasn't interested in catching him, but simply wanted him to fuck off and pose no threat to Vicki. As he stepped back, hands held palm out, the cheeky cunt just gave him a nod as if to say 'good boy' and then he gave Vicki a final stare and fucked off out the back of the alley.

Matt gave it a couple of seconds before turning back to Vicki. She looked okay but he checked anyway.

"Alright, pet?"

She gave him a nod and then Matt could put it off no longer, he approached the fallen man.

"You alright, mate?" he said.

Getting no response, he bent down and checked him over, all the while keeping a wary eye out for the mugger.

"This poor fucker's in a right state, Vick."

"Put him in the recovery position and check he can breathe okay, but don't touch anything with your fingers if you can help it. The switchboard woman said the coppers are on their way."

As Matt rolled the man onto his side he remembered the sick on his tongue and jumped back to avoid getting it on his jeans. He was puzzled when nothing came out despite the man's mouth being open so bent right down to look in and came back up retching.

"What's the matter, pet? Is he still breathing?" Vicki ran over, all thoughts of her safety forgotten now she'd seen her man in distress for the first time.

Matt, still in Sir Lancelot mode held her back with one hand and covered his mouth with the other as the blue lights approached.

"Don't look," he said. "The sick fucker's stapled a business card to his tongue."

70

The Long Game

Falcus checked his watch; ten thirty. Lozzo must be having a very good night as he'd normally be here by now. He knew the score, though… payment by last orders and he'd never let him down before. Rubbing his hands together, Falcus got two more pints for him and Terry and mentally ordered the Indian takeaway he'd be splashing out part of his commission on. The thought of Shami Kebabs followed by a nice big Beef Dhal had his belly doing somersaults. Fucking belter.

Back in the cut through Barney was engaged in a quiet conversation with Suzie about the man they'd just put in the back of the ambulance. There was something nagging him about it, there was something he was missing here.

"Right Suzie, from the top. Who's the victim?"

"Lawrence 'Lozzo' O'Brien, career mugger. He's done plenty of time for it. Never normally gets too violent, just cuts and bruises if the lads get brave. I think the knife's just for show to be honest."

"And we had reports of muggings earlier in this very alley?"

"Yes and all descriptions related to the unfortunate Mr O'Brien." Suzie couldn't stop smiling, O'Brien was scum and now he'd got back a bit of the fear he'd given out over the years.

"Does the mighty Falcus not mind someone working his patch?"

Suzie smiled at Barney's naivety. "No way of proving it, obviously," she said. "But Mr O'Brien here will be passing on a percentage of his earnings to someone in exchange for being allowed to work here unmolested."

"Right, now that's established… what about those two?" Barney asked, nodding in the direction of the patrol car.

"Matt Blake and Vicki Hughes. Basically, they were just going

71

out for the night and noticed an altercation. Mr Blake tried to help and scared off the attacker."

"Any possibility of Mr Blake being the attacker and the masked man just a red herring?"

Suzie laughed. "I always had you down as more of a CSI man than Columbo, Barney. Masked men and red herrings? You'll be smoking a pipe and calling me Watson next."

Barney's discomfort at being mocked by Suzie was revealing itself in his big red face, he just knew it. He could physically feel his face getting rosier while he struggled for a smartarse answer.

"These questions have to be asked."

"It wasn't him, Barney. There's no blood on him at all. We'll take samples obviously, but it's not a line of enquiry I'd pursue." Suzie was of the opinion that Matt looked more like a lover than a fighter and that Vicki was a lucky cow.

'Marks out of two,' she thought. *'I'd give him one.'*

"Yes, well," Barney had recovered his composure now and his policeman's instinct told him he didn't like the way Suzie was looking at Mr Blake. "We must follow all avenues, Suzie. You know that."

Suzie just smiled at him. He was a strange bloke, really. Lots of little moods and that, very deep though and she liked that. She liked that a *lot*.

"Barney, we did get a major piece of evidence to suggest it was the vigilante, remember?"

Barney, still in a huff even though he wasn't sure why, just sniffed and shot back with, "And what was that then?"

Suzie, quite enjoying his performance, smiled sweetly again, leaned in close and whispered huskily into his ear.

"That'll be the business card that was stapled to his fucking tongue."

Barney snapped backwards at the pleasure of her breath in his ear and the closeness of her body nullified by the fact she'd just sworn at him... and the realisation she was taking the piss. Add that to the knowledge that in his haste to try and find a way to try and associate Blake with the crime, he'd forgotten about a large piece of evidence and he was more than a little discomfited.

"Y-y-yes," he mumbled, staggering over to the first responding officer and away from Suzie. "I'm just going to discuss this now, actually."

Making a mental note never to make an arse of himself in front of Suzie again, he strode purposefully over to the clutch of plods at the scene of crime.

Watching him go, Suzie smiled to herself. Barney liked her, she just knew it. Looking back at Matt she sighed. It had been a long time and he would have been handy just for one night. Looking back at his retreating figure she decided that she may well have to play the long game. He was definitely interested though, *definitely*.

MONDAY

Under Pressure (1)

Barney was at the back of the briefing room, Chief Inspector Pascoe himself was going to speak to everyone today, and every copper on every shift was having this conversation apparently.

"Gentlemen, if we're all here then let's begin."

The whispering, coughing and general hum of noise quietened immediately and the most coppers Barney had ever seen in one place turned to look at the Chief Inspector.

"It appears that we have a vigilante on the loose in the Byker area. Thus far he has assaulted a burglar, two shoplifters and now a mugger. The injuries sustained by all were quite severe; particularly the mugger, and I want it to stop. Not only is this man committing quite serious crimes but he is making us, the police force in this city, look bloody stupid.

"Also, as part of his modus operandi this man always leaves a calling card, the press hadn't picked up on this before last night but I had a call this morning from the Scottish gutter rat at *The Chronicle,* Mr Docherty, and he is now right on the case. This will undoubtedly result in the nationals getting wind of this, courtesy of Docherty again as he seeks his big move South. Once that happens we will have to endure a spate of copy cats and more questioning about why this man can catch these criminals when we can't."

Barney thought that was a fair comment, really. If the vigilante knew who to target then why did the police not? He also considered that maybe it wasn't the reporter's career that Pascoe really had in mind. After all, a vigilante running round cutting people up on his patch couldn't look good for the Chief Inspector, could it?

"In fact," Pascoe continued, "the mimicking has already started, to an extent. As the night-shift will testify, a number of individuals in the city centre were accosted last night by a group of men in Alan Shearer masks. Whilst the young persons attacked were all of the lower classes and engaged at the time in begging money from passers by, this does not excuse the fact they were assaulted."

Barney had heard about this already. The lads that had been chased through town and set upon were what was known up here as charvas or down South as chavs; tracksuit wearing hooligans who spent their time abusing ordinary decent people. This particular mob had been harassing people for 'fifty pence to get the bus home, mate' when the attacks had happened. In Barney's opinion it wasn't the end of the world, really.

"Now then," Pascoe went on. "In order to catch this man I have decided that our new recruit and highly-qualified criminalist, Barney Netherstone, will be heading up the team of detectives that will, as of now, drop everything else until this nutter is caught. I also wish to make it clear that I expect every resource to be made available to him. Okay, Barney?"

Barney hadn't seen that coming and gulped hard as every pair of eyes in the room swivelled his way; he could feel his face start to redden and quickly fired off a positive response before it got any worse. Luckily Pascoe, relishing the spotlight like a bad actor in an amateur dramatic production, quickly made himself centre stage again.

"Right then, team. Never forget, we're the biggest gang in this city and no one, but *no one*... messes with us. Now go out there and KICK SOME ASS."

There was an embarrassed silence until Pascoe's mortified assistant started to applaud, looking pleadingly at the rest of the dayshift, who followed suit slowly and unenthusiastically. Barney just leant back against the wall and thanked God that there was someone more inept than him in the room at that moment and then turned his mind to the matter of catching the vigilante. He needed someone he could trust working with him, someone with no political axe to grind over his appointment, someone with no hidden agenda, someone who would play it by the book. In short, he needed someone with great tits that he would love to sleep with.

"Suzie, have you got a minute?"

* * *

Matt waited nervously in the reception area at German Wizard Distribution, his disciplinary hearing was at eleven and he had a few minutes yet. He'd been in enough of these as a witness for the other lads so he knew how they worked. Latimer would have already decided what he wanted done with Matt, but would go through the motions for the benefit of the Human Resources woman who would truly believe that all companies followed the rules of recruitment and dismissal. He knew his only chance was to somehow make the HR woman think he was being harshly treated and get her backing him against Latimer. There would only be one winner if he could get her scared about sacking him and the costly compensation claim that would follow.

"Mr Blake?"

Matt looked up at the receptionist and she smiled. "They're ready for you now, if you wish to go through."

Matt gulped and raised his eyebrows at her, she mouthed 'good luck' at him as he straightened his tie and then it was time for kick-off. He headed to Latimer's office, going over his story one last time.

Under Pressure (2)

View from the Doc

So it seems we have a vigilante running around Byker at present. Is this any surprise to the residents of that famous old area? The police have made their priorities clear in their policy of running down foot patrols and bobbies on the beat in favour of directing resources at the hard-pressed and mainly law- abiding motorist. Inevitably, this course of action has left normal residents living in fear in their own homes and unable to walk alone down the streets where they live as the criminal scum amongst us realise that it is open season on normal society.

Indeed, if you challenge one of these anti-social miscreants you run the risk of being prosecuted yourself for assault, regardless of whether you were being attacked or burgled.

While this newspaper cannot condone any ordinary member of the public taking the law into their own hands I have to admit from a personal point of view that it gladdens my heart to see the criminal fraternity being put in hospital rather than law abiding, tax paying citizens.

It's just a thought for the man who runs the police force on the East side of this city, but maybe if you put some effort into catching more criminals then ordinary people would not feel that they had nowhere else to turn and there would be no need for them to take up the cudgels, metaphorically speaking, on behalf of their community.

Not that the blame can be shouldered by the police alone; there are times when they do catch the petty criminals who make life a misery for some people and they actually get them to court only for ludicrously light, or even non-existent, sentences to be handed out which have them back on the street and committing crimes again within minutes.

Oh for a valid successor to the sadly deceased Judge Maxwell, a man who never sentenced one year when he could give five, he has never been adequately replaced and the criminals are positively loving it. Furthermore, why oh why...

Pascoe could read no more, his superiors would be reading this as well at some point today and then be on the phone demanding to know what he was doing about it.

'Damage limitation now,' he thought. *'Careers can always survive little stains as long as they're handled correctly. My best move was to give the case to Netherstone, his dad was well thought of and it'll buy me some time when I explain he's still bedding in. If he doesn't come up with the goods then I've always got the perfect fall guy. I can cope with that kind of collateral damage as long as it gets me to the top job someday.'*

The shrill ring of the phone dragged him from his thoughts, his heart skipping a beat until he realised that it was only his secretary

"Yes, what do you want?"

"Sorry to disturb you, Sir, but it's the Chief Superintendent. He says he wants to speak to you urgently."

Pascoe looked back at the picture of the blood spattered mugger on the front of the paper and audibly gulped. Then, turning back to the phone, he whispered, "Put him through."

Small Victories (1)

"So then, Mr Blake. Just to reiterate; you have declined a witness for this hearing. Ms Latif is here as the company witness and is also the company's human resources representative whilst I am here as the chair of this hearing. Do you understand all of that?"

Matt had heard all this before in numerous disciplinaries for the other lads and knew it was all bollocks. It didn't matter if you had a witness in with you or not as they couldn't say anything and weren't really needed anyway. The company wouldn't dare lie in the minutes of the hearing as that would be easily proven and cost them a fortune in claims at industrial tribunals.

"Yes, I understand, Mr Latimer," he nodded at the HR bird and continued his spiel. "Ms Latif, I would like to point out that I haven't brought a witness along as I don't wish to disrupt the work pattern or output of the company and, having attended a number of these hearings as a witness for other employees, I believe very strongly in this company's fair and even-handed approach."

Utter shite. He knew that Latimer wanted him sacked and that the HR bird was just here to see if it was feasible beyond reasonable doubt. However, all this would be in the minutes so, if he had to go to a tribunal, then it would look good. Latimer knew he was talking nonsense as well and smiled at him, it was like a game of fucking chess this... and Matt was good at chess.

"So, Mr Blake. Can you begin by telling me what you were doing in the restricted area of the warehouse that, as you very well know, is sublet to Rivisco Stationery?"

You had to hand it to him; there was no fucking about with Latimer.

'Straight to the point with this twat. Right then, here goes...'

"Well, Mr Latimer... as you know, I've been here a while now and if you look through my record you'll see that I've never taken any time off sick or indeed have never even been late for work. A record that I'm sure you'll agree puts every one of my co-workers at German Wizard to shame."

The HR woman was nodding and even Latimer had to concede it. "Yes, yes, you are very reliable. What has that to do with you being in the restricted area?"

"Well," Matt continued, "as you also know, because of this record and my length of service, I am the most senior person on the shift and am also considered to be an unofficial team leader by both my colleagues and yourself, Mr Latimer. I believe the conversation we had about my being seen in this way has also been recorded on my file?"

Ms Latif was thumbing frantically through the file and nodding her head while Latimer sat looking blankly at him. Either he was very good at looking poker-faced or he couldn't see where Matt was going with this.

"Yes," he retorted. "You asked me for more money in light of this *seniority* and I told you we'd review it in six months if you continued being the first point of contact for the staff."

Matt was laughing inside, this had all been recorded on the minutes and was now, as far as any tribunal was concerned, fact. In reality, it was bollocks. He'd just tried his luck for more money and Latimer had basically told him to fuck off, but the HR woman was realising the implications of what was being said and had started looking daggers at Latimer. He in turn hadn't realised that Matt had just cornered his King.

'That's you in check, bonny lad,' he thought.

"Well," Matt went on, "with this in mind you have to understand that, when I was walking past the stationery area and heard a noise, I was in two minds what to do. You've mentioned pilfering in there in the past to me so I checked your office but you weren't there. If I had gone to look for you then whoever was in there might have got away, so I made a split-second decision to catch the culprit. You're always telling me to be pro-active, aren't you? In fact, I think that was one of the major points you made on my last appraisal."

The HR bird was blushing red and leafing through his file again.

'Can't see you escaping this attack. Your King is about to be dethroned, my good man.'

Latimer looked shocked, like he'd never considered Matt would have a defence, "You heard a noise in there... and *that's* why you went in?"

Matt did his best to look sincere even though he was mentally doing the victory dance all over Latimer's desk.   "Why, yes. Why else did you think I was in there? I could understand you suspending me, John, procedures and all that, but did you honestly think someone with my record and position of responsibility would have any other reason to be in a restricted area?"

'Checkmate, you twat.'

Latimer was fucked and both he and the HR woman knew it. She looked furious at him and Latimer himself looked like he was about to start clutching at straws.

"Well, who did you find in there then, Mr Blake? There must have been somebody if you heard a noise?" Latimer looked triumphant, like his King had found a way out. He and the HR bird both leant forward assuming Matt had talked himself into a corner and they were anxious to make the most of this lifeline that had come their way, but Matt had been building up to this and drawing him in ever since the hearing had started.

He paused for effect and then finished them off.

"It was a pigeon, John," he said smiling and shaking his head in mock surprise. "I mean, can you believe that? You've mentioned a nest of them in there somewhere a couple of times now and I nearly put my job on the line by forgetting about them. Bloody ridiculous, isn't it?"

Matt knew that Latimer was properly fucked now, he'd put a maintenance request in to have the nests removed a few times and couldn't deny their existence. He was beat and he knew it.

"Right, Mr Blake," he said. "Now we've heard all the evidence I'd like you to wait in reception please, whilst Ms Latif and I discuss how to proceed with this."

"Certainly," Matt replied, his smug smile leaving Latimer in no doubt that he knew he'd done him. *'Small victories,'* he thought. *'That's what makes life worth living.'*

Take a look at the Lawman

Barney flipped over the business card in his hand, the bag that enclosed it creased with every flip and the sunlight from his office window reflected off the shiny plastic.

'Why?' he thought. *'Why leave this every time? What relevance is there in it?'*

His training had also included basic psychology, which, at the time, he'd thought was pointless. He was now beginning to realise that it may just have a bearing on this case.

'There must be a reason why this person feels he has to clean up the streets. Was he a victim of crime maybe? Burgled? Mugged? Raped?'

Rapping his fingers on the desk as he pondered, *'This man wants to impose law in an area he believes is lawless. He has to leave his mark in some way other than his present situation allows.'*

Then, looking at the card again he suddenly exclaimed, "Bugger it, and forget the shrink stuff... we'll concentrate on the physical evidence. Someone, somewhere has printed these cards for him."

Special

Jumping up, he opened his office door and scanned the Operations room until he saw what he was looking for.

"Suzie... *Suzie*, have you got a minute? I've got a job for you..."

* * *

John Latimer was not happy. He moved the Hoover around his already immaculate living room floor with a violent intensity as he considered the punishment he was directed to give in Blake's disciplinary hearing.

'Written warning? A written-bloody-warning? He should have been sacked, we know he's been thieving from that chamber, we just know it and now he's back at work tomorrow. Bloody politically correct Personnel Department. Oh, no. I must remember it's called Human Resources now, isn't it? Stupid Paki cow fell for everything he said, she fucking loved it, hung on his every word. She probably wanted to shag him, the stupid Paki cow. Ginger Biscuit agreed with her as well, useless bloody twat probably wants to fuck her as well.'

He was ramming the Hoover against the settee now in an effort to pick up the solitary piece of fluff that had survived yesterday's cleaning frenzy, but it was just out of reach so he forced it harder against the settee.

'Saying it was our own fault, that we'd given him a way out by documenting all those conversations. We've got to document them and she knows that, her own bloody department tells us to do it. Fucking liar, she probably wanted him to fuck her there and then. Probably wanted to do it in front of us dirty, Paki cow. I bet she couldn't wait to suck his cock either, get a bit of man fat down her, fucking slut.'

Bits of plastic were flying off the Hoover's casing as the settee was being pushed back against the wall.

'She probably would have let him take her up the arse as well. Oh, yeah... bum fun for Matt. That's probably what he's used to

83

anyway. "Ooh, Matt you're so sexy not like old Latimer there, I wouldn't let him touch me but you can do anything you want and I'll forgive you. Do you want to steal the computers from the offices? No problem. Do you want to sell all the pallets off? I don't mind as long as you go harder, Matt. Go harder, Matt. Harder, faster, Matt. Faster, Ooh, ooh, yess... yess." Slut, SLUT, SLUT.'

The Hoover slewed forward, somehow bringing the offending fluff into range and sucked it up, saving it's own plastic life in the process. Latimer, pleased that he'd got what he wanted and out of breath a little, unplugged the machine. Putting it away his eyes alighted on his dad's picture again and he instantly calmed down.

"It's not like the old days, Dad," he said sitting down. "There's no respect anymore. No one respects anyone else at all."

Taking some fruit juice from the fridge he got himself a glass from the cupboard and held it over the sink while he poured it in. Satisfied that he'd not spilt a drop he wiped the bottom of the glass just to make sure and then returned to the table, placing his glass on a coaster as he did so.

"Nothing's like it was, really," he said looking back at the picture. "The streets are filthy with discarded junk food and sweet wrappers. Women have no modesty anymore; if they're not in the street baring everything then you only have to open a newspaper to see bare breasts. A newspaper, for goodness' sake.

"And the young people... don't get me started on them. Drugs, drink and sex; that's all they're interested in. It's just preposterous, go into any town or city at the weekend and you'll see them. They'll be out of their heads, falling about, vomiting, fighting, urinating, and that's the women as well as the men. And having sex. They're like a pack of wild animals, Dad. They really are. No respect for anybody.

"I remember when I was young before I went to live with that other family and it was just you and me. We could go out at any time of the day or night and people would be respectful. If there

84

was a fight when the pub closed, it would be two men with their shirtsleeves rolled up and a handshake afterwards, no weapons or mates involved. Women kept themselves covered up and had some dignity. Not like now, being a slag is a career choice. Want to be famous? Want to be on television? Well get your vagina out for the tabloids and you never know, you might get a date with a footballer. Their mothers must be so proud."

Moving to look out of the window, but carefully keeping the tea towel under his glass so as not to spill any on the clean floor, he looked wistfully at the local park.

"Look at that... school's finished for the day and the park's empty. When I was a lad we'd be flying kites, playing football or making dens. Now they're on their computers or watching television and becoming fat, pasty-faced loners who don't know anything about healthy competition or survival of the fittest. We're raising a nation of whiners and morally bankrupt; spineless kids who get everything they want because their parents are too gutless to say no and risk a tantrum. They're bloody illiterate as well; they think everything's spelt the American way because they spend so much time on their computers. Actually it's not just kids; I saw a mistake in *The Express* the other day. *The Express* for goodness' sake, that's how far standards have slipped."

Turning back to the table he retook his seat and stared into his dad's eyes.

"Mind you, Dad. I think things started going downhill when you went and I was taken in by the Latimers. They were a good, hardworking and God-fearing couple but they weren't as strict or as fair as you and that's when I started to notice what was wrong with the world. Their kids would look at filthy magazines, the kind you would never have had in the house, and when that Channel Four started they would watch programmes that were almost pornographic every time Mr And Mrs Latimer were out of the house, even the girl. She was a telltale as well; making things up about me to get me into trouble with Mr Latimer, the bloody harlot. That was innocent though compared to now, Dad. The scum have taken over and they're running wild; the police have given up."

Sighing to himself and standing back up he looked out of the window again, the moistness of his eyes blurring his vision so the setting sun looked like a big light shining right at him, he turned back to the photo.

"I've always lived by your standards, Dad. Always. I did what you said as well; never let anyone get too close, never show a weakness and the buggers can't get you. They can never touch you if you don't let them. I've never even told anyone about you and what happened to you."

'Anyone, John?'

"Well, yes, Dad. I did tell Reg about you but he's a good man. He has the same morals and principles as us."

'Did you tell him everything John?'

"Oh, no, Dad. He knows about you and how you went but I haven't told him the other thing. I can't tell anyone about that. Not until the time's right."

'Good Boy. Remember, Son... never give up. Never.'

"I know, Dad. You kept going right to the end and you taught me well. I'm from the same blood, remember? I'm proud to be a copper and I'll fight lawlessness with every breath in my body."

Every Cloud

Matt was in the mood for celebrating; he'd got away with it and kept his job.

'That deserves a small celebration,' he thought to himself while

he ironed a shirt. *'I'll take the lovely Vicki for a drink and a curry, I think. I can use some of the money I was saving in case I got the bullet. I'd best not get pissed though, Latimer was fucking furious at not being able to sack me, I could tell. I can't turn up tomorrow smelling of drink or being late as that'll be just the excuse he needs. Still though, that was a great result and I'm definitely having a couple tonight.'*

Hanging his shirt up he moved across the poky flat and picked his jeans up from the back of the chair they'd lain on for the best part of a week. Placing them carefully on the ironing board he noticed a beer stain on the leg and sighed as he headed to the sink.

'I need to sort my fucking life out,' he thought, dabbing at the leg of his jeans. *'I'm nearly thirty-years-old, I live in a tiny council flat and I've got a dead-end job. Some of my old schoolmates have got careers, houses with gardens and wives and kids. Fucking Biggsy goes on holiday three times a year and has got his own villa in Spain; he was a thick bastard at school and now he's an IT guru. I used to do the prick's homework for him.'*

Switching the iron off he flopped back into a chair and looked at his photo board; the collage of pictures from his past seemed to hold a success story no matter which one he looked at.

'Little Daz... we all took the piss out of him when he said he was joining the army now look at him; nearly fifteen years on and he's running his own gym, he's got arms like my legs and he's making a fortune. Granted, he spends it all on his teenage glamour model girlfriend and had to suffer the indignity of finding out through the Sunday tabloids that Peter Stringfellow had broken her in, but still, it's better than stacking fucking fridges for a living, isn't it?'

Standing to look out of the window at the view below, he noticed the flashing lights of a car alarm just before the sound reached his high-rise abode. Looking carefully, he could see the fleeing shadow dashing across the car park to another motor parked behind the bushes as a door opened below and a shape that obviously belonged to the car owner came fleeing after him. A wry smile formed on his lips as he remembered a couple of lads that weren't quite as successful as the rest of his classmates.

"Eggy and Gonch," he whispered as he prised some cheap corned beef from the tin onto the buttered bread, and started spreading it around. "Currently detained at Her Majesty's pleasure. They were fucking useless those two."

Shaking his head in amused disdain, he added tomato sauce before cutting and licking the knife clean before he sat back down with his sandwich and sought their faces on his photo board.

'There's big George as well,' he thought, mouth full of corned beef and onion. *'Runs a pub down near Oxford now. Haven't seen him since I last visited a couple of years ago. Nice place though. Banbury it was. Ride a cockhorse and all that. I might give him a ring actually and arrange a little holiday for myself, be the closest I get this year anyway.'*

Then his gaze alighted on the two faces he was searching for, the two clowns who could make him feel that he alone wasn't the class failure: Eggy and Gonch.

'Absolutely shite them two. The worst pair of thieves I've ever seen.' Even from a distance of five feet and while he was distracted by the tomato sauce dripping out of his sandwich, Matt could still see Gonch's bright red hair and could remember his face flushing with embarrassment whenever attention turned to him, particularly when crimes were being investigated. This was not a good thing for someone who had embarked on a career as a professional criminal.

'Mind you,' he thought, *'teaming up with Eggy wasn't the best idea either. It's bad enough that one of you stands out like a beacon to anyone but a blind man without the other team member stimulating any potential witnesses' sense of sound. Aye, great fun*

we had at school with Eggy and his Tourettes, probably fucked his earning potential though.'

Chuckling to himself Matt took the empty plate back to the kitchen part of his flat-cum-bedsit. The story he'd heard of Eggy and Gonch's last criminal enterprise had been that they'd decided to rob a sub post office but had disastrously mixed up their roles in the job. Leaving Gonch outside as lookout was bad enough as the locals had him spotted and the law informed within five minutes of their arrival, but they'd still have got away if Eggy hadn't spent vital minutes shouting 'bigtitsmanfuckus' and 'smellygashdortygob' at the old biddy behind the counter before telling her to give him the money. They'd been knocked down and locked up before they'd even got to their getaway car.

Buttoning his shirt, Matt smiled again, musing, "It's true there's always someone worse off than you."

Then he headed for the door, he was looking forward to a pint.

Win Some, Lose Some

Barney swallowed hard then opened the door to Pascoe's office.

"Yes, Mr Netherstone. What is it? Good news about our vigilante maybe?"

Pascoe had his feet on the desk and his chair tipped back. It was fair to say he looked relaxed, maybe now was a good time to do this after all.

"W-well, Sir," Barney began, "It's about this case. The truth is, Sir, I'm not convinced it's a local man as you seem to think. I've been speaking to some psychologist friends in London and—"

"Hold it *right there*," Pascoe butted in and sat bolt upright. "You've been discussing this case with people not directly involved in it?"

Barney wasn't expecting this and attempted to play for time as he quickly considered the ramifications of every possible reply.

"W-w-well... I sought a second opinion from some very qualified university friends and they—"

Pascoe had gone red in the face and looked ready to explode. "YOU *DO NOT* DISCUSS THIS CASE WITH ANYONE OUTSIDE OF THIS POLICE FORCE WITHOUT MY EXPRESS PERMISSION MR NETHERSTONE. DO I MAKE MYSELF CLEAR?"

Barney sat head down and cowed in the face of this withering blast from his boss and just nodded, then quietly whispered, "Yes, Sir."

"So, Netherstone. What did these friends of yours have to say, anyway? Have any of them ever done a real job?" he sneered. "Or have they just sat behind desks for years pontificating on getting their hands dirty?"

"W-w-well, Sir," Barney responded, unable to look Pascoe in the eye, "they were of the opinion that the vigilante fits the profile of someone in authority, maybe even a policeman... s-s-someone who maybe is disillusioned with the punishing of criminals these days."

"Oh, do they indeed?" Pascoe cut in again sarcastically. "And how many criminals have they punished in their academic careers then? Answer me that, Netherstone."

Ignoring his last comment, Barney tried gamely to press on with his original theory. "They also thought, Sir, that it may be someone who has suffered some kind of crime themselves that was probably never punished. Something violent or shocking..."

"Ridiculous, Netherstone. Absolutely *ridiculous*," Pascoe leaned in, almost hissing with anger. "Now listen to me; this is *not* a television detective show, there are *no* convenient butlers or wronged women here who will have committed these crimes. This is a rough town populated by rough men; one of them will have taken exception to the scum that surrounds him. Your job is simple, find the bastard and make an example of him. UNDERSTAND?"

Barney, realising he was beaten, mumbled, "Yes, Sir," and headed for the door.

Pascoe, watching him leave, just shook his head. *'Does this man not know what he's doing?'* he thought. *'A position of authority indeed, preposterous. If it was to get out that it was someone under this command then the fallout would be enormous, my career could be stalled indefinitely all on the whim of some bloody student down South.'*

Getting out Barney's file from his cabinet, Pascoe pulled out the probationary report he was meant to fill in weekly.

'I think I should start the official documentation of Mr Netherstone's incompetence, so there's a solid auditable trail should this thing blow up.'

Then, using a red pen, he started to fill in the report.

* * *

Barney had had enough for the day and was on the verge of heading home. Spotting Suzie he decided to seize the moment, reasoning that not much else could go wrong.

"Suzie, have you got a minute?"

She turned to face him, she looked different. He couldn't work out what it was. Different but still lovely.

"I was wondering if... if you fancied... g-going... going for a drink."

"Oh, Barney. I'd love to..." she started.

Barney's heart jumped, he knew his day would pick up eventually.

"Right, then," he said. "Shall we go into town?"

"But," she continued, wincing, "I'm already meeting someone. I'm sorry. We could do it at the weekend?"

'Bollocks, bollocks, *bollocks*. Made a tit of myself again.'

"Ehhm... I'll come back to you on that. You look nice anyway, I hope he appreciates it," Barney managed to reply, before bundling himself through the door and heading for the chip shop at the top of the road.

Suzie stood and watched him go; she looked forward to her fortnightly bingo sessions with her mam and sister, but would have gladly forgone it for a drink with Barney. He'd seen her made up for the first time and assumed she'd been going out with another bloke. The two of them were fucking tragic.

* * *

Vicki was knackered; it had been a long time since she'd done a full week's work and she was feeling it a bit. Getting in at half five and then doing a load of washing and ironing had just about drained her and she really couldn't be bothered to do anything else tonight. Having said that she did enjoy her job and the people she had met since starting it, particularly Vi and Gladys. It certainly beat sitting watching daytime television all day and the money would be handy once she'd finished her first month.

Putting the last load of ironed clothes into Nick's cupboard she smiled to herself; they were so excited today because Gladys's grandson, Robert, was visiting tonight and they were getting their tea from the chip shop. Vi had kept telling her how much she loved fish and chips and how it was her weekly treat. Bless.

Heading back down the stairs she hoped that Matt wouldn't come round tonight as she could do with a rest and quite fancied curling up on the settee and spending some time with Nick. Since his arrest she was determined to keep him on the straight and narrow.

'No way is he turning out like that wanker who spawned him,' she thought to herself. *'No way.'*

She'd just got her feet up when there was a knock at the door. *'Fucking sod's law,'* she thought. *'Oh, well. At least it's given me a reason to get up and close the kitchen window before it gets too cold in here.'*

The dark blob at the glass looked suspiciously Matt-shaped and her heart sank as she unlocked the door and pulled it open... all thoughts of closing the window and retaining heat forgotten.

"Alright, pet?" he entered the kitchen like an all-encompassing whirlwind, taking her in his arms and twirling her round. "How's my favourite checkout girl, then?"

Normally his smile and enthusiasm would have been infectious on Vicki and she would have been dancing round the room with him, but her tiredness had just left her bereft of energy and she couldn't be bothered to play tonight. Pushing him gently away from her she leaned towards the kettle and pushed the switch.

"Cup of tea?" the flatness of her voice was meant to convey to him that she was fucked and wouldn't mind a quiet night but, she realised too late, it had in fact left him under the impression he had done something wrong.

"What's the matter with *you*?" his voice too had now lost its cheery tone and he sounded concerned.

She smiled back at him, hoping to allay his fears a bit. After all, she was just tired and not pissed off with him. She stifled a fake yawn. "I'm just a bit tired tonight, pet. It's been a heavy week. Loads of overtime as well."

"Ah, well," he jumped in, his grin returning. "I've got just the thing for that... a curry and a couple of pints on me."   Then he lifted his arms like he'd won the FA Cup, ran into the living room and did a lap of honour.

Despite herself, Vicki grinned and followed him. "What are you doing, you plum?"

He didn't stop jogging with his imaginary cup above his head, just turned to her and said, "It's the victory dance. I had my disciplinary today and got away with it. I'm back in tomorrow and we need to celebrate."

Vicki considered it for a second and then shook her head slowly. "I can't, Matt. I'm knackered and we've got a big delivery tomorrow. It's my job to sort it all out and I need a rest tonight. There's Nick as well, he'll be back from his computer club in a minute and I don't really want him in on his own too much. Can't we leave it 'til the weekend?"

Matt had stopped running and was facing her now; this was the downside of having a bird with kids. Any other time and he would have just fucked off out and stopped ringing her but this was different. For the first time in his life he actually cared about how someone else felt; Vicki was special.

'It must be love', he shivered. *'Or presumably, anyway.'* He'd never felt like this before and he didn't really have anything to compare it to. The only thing he knew was that he didn't want to go back to his flat and not be with her.

"Come on, man, Vicki. We'll only be a couple of hours and you don't have to get ready or anything, it's only an Indians. Nick'll be alright as well, he's not a little boy anymore."

Vicki felt herself wavering a little. She was in love with Matt and reckoned that, even at this early stage of their relationship, she would happily spend the rest of her life with him. Not that she was telling him though, he'd run a mile. Fuck it; surely she was still young enough to go out at night and then go to work the next day wasn't she?

Sensing her indecision Matt moved in for the kill, "At the end of the day, pet – and don't take this the wrong way – I think you baby him a bit too much, he needs to be allowed to grow into a man. He's a good lad."

"You're right," she replied. "Make yourself a cup of tea while I put some make up on and give him a ring. I'll be as quick as I can."

Battered

As Nick approached the house he tutted under his breath. 'She's left the kitchen window open and the house is in fucking darkness, it's an open invitation for fuck's sake.'

Turning his key in the lock, he thought about how he'd like Matt to move in with them and absolve him of man of the house responsibilities. His mam reckoned he'd dealt with the mugger situation really well, keeping her safe at all times and not panicking the bloke into attacking them.

He reached for the light as he opened the door, not wanting to walk fully into the dark, just in case, but even this precaution didn't save him from the half pickaxe handle that was wrapped around his chin a second later leaving him spark out on the kitchen floor, legs half out of the door and on the garden path.

He was unceremoniously dragged into the kitchen from inside and then a masked face peeped out and looked up and down the street. Seeing nothing to alarm him, the burglar known as Ghostboy hauled his sports bag full of electrical items and money over his shoulder and headed for the lock up. Time for tea now, another day over.

* * *

Barney, having decided that his day had been officially shit, was now looking through the mouth-watering selection of pies, pasties, fishcakes and sausages at Taylor's Chippy while the queue went down. The packed interior was testament to the assumption that this was the best chip shop in the East End if not the city. Luckily, Barney was in no hurry and had used the waiting time to decide and, now the shop had emptied, he was ready.

"I'll have a chicken pie, a jumbo sausage, a fishcake and a portion of chips, please," he said jovially.

The big woman behind the counter gave him a smile and replied, "That's what I like... a man with an appetite."

"Ah, well," said Barney making an attempt at flirting. "You'd better give me a couple of buttered buns as well then."

She laughed and replied, "My kind of man, pet. My kind of man. I bet you like your sausage battered, eh?" and then busied herself with his order.

Barney wasn't fucking about tonight, he was getting a taxi straight home and eating this while it was hot, his mouth was dripping at the thought of it.

He remembered seeing a taxi office down the road and stuck his head out of the door to see if any cars were hanging about, when a huge man walked straight into him and bumped him out of the way before carrying on into the shop. Barney turned and stepped back in away from the door frantically patting his pockets in case he'd been done again. Feeling the lump of his wallet he sighed his relief, the man was just ignorant rather than criminal. Then, sensing rather than seeing the man look him up and down Barney raised his head; the man mountain was looking straight at him. He couldn't break the eye contact, it was almost hypnotic and he was almost grateful when the man spoke.

"Why did you check your pockets after I bumped you?" The man took a step towards him. "Are you calling me a fucking thief?"

Barney frantically fished in his pocket for his police ID while at the same time trying to remember his self-defence training at university; his hands were bouncing off keys and coins in his pockets.

The bloke was right in his face now and hissing at him "Because if I was a pickpocket and I got your wallet and you then got me nicked and decided to testify against me, then I'd be really pissed off. People who grass and then grass some more in court, well... they're fucking scum and they deserve to die. Know what I mean, copper?"

Special

Barney was shaken now and stopped looking for his ID. It was pointless, the bloke already knew and wasn't bothered in the slightest.

"Listen, I think you should know that—"

The man mountain just continued unabated, "Yeah, I think anyone who grasses should just be killed on the spot, me. Anyone who would be stupid enough to lose their wallet to a dipper and then cry about it to the judge, well, that's execution time for me that is."

With this he pushed his coat aside so that Barney could see the huge machete sticking out of his trousers. Barney was frozen to the spot and could feel his head swimming. The fear was making him shake and he felt nauseous, he had never been this scared in his life. This man was warning him he would be killed if he went to court about the pickpocket last week. He tried to speak but his voice simply wouldn't work.

"Eeh, leave him alone, man. It's not his fault he's a bit slow."

"Gladys's right, you big bully. He's only come for some chips, he's not hurting anybody."

Barney had heard these voices before and turned to see a couple of older women pointing at the big bloke who was just laughing and holding his hands out in mock defence.

The big woman from behind the counter was holding his order out so he took it and headed for the door. As he got there he took one look back at the man. He was smiling and holding a finger across his lips and then he made a slicing motion across his throat and nodded. Barney couldn't get out of there quick enough but didn't want to leave the relative safety of the chippy without checking there were taxis at the office. Satisfying himself that there were a couple free, he made to go.

"Honestly, Gladys. I'm writing to the council, me."

"Why, Vi?"

"That lad, man. It's not his fault he's the way he is but they

97

shouldn't let him loose in the community. He's gonna get hurt one of these days, it's all wrong."

*   *   *

Matt handed the coffee to Vicki who took it without a word. She was still fuming over what had happened to Nick and inside, she was scared that someone could come in and violate their home. She'd always been her baby's protector, always kissed away the dark when he was little and scared and now when he'd needed her she wasn't there. She'd been out with Matt; he'd persuaded her when she didn't really want to go anyway. Glaring at him as he looked away guiltily, she knew it was wrong feeling like this, knew it wasn't fair and that he was a nice bloke and knew that she was being a bit irrational... but she didn't care. Her little boy had a broken jaw and her house had been robbed; *someone* had to pay and the only person here was Matt, the bloke who'd taken her out tonight. Biting her lip to keep her thoughts to herself she started to drink her coffee.

Thoughts of Nick as a baby flashed into her mind like snapshots from a photo album. Her eyes moistened even as she smiled at some of them when he was small and cute. Her baby had been set upon trying to defend his home. The first tear fell onto her lap. They'd found him unconscious and covered in blood, slumped on the kitchen floor. He'd looked dead at first and Vicki had screamed and screamed until Matt checked his breathing and got an ambulance; only when the paramedic had re-assured her he was alive had she calmed down and now her mind was racing with pictures of him as a two-year-old in his little Newcastle United tops interspersing with the image of him beaten and broken on the kitchen floor. It was too much and the tears came flooding out, Vicki sobbed at the unfairness of it all and Matt put his arm around her.

She stood up and pushed him off. "Don't touch me. This is your fault."

Special

Even as the word spilled from her mouth with a bile that surprised her, she knew she was wrong but she just couldn't stop herself.

"You made me go out when I didn't want to, you bastard. And my Nick paid the price. This is your fault."

Matt held his arms out in surrender and tried to plead but Vicki didn't want to hear him, she knew he would talk sense and didn't want to hear that at the minute, she just wanted to lash out.

"Let him grow up, you said," she sneered, tears clouding her face. "Well is a broken jaw fucking grown up enough, Matt?"

Matt tried to cuddle her, "It's alright, Vicki. He'll be alright. You know I lo—"

She didn't let him finish the sentence, she couldn't. Throwing his arm off violently, she felt her voice rise and couldn't stop herself shouting at him.

"YOU NEED TO FUCKING LEARN ABOUT RESPONSIBILITY, MATT. HE'S MY FIRST PRIORITY, NOT YOU. I FAILED HIM BECAUSE I LISTENED TO YOU AND I WON'T DO IT AGAIN. JUST FUCK OFF AND LEAVE US ALONE."

"Vicki, don't do this. Please don't do this."

Vicki couldn't be stopped now, her eyes were blazing and she screamed at him again "I MEAN IT. JUST FUCK OFF AND DON'T BOTHER US AGAIN."

Matt wasn't used to being dumped and, not knowing how to take it, he just slunk off shaking his head. Vicki, not caring about the looks that were coming her way from everyone else just sat back down and continued sobbing.

TUESDAY

Only his fucking Mouth

"It's like she thinks I robbed her house and broke the lad's jaw myself. I fucking like the kid, she knows that."

"Women, man, Matt. You know what they're fucking like. She'll probably calm down in a couple of days, spur-of-the-moment and all that."

"You should have seen her though, Tonka. I thought steam was gonna start coming out of the top of her fucking head. She said we were finished an all, I think I fucking believe her as well, like. Fuck her anyway, the stupid cow, I can't be doing with fucking drama queens me. I'm probably best off on me own."

"Aye, I can see your point. At the end of the day it was only a broken jaw, we've all had worse when we were younger; it'll probably do him good in the long run. Was much nicked?"

"Just the DVD player, telly, video and a couple of shitey ornaments. Nowt with sentimental value and nowt that can't be replaced. Fucking right over the top that reaction, if you ask me."

Even as he was saying it Matt knew that he was wrong and that Vicki had reacted as you would expect someone to do when their son was assaulted and their house robbed. His frustration in their parting had manifested in moaning about her and saying stupid things that he instantly regretted; especially as he'd been spouting off to big gob Tonka and he knew it would be all around the warehouse by the end of the day. They couldn't really be finished, could they? He'd give it a couple of days before finding out for sure. Let her calm down a bit.

'I've never been in this situation before, it's normally me that does the finishing without a second thought, but if it's over with Vicki I'll be absolutely gutted.'

Tonka tapped him on the shoulder. "Break time's nearly up mate, we'd best get back; owld Latimer's keeping an eye on you, remember?"

Matt looked up from his thoughts and saw the boss sitting a couple of tables away smiling at him. It was a strange look; he didn't think he'd ever seen him smile before.

'Only his fucking mouth smiles, mind. Not his eyes, the prick's dead inside, I reckon. He should've been in the Thriller video. '

Walking out of the canteen, Matt turned to look back and see if Latimer was following them out but he was scribbling into his notebook.

I wonder when he came in,' he thought. *'He wasn't there when we started our break and I never heard him sit down. Fuck, I wonder how much he heard? He'll make my life a misery if he knows I've been dumped.'*

His heart, which he'd thought had been ripped out of his chest when Vicki binned him, suddenly re-appeared and sunk as far down his body as it was possible to go at the thought of this and he gloomily made his way back to work.

Memories

'So the mighty, all-knowing and untouchable Matthew Blake has just had his heart broken, has he? He might think it hurts now, but we know how to twist the knife and then rub salt all over the wound.

'What would really, really upset him, Johnny? What would maybe even make him think it wasn't worth staying around here anymore? What would drive him to despair so he just went, left his job and wasn't around to make your life hard anymore? Obvious, really: if the woman he loved started seeing the man he hated most in the world... his favourite boss. Ha-Ha!

'Let's face it... she's a bit of a slag: single mother, her son's a troublemaker who's known to the police and mixed up in drugs. She'd be grateful for a moral, upstanding citizen like you to even take an interest in a fucking trollop like her. She'd probably welcome the discipline you'd bring to her son as well, give him a bit of moral guidance and direction. Yes, I think her gratitude would be such that she'd probably do anything you wanted.

'Mind you, it's best not to be too hard on her; we all do stupid things when we're young. She made a mistake and has paid for it with the hardships of bringing the boy up alone. Predictable consequences to that obviously; running wild with a gang and taking drugs, but nothing a firm stand couldn't bring into line. She probably sponged off the state for years as well, milking the taxes from decent, law abiding people like yourself, but I've heard Blake say she's working now, so she's obviously got some morals and is trying to put things right. No, you can't fault her for trying. She obviously just needs some help to take the next step and who better to help her than John Latimer; role model for the community and all round good egg.'

Latimer got another cup of coffee and took it downstairs to his office. Sitting back in his chair he clicked the closed circuit television system onto multi-screen so he could watch all aspects of the warehouse operation at the same time and then tuned his walkie-talkie into the general channel frequency so he could hear all the instructions and requests being made. Then, putting his feet up on his desk, he drifted back into the half formed idea in his head.

'Yes, we all make mistakes when we're young, particularly

*with members of the opposite sex. It's difficult when you know
nothing about them, so you have to play it by ear and learn from
your elders. That's where you were at a disadvantage; not having a father to advise you and having to listen to your surrogate
elder brother... good for nothing chancer that he was. Still, he
learned his lesson.'*

Smiling to himself he remembered his first ever date when he
was sixteen-years-old.

*'Doreen Walkinshaw... her dad owned the local grocers shop
and I used to see her on a Saturday when I went for the messages
for Mrs Latimer. She was such a pretty little thing and had gone
out with a couple of lads already so I was a bit in awe of her,
really. I was shocked when she came up that day and asked if I
wanted to go to the pictures with her that night. I quickly stammered out a yes and ran all the way home.'*

Getting out of his chair and walking round the room Latimer
fractionally straightened the motivational picture on his wall and
stepped back to look at it. It was one of those 'together we can
do anything' jobs with a shot of a flock of cranes or something.
Looking at the picture made him frown as he recalled the cinema
trip in vivid detail.

*'The Hitchcock film, The Birds, it was meant to be a great
picture but I never really watched it. I spent all my time looking
at Doreen and worrying about whether to put my arm round her
and when to make a move to kiss her. Bloody Clive had told me
all about it though.*

*"'Buy her loads of sweets and pay her in," he'd said, "then at
a scary bit, put your arm round her. When she cuddles into you
blow in her ear a little bit and she'll melt. You can kiss her 'til to
your heart's content then. Honest, Johnny, I promise you that's
how it works with girls."*

*'So that's what I did. I took half my savings from their special
hiding place and blew it on taking her to the pictures and buying a*

load of sweets. Then, after waiting and worrying for what seemed like hours, the birds in the film attacked and she jumped and gave a little squeal. Thinking it was now or never I put my arm around her and she smiled at me and snuggled up, it was brilliant. Having a quick glance around the cinema I could see everyone else doing the same; hundreds of female heads resting on hundreds of young men's arms and it made me feel normal, like I belonged. For the next ten minutes I was content and all was right in my world, I blew softly into her ear and she shivered gently, turning to me and smiling sweetly while I surreptitiously licked my lips in preparation for my first ever kiss.'

Latimer could see a Daddy longlegs that had invaded the sanctity of his office. He moved towards it as it sunned itself on the windowsill. Cupping it in his hands he could feel the frantic wing beats bouncing off his fingers as it tried to break free from this man-made prison.

'Then, as I was mentally praising Clive and thinking how we'd obviously put the incident with his sister behind us for him to help me out like this, Doreen jumped up in the middle of the auditorium and screamed.

"GET YOUR HANDS OFF ME, JOHN LATIMER. I'M NOT THAT KIND OF GIRL."

The whole cinema stared at me as she stormed out; I could hear them laughing and, even in the dark, I'm sure they could see me blushing. I knew I would be teased mercilessly at school because she'd even told them all my name. I couldn't understand it though; it was all going so well, just as Clive said it would.'

The Daddy longlegs had stopped struggling now and lay spent on Latimer's opened palm, he moved his other hand over it and held it there motionless.

'I gave it five minutes and went outside to see if she was still there and to find out what was wrong and that's when I realised...'

104

Latimer slowly used two fingers on his free hand to grip a wing of the insect and tugged.

'She was with Clive, eating the sweets I'd paid for and laughing. When they saw me he made a big show of kissing her and then they walked towards me.'

Pulling off the other wing, Latimer broke out of his nostalgic trance and looked down at the wriggling insect. The veins in his temples throbbed as he dropped it onto the floor and then brought the sole of his shoe down on it hard.

"Freak," they shouted at me.

'Clive told me he would make my life a misery if I ever looked at his sister or Doreen, who it turned out was his girlfriend, again and that I should consider myself paid back and leave it at that.

'That pair of fucking bullies? Even though Clive lived in the same house he didn't know us very well, did he, Johnny?'

Picking up the phone and smiling wryly at a long forgotten some long-forgotten memory, Latimer spoke into the receiver "Hello, hygiene, there's some kind of squashed insect on my carpet that I want cleaned up right away."

Man Management

Rob Lawrence warily entered the house at Axel's request. Stepping over the assorted children's toys he found a chair in the corner of the living room that seemed untouched by sticky toddler hands.

Falcus looked him up and down on his way to the kitchen; young Rob was one of his best money getters and, as he was still young, he didn't yet have the nous to realise he should be making more money. Falcus knew that the days of the Ghostboy accepting only twenty-five percent of what he stole wouldn't last much longer and he had called Rob to his house to ensure that he maximised his earnings from him while he still could.

"Cup of tea, son?" he called into the living room.

"Aye, Mr Falcus" Rob replied.

"Call us Axel, son. Call us Axel."

"Ehm... aye, Axel. One sugar please."

Rob scanned the room, his trained housebreaker's eye appraising the profit in doing this house. He could make a few quid in here and no mistake.

'I'd have to be the stupidest fucker in Byker to do that, though. He'd find me and kill me in about ten minutes.'

Just then Falcus's youngest daughter walked in, wearing only a g-string and a skimpy crop top.

"Oh," she exclaimed in mock surprise. "I didn't realise we had visitors."

Making a token effort to pick up some child's toys and exhibiting everything she had in the process, she smiled back at Rob and winked.

"When will you be sixteen then, Rob?"

Rob gulped and tried to ignore the fast hardening bulge in the crotch of his jeans as Axel Falcus walked back into the living room.

"GET BACK UP THEM STAIRS AND PUT SOME FUCKING CLOTHES ON, YOU FILTHY BITCH."

'Fucking hell,' thought Rob. *'The house isn't the only Falcus possession I won't be screwing.'*

Falcus's gaze turned from his daughter's rapidly disappearing arse back to Rob as he put the cups on the coffee table.

"Do you like our Lindsey then, Rob?" he asked.

"Ehhm, aye. She's alright, Axel," Rob gulped.

"That's, Mr Falcus, son," he said quietly as he walked to the dresser at the far end of the room. He paused. "So... are you thinking about fucking her now, are you?" he demanded, his back still to Rob.

"I... I don't really know her, Mr Falcus. I've only met her once." Rob didn't like the way this was going and the change in Falcus's tone.

Falcus straightened up and suddenly turned. The sun shone in through the window and for a second Rob thought he saw an evil glint in his eye. Then he realised it was from the small axe that he had in his hand and he flinched as the main man in this part of town jumped towards him screaming.

"YOU WANT TO FUCK MY DAUGHTER, DO YOU, SON?"

Grabbing him by the throat, he held the axe at Rob's crotch.

"MAYBE I'LL JUST USE *MY* CHOPPER TO REMOVE *YOURS*. YOU COULDN'T FUCK HER THEN, COULD YOU? WHAT DO YOU THINK OF THAT, YOU WIDE LITTLE CUNT?"

Rob was squirming, the fear overtaking him, holding him to the chair. The damp patch on his jeans betraying his state of mind as he jabbered away trying to talk Falcus out of ending his life.

"Really, Mr Falcus. I've got nee intention. I've ownly met her once. Honest... it never crossed me mind... please, Mr Falcus, man. Divvent... please."

He was crying now and had lost all façade of the streetwise young crook.

Falcus let him go and straightened up. That was just the softener he needed. The boy would do as he was told now and increase the jobs without a murmur. It was worth the fifty quid he'd had to give to Lindsey to parade herself; still she normally did it for nothing so it was no skin off her nose.

"Drink your tea, son... and let's talk business."

Best Served Cold

Latimer was in his back garden. The sun was shining and he was performing a few mundane tasks before going for his evening shift at the station. He had a special job to do tonight, once he was in his official capacity, but that could wait a couple of hours while he sorted his garden out.

Thinking back to earlier, the episode with Clive and Doreen had upset him a little but he'd had a good chat with his dad when he'd got in from work and that had reminded him of their old maxim: revenge is a dish best served cold.

'Oh, yes,' he thought. 'They'd got theirs alright.'

The Latimers had thought it strange when their normally athletic eldest son had started crying off school with headaches and slothfulness. His teachers had remarked to them that he'd seemed almost slow and backward in his lessons and they'd been at pains to find out why. At first they tried to 'beat it out of him', as it was assumed he was swinging the lead, but this hadn't worked. He continued his slide down the sets at school until he ended on the bottom rung of the ladder with no prospect of the school even letting him take exams and his life being consigned to a series of manual jobs for poor pay.

What they all didn't know, least of all Clive, was that young John, who since the cinema incident had withdrawn into himself but had continued his excellent studies to keep everyone from looking to closely at him, had been spiking Clive's night-time glass of squash, that was kept beside his bed and drained by first light, with gin. The Latimers never noticed that their drinks cabinet was being slowly depleted and were at a loss to explain their son's deterioration.

He had slowly built up Clive's dependence on what John's

father had often referred to as 'the demon drink' with the cheap bottles he started acquiring with his savings when it was too dangerous to use any more of the family bottle. At first, Clive was just suffering from hangovers at school and was unable to work and then progressed to subconsciously craving alcohol so that eventually John was virtually pouring a full glass of gin at night-time and throwing the squash away.

Then, as Clive was preparing to leave school, John abruptly withdrew the supply, leaving him in an agitated state and unable to function which resulted in him being fired from jobs and spending great portions of time living off the state. He'd soon developed his own full-blown drink problem and ended up in the gutter. As the years went by John made sure he had nothing to do with him – save the cases of gin he'd regularly leave anonymously at his bedsit – until one day about ten years ago when he was crossing the road to work. John could see a figure asleep against a shop window, big beard, Oxfam coat, that type of thing, and had glanced as he walked past. The voice had stopped him dead in his tracks.

"John. *John,* is that you? Help me," it whispered.

John had looked back and recognised some old forgotten face. Stepping back to the tramp, he'd leaned in and stared him straight in the eye.

"Is that you, Clive?" he'd asked.

The tramp had nodded, tears rolling down his face.

John had smiled at him; pulled his wallet out of his pocket and removed five twenty pound notes then, holding them at Clive's face, he'd asked, "Remember that day at the pictures with Doreen? Well, I put you here freak"

Putting them back in his pocket he'd walked away without a second glance. Life was good.

Taking the boiling kettle from the holder, John went back into the garden and approached the patio. Lifting a slab he could see all of the ants scurrying around, thousands of them. Pouring the water onto them and watching them boil and scald he fancied he could hear them scream and he smiled. It reminded him of how he'd gotten Doreen back.

That Ghostboy Twat

Vicki was on the sofa staring at the space where the telly used to be. Drawing on her last tab was helping but she was still a bag of nerves. Nick was still in hospital; kept in for observation and groggy from the effects of the pain-killing drugs combined with the last vestiges of shock from his beating. As soon as she'd got in from work she'd made sure that all the doors were locked and the windows closed and had just patrolled the house constantly. Every noise from outside had her up at the window staring out.

'It was that Ghostboy twat,' she kept thinking. *'I know it was that little bastard.'*

Her mind wouldn't let her contemplate the wider issues of finding and hurting him however; she knew she could do nothing about it. The impotence that all the tough men on the estate must feel when confronted with the reality of being burgled by that twat was threatening to overwhelm her now.

'He works for Falcus.' The words just kept echoing through her brain as the tears dripped from her eyes.

'Even if I knew who he was I wouldn't be able to do anything. I daren't ask Matt as he'd probably have a go for me but he could end up dead. That's if I ever see him again, anyway.'

The sheer frustration of her situation coupled with the feeling that she'd probably driven Matt away for good caused her such pain that she had to sit down as big tears flowed unhindered down her face. Burying her head in her hands she sobbed uncontrollably, her body heaving.

Then there was a knock at the door and she rushed to it hoping it was Matt with a bunch of flowers.

"Miss Hughes?"

It was that arsey copper from the other night, probably here about the break-in.

"Yes. Come in, officer."

He smiled at her but it wasn't a nice smile; not sympathetic or anything, more of a leer really.

"Do you want a cup of tea or anything?" Nice to be nice anyway.

"That would be lovely Miss Hughes," he replied. Then, "I'm here to give you the formal caution for your son following the incident with him last week."

So they still hadn't been round about the break-in, obviously didn't give a fuck and just wanted to chase a criminal they could easily catch without any effort. Suddenly she felt very alone and vulnerable; a single mother on this estate. The tears started to moisten her eyes again. Where the *fuck* was Matt when she really needed him?

The copper had his arm round her now, it felt so nice, so comforting that she couldn't hold back the sobs that emanated from deep in her chest.

"Now, now, Miss Hughes, don't worry. He's not in any more trouble."

"It-it's not that, off-officer," she gasped out between wracking sobs. "It's the break-in. It's left me so shook up."

His eyes flared and his demeanour changed. He stood up straight and moving to the sofa he sat her down and then headed for the kettle.

"I'll make the tea, Miss Hughes, and you can tell me all about it."

'Maybe he's not so bad after all,' she thought as he gently probed her about the break-in, *'and he's taking an awful lot of notes.'*

WEDNESDAY

Small Victories (2)

John Latimer had a smile on his face. A big smile. The type of smile that said, *'I had your girlfriend last night, Mr Blake, and she bloody loved it.'*

He had the walk on as well, light on his feet, just floating over the floor, it screamed out, *'I haven't emptied my scrotum for twenty years but your lass took it all last night and I feel a stone lighter.'*

In reality, she'd simply cried on his shoulder for a while and he'd stroked her head, but Blake wasn't to know that. The constant smiling was becoming an effort, though. Moving into the canteen he noted, with a little shiver of pleasure, that Blake had his reprobate friends in attendance. That was good, humiliation only worked if it was public.

"Good morning, gentlemen," he ventured in their direction.

They all nodded and grunted at him with the exception of Blake who sullenly and under silent protest just looked at him. None of them quite brave enough to simply ignore him.

"Isn't it a good morning?" he continued, moving to within a couple of steps of their table.

"What's good about it, we fucking work here don't we?" Blake mumbled, more to himself than Latimer.

His workmates, caught between the desire to laugh at this perceived insult to Latimer and the desire to avoid his wrath just sneered and snorted, most of them fixing their eyes on the table in front of them.

* * *

"Well," Latimer continued unabashed, "It's a good morning for me, it always is after the night before... if you know what I mean."

With that he winked at them and headed to the service counter for a bacon roll and a coffee and listened to the buzz of whispered conversation on the table while his back was turned.

"That bastard got a shag last night."

"Fuck off! Who'd shag that owld twat?"

"I'm telling you... look at him, man. He's like the fucking Cheshire Cat."

"Keep it down, he'll hear you. Anyway, doing some pensioner from behind for fifty quid and a new set of teeth doesn't qualify as a proper shag in my book."

"Matt man, you're just jealous cos he's getting some and you're not."

"Fuck off, Tonka. I know you're getting nowt as well. Your lass told us when she was picking her knickers up off my floor last week."

"Hadaway and shite man, ye daftie. Say nowt, he's coming back."

Latimer sauntered towards them again and brandished his bacon roll at them saying, "Got to keep your strength up lads, eh?"

"On the job last night then, boss? Anyone we know, eh? Not that I know many owld dears down the bingo club, like. Ha-ha."

As he walked past them to an empty table Latimer smiled, giving them all the thumbs up, and then looking at Matt, he said, "Someone *he* knows very well. Mind you, so do *I* now."

He could hear the whispers again as he turned his back to them and sat at his table. Blake's voice could be heard most clearly saying, "No chance, man. Get fucked."

Looking back around at them he looked straight at Blake and said, "No need to worry about young Nick Hughes, Mr Blake. His little incident has been dealt with now." And he gave him a big theatrical wink as the table exploded with mirth. Affecting non-chalance he turned back to his roll, pausing just long enough to gauge Blake's reaction. He wasn't disappointed. With his face a dark shade of beetroot and his fists clenching and unclenching Blake strode out of the room, slamming the door behind him.

Anyone not observing the exchange and not knowing the history between the two men would have been surprised to hear, in between bites of his roll and gulps of his coffee, the barely audible chant of, "One – nil, one – nil" emanating from Latimer's lips. The smile, however, had gone.

* * *

A mile away Barney was also feeling quite mirthless while he sat at his desk staring at the pile of statements stacked next to the many bags of various items that comprised the entire haul of evidence in the vigilante case. Despite the volume there wasn't actually a great deal to go on. Looking across at his so-called incident board, he gently tugged at his hair in an effort to stimulate his brain into action.

'There's something I'm missing here. What the bloody hell is it?'

The pile of statements seemed to mock him; he knew them all word for word. He could tell you that the majority of people questioned seemed to think that Falcus was behind the beatings of Collins and Donnelly. This was obvious by the way they were at pains to stress that they didn't think that. Suzie had pointed out that the criminals in question actually worked for Falcus, as did the two shoplifters who were beaten in the car park.

The board had a map that was ringed with the three incidents, all of them in Byker.

'No real geographical or physical pattern, just the fact that they were local criminals working their own patch. That would suggest a local man but that's all.'

Looking through the plastic wrapping that enclosed them, he stared at the various business cards that had so far been collected from each victim.

'All exactly the same; so where were they printed? If he's done them at home, where did he get the card from?'

Holding one up to the light, Barney squinted as the plastic reflected the glare. The card was obviously good quality, thickly cut and dense between the fingers. Staring at it for a second longer, he suddenly slapped his forehead.

'It's got a watermark. It's got a bloody watermark. You dolt, Netherstone.'

This was, without doubt, a solid lead. Lifting up his telephone receiver he quickly punched in a number on the keypad.

"Put me through to Forensics at Market Street."

The Finer Points of Etiquette

Matt lurched forward as the bus hit a pothole then righted itself. The quarter bottle of whisky in his pocket clinked against the seat as he attempted to straighten up, leading an older woman alongside him to tut in his direction.

He knew he looked a bit shit. He hadn't had a wash since leaving work and had just got straight on the drink before deciding he was going into town. Fuck it though, he'd had a hard day and he was stressed out. It was fair to say he was usually quite a laid back bloke, but that shite Latimer had come out with today had surprised him. He'd even been booting lockers in the bogs and threatening to kill the twat this afternoon... not like him at all.

'Fucking driver's in a hurry, must be late for his tea or

something. His lass probably nags him to death if he's late. Fucking women. This mardy cow next to us is the same I bet; coming over all holier than thou cos I'm having a fucking drink. What's it got to do with her? She's probably single, left on the shelf and all that, full of bitterness and taking it out on a hard-working bloke who happens to want a drink tonight after some very bad news.'

Shaking his head he reached into his pocket and undid the screw top on the bottle, noting uncomfortably that there wasn't a lot left, he lifted it to his lips slowly, checking from the corner of his eye that she was watching him. Taking a long swig, he smacked his lips exaggeratedly and then quickly turned his head to the window so she wouldn't see him wince when the firewater hit his chest.

'Latimer shagging Vicki? That cannit be fucking right in a million years. I know she's not a slapper; fuckinell it took me weeks to get into her knickers and that horrible owld prick reckons he did it in a couple of hours. Bollocks did he. I wonder if she knew he was my boss or if she just knows him as a copper? Fuck it, either way she still wouldn't do him... or would she? She was really pissed off with me about Nick getting a hiding and, if she knew that he was the bloke who tried to sack me, well, she might think it's worth opening her legs to the twat just to get back at me. They'd be some pretty serious mind games if that's what she did, though.'

Forgetting about the woman opposite for a minute, Matt took another hefty slurp from the bottle before catching the evil looks being thrown his way.

'Fucking birds, man. Think they can control you. She thinks I'm an alcoholic, does she? Well, maybe I'll play the part for her. Then she can tell all her friends how she's always right and it might just make the sour faced owld boot happy for once.'

"HOO, DRIVER. IS YA TEA READY OR HAVE YOU JUST GOT TO GET TO THE TOILET OR SOMETHING? HA-HA."

'She's tutting again... good. She'll be happy now she's outraged.'

117

Taking another swig, Matt reflected that it didn't really take a lot to make people happy, just let them think they were right and that was them content.

'Mind you,' he thought, finishing the bottle off, 'I don't even need that. A quarter bottle of cheap booze and I'm happy.'

The effects of the whisky and no tea were hitting him now and he was enjoying the fuzziness. The woman opposite had paled into insignificance as his thoughts turned to Vicki.

'I am gutted she's finished with me. I really want her back. Even if she's shagged Latimer, though? Well, I'd have to discuss that with her, but I really miss her. It was the bastard who robbed the house that's caused this. It'll be that Ghostboy twat. I know who he is an all, everyone does. Little fucking prick thinks he's untouchable cos he's backed by Falcus. He'd better keep out my way. The arsehole's ruined my fucking life.'

"Ruined my fucking life!"

To Matt's surprise he realised that he'd actually said that out loud and that he could feel tears on his cheek. He felt a hand on his shoulder; it was the tutting woman, she looked down at him kindly as she was getting off the bus. "You won't find the answer in the bottom of a bottle, son. Good luck with whatever it is, anyway."

Matt, slightly humbled and feeling ashamed of himself, watched her get off and thought back to the Ghostboy; it was all his fault. The adrenalin raced through his body as he visualised making the prick take everything back to everybody on the estate and then smashing his head to a pulp in front of them all.

"Aye, pet," he said in a low growl to no one in particular, "It's not me that needs luck, though; it's that Ghostboy cunt, he's fucking well *claimed* he is."

* * *

Jimmy was starting to panic; twenty past he was meant to finish and it was twenty-five past now. Fucking Bucky was always late, the prick. He wasn't even on shift today, this was fucking overtime.

'Not tonight,' he thought. 'Please not tonight.'

By a Herculean effort he had managed to get Falcus's money together and could pay him off for this month, thus avoiding any chance of being pinned to a dartboard again. Now though, he was risking being late because of this wanker and Falcus would enjoy slapping him for that and probably increase the debt.

"Interest he'd call it, the fat, greasy cunt," he muttered to himself.

Drawing heavily on his super strength tab he looked hopefully up the empty road at where Bucky's ambling, laid back form should be and then started to work out exactly how long he had.

"Right, he's expecting me in The Hare at twenty to. It takes ten minutes to walk there meaning, as I've got the cash on me, I need to leave at half-past latest."

Scanning his watch again he mentally pleaded for Bucky to appear. His watch, never one to appreciate things like compassion, simply read twenty-seven minutes past.

Fuck it,' thought Jimmy, *'my shift's over, I've radioed them useless twats at base twice now. I'm going.'*

With one last look up the road – empty save for the sweet wrappers – and a touch of the money in his pocket, Jimmy sighed. He ditched his tab, threw his bag on his shoulder and stepped off the kerb to cross the road.

"HOO, YE FUCKER. WHERE DO YOU THINK YOU'RE GANNIN?"

* * *

Matt couldn't believe it; the driver was deserting the bus. He was just leaving them at the bottom of Shields Road with no relief driver.

'This fucking country,' he thought. *'There's no such thing as*

customer service, really. Everyone just pays lip service to it with their call centres and silky-voiced operators reading from scripts, but they don't give a fuck once they've got your money.'

"HOW AM I MEANT TO GET INTO TOWN BY SITTING ON A BUS THAT'S NOT FUCKING MOVING?"

It occurred to Matt, even through his drunken state, that the driver was looking agitated and anxious but that was no excuse for poor standards. He looked torn between coming back to the bus to talk to Matt or just walking straight off. Matt wasn't giving him the choice. Swinging off the bus door he headed shakily towards the unhappy-looking driver.

"I've paid a quid to get into town, not to sit here like a lemon at the mercy of every passing charva. Where the fuck are you going?"

The driver seemed to pause for a second before looking at his watch and cringing. Then, he straightened his back, moved his head towards Matt's and stared at him eyeball-to-eyeball before replying.

"My shift's finished, son, and I'm going home. I've got things to do and the relief driver's on his way so you don't need to fret. Now, I don't appreciate being sworn and shouted at but I don't have time to debate the finer points of etiquette with someone who necks whisky for fun on public transport. So, if you'll take your seat back on the bus the other driver will be here any minute."

Matt wasn't having that, he could appreciate the bloke's shift being finished, he was that way inclined himself and didn't hang about a second longer than he had to once the working day was over, but, for the cheeky get to imply he had some sort of drink problem... well, that wasn't on.

Grabbing the bloke's shoulder as he started to walk away Matt growled. "Hold on a second, bonny lad. Who you calling a fucking alcky?"

Something seemed to have snapped in the driver. Whatever problem was agitating him had gone past the point of no return and he swung round grabbing Matt by the throat.

Special

"DON'T EVER TOUCH ME, YOU PRICK. I'VE HAD ENOUGH OF PRICKS LIKE YOU PUSHING ME AROUND. I'M SICK OF IT. DON'T EVER FUCKING TOUCH ME, SON. UNDERSTAND?"

Matt sobered up swiftly as he was pushed back hard against the wall. The thump of cold brick against his spine was the equivalent of a gallon of strong black coffee and he mumbled his apologies as the driver sprinted off looking at his watch again.

Taking his seat back on the bus he noticed the other driver was in position and ready to go. Fuck it, he was buying some drinking powder in town as well, make a session of it.

Fuck them all.

Six Hundred Seconds

Jimmy was sweating and feeling sick as he rounded the corner of Raby Street and approached the Hare and Hounds.

'Ten minutes late, fuck! That Bucky is a useless bastard, the thing with the drunk wouldn't have happened if that twat had been on time. He's getting it tomorrow.'

Getting his breath back, he paused before entering the bar. It didn't sound like there was much noise in there... hopefully it meant there wouldn't be many people to see his public humiliation; and it *would* be public, Falcus liked to extract his pound of flesh from late payers, even if it was only by ten minutes.

'How did it come to this? Forty-eight-years-old and I've got a shit life. When I was eighteen it was great; decent pay, loads of birds, holidays to Blackpool and Ayr. Now I live in a tip of a council house with a wife who barely speaks to me – not that she

*has her mouth empty long enough to speak, the fat cow – kids
that embarrass and appal me, no money cos I'm the only one that
works and no break at all from the routine. Even Newcastle are
shit these days; fucking useless cockney prick in charge.'*

Sighing, he put his hand on his right leg to stop it trembling
then took a deep breath.

'Best get it over with,' he thought, then he entered the bar trying to look as subservient as possible.

The cunt wasn't there. *He wasn't fucking there.*

Shaking with a mixture of happiness and rage at his situation,
he approached the bar.

"Has Falcus been in, Marion?"

"Nah Jim, he rang about half an hour ago though to tell you
he's been unavoidably detained and to leave the cash behind the
bar in an envelope. He says he'll get it later. Do you want a drink?"

'Do I,' thought Jim. *'Fucking right I do.'*

* * *

Rob Lawrence knew he'd had a crap upbringing. He wasn't
stupid like people thought he was either, despite not going to school
since he was thirteen-years-old. He knew, for instance, that a five
pound bet on a five to two shot would give you twelve pound fifty,
plus your stake back. He knew that screaming about your human
rights while under arrest would usually get you out of the nick fairly
quickly or at worse, a telling off and a slapped wrist. He knew that
working forty to fifty hours a week for shit money was a lot harder
than burgling houses, particularly ones he could be in and out of
in ten minutes. And... he knew for an *absolute fact* that even if he
wanted to – which he didn't – he couldn't now cross the mighty
Falcus and stop working for him or he'd be on the end of a savage
beating, maybe even death.

He knew as well that his granny worried about him; she told

him all the time so it was an easy one to work out. He often went to hers for food as there was usually no one about in his house; his dad was still inside and his mam, well, if she wasn't 'entertaining' then she was in the boozer spending her commission on her previous night's 'work'.

He loved going to his granny's house though; the heating was always on, it was always clean, she loved seeing him and made a big fuss of him which felt good and, above all, she always had a fridge groaning with food as she worked at Iceland and got a big discount. Walking along the top road back into the estate, he patted his stomach contentedly; it was class going to granny's, it was even worth listening to her going on about him going back to school or learning a trade.

"No trades about now, Gran," he'd said through a mouthful of Alabama Mud pie.

"You need an education though, son," she'd replied, "or you'll end up with nowt and working in a dead-end job. No prospects, nothing. Look at me and Vi; still working at our age when we should be putting our feet up."

Rob had thought on this and quietly decided that his granny was past it and not really in touch with modern life. He didn't need a job at all, the Social would happily give him money for the rest of his life, give him a house, pay his rent and throw money at him for all the kids he would knock out via whichever fat slapper he got caught by first; add that to the money he would be making himself by screwing houses and he was in easy street. Fuck getting up at six o'clock every morning to get a bus in the rain to a grimy horrible shithole where the bosses treated you like a slave; he'd heard enough about that from his granddad, God rest his soul; thirty years down the pit, man and boy, then that horrible politician bird had taken over the country and they were all out of work... just like *that*. She made sure the southern bastards were alright but hadn't given a fuck about people like granddad, on the scrapheap in his fifties and he couldn't get work anywhere. His dad had told him that's what killed granddad in the end. Shame at being unable to support the family and having to send his wife out to work. Rob hoped that politician bitch died in pain, the same way granddad did out in the corridor of the hospital. His dad had told him that's why he never bothered working; they just got rid of you in the end when you were knackered and old and gave you fuck all. His granny still had to work now at the age of sixty cos her pension wasn't worth a light. Rob read the papers as well; he knew that the posh bastards in suits ripped pensions off left, right and centre leaving nowt for the ordinary people. Nah... fuck working, that's a mugs game.

He didn't say any of this to his granny, though. After all, she had just fed and pumped endless cups of tea into him, so he kept his mouth shut. It was only now as he wandered home through the estate that he wondered about how different his life was from granddad's at his age.

'That poor old bastard would have been underground now choking on coal dust for about twenty pence a day.'

Shivering slightly at the thought, he scraped his brand new trainers against a kerb to make them look a bit more dated; new ones looked shit so you had to scratch them up a bit or everyone took the piss and you looked shan. Then, looking up from his trainers he noticed it; the previously empty house at the end had curtains up and an upstairs window was open. The music blasting out of the house suggested someone was in at present, but that wasn't a problem to Rob, he was a very patient boy.

'New neighbours, eh? Only polite to say hello,' he thought as he turned to head for home.

Job Done

The house had indeed stood empty for quite some time; the previous occupants had been drug dealers. Using their three toddlers' pushchairs as cover they had moved around the estate making deliveries all day. It had been the perfect front as, to a neutral observer, they were simply concerned parents who made sure that their children got enough fresh air and exercise. In reality, the children's father, petty criminal Spugger Samuels, was concerned only with feeding his own habit; a habit he had generously shared with his sixteen-year-old girlfriend before getting her pregnant three times in as many years. The debts this had brought them had forced them to start dealing just to prevent physical harm occurring in lieu of payments and, as Spugger would tell you himself, "I'm the only person that matters to me."

The couple had for a while made a profit from their narcotic activities, keeping themselves in smack and making enough to buy some more of life's essentials such as the wide screen television, the dodgy sky box and dish, snide DVDs and, of course, the obligatory sovereign rings.

Spugger himself had started to live the high life as befitted a man of his social standing; he would drink chasers with his pints and Stella instead of Carling, have pie and chips at closing time instead of one or the other and buy his clothes from shops rather than the pub. The local slappers and tarts benefited from his generosity on more than one occasion also. Well... a man has needs, doesn't he? And Spugger would never deny himself.

Unfortunately for him and his not-too-bright partner in crime, a few people noticed this upturn in fortune and change in lifestyle. One of those people was Falcus who, as he would tell all and sundry in The Hare, did not like the idea of smackheads pumping shite into the veins of his grandchildren. Privately, he would concede to himself that it was just the fact he wasn't making any profit from it that rankled; a fact that would one day be rectified. One day when the hapless Samuels family were out on their rounds, the house was screwed and they lost the lot, including their stash, which they hadn't yet paid for. On top of this, there was a delegation from the police and Social Services waiting for them who promptly took their kids away as it turned out that due to mummy's little habit they had been born heroin addicts also and just wouldn't go to sleep at nights if mummy didn't give them a little milk/smack mixture.

This wasn't what drove them away from the estate though, they figured they could make the money back and weren't that bothered about the kids anyway. What got rid of them was the reception committee formed by local residents, arranged by Falcus, obviously. They'd been informed that, as well as being a dealer, Spugger was also part of a child porn ring and had been drugging his kids before making videos with them.

As with all of these things, it only took a couple of hours for a small whispering campaign to snowball into a hysterical mob of tabloid fodder. Some of the vengeful parents had separate agendas, as they knew that Spugger had in fact, over the last couple of months, shagged their teenage daughters. They saw their chance for revenge, declaring this as proof of his paedophilic tendencies and, hinting that he was also a police informer, they dealt with him appropriately. As is also usual with all of these things, the law were a couple of steps behind events at all times and when they finally caught up and came to interview the unfortunate Spugger in hospital he wouldn't say anything. He couldn't with no tongue. His girlfriend had fled, never to be seen again, and the local housing officer rubbed his hands with glee; another problem family relocated off his patch. *Job done.*

Special

Go call the Vigilante

Rob approached the house from the side, as an end house it meant he could loiter in the alley without being seen. Obviously as a professional he'd waited until darkness and was now just waiting for the telltale signs that would let him know if the job was on. He scouted round the front, moving slowly and aimlessly to the untrained eye. Looking to all the world like a bored kid he kicked at the kerb and bobbed his head, all the while staring through the corners of his eyes into the living room window. The curtains were shut and there was no light on in the house.

'The stupid bastards have gone out and left the place in darkness, fucking idiots.'

Just to be on the safe side though, he wandered round the back to see if the bathroom light was on; it was always possible that the occupants had gone for a bath or even a shag without realising it was dark outside. He chuckled, recalling the time he'd blundered in on a girl getting ready for a night out.

'Aye, I'll never dee that again. Twelve-years-old and I'd screwed more houses than lasses; that was the first time I'd ever even saw a pair of tits that. I was wanking for weeks. Professional and experienced these days, though. And I reckon this is all systems go.'

Moving quickly back to the side of the house, he retrieved his holdall from the bushes and climbed the garden fence.

'The good thing about these houses is that people build big garden fences to keep their fucking kids in and paedos out. What they don't realise is that I can reach the upstairs windows from them and, that being a smallish young lad, I can squeeze through tiny windows if I have to. Windows such as this bedroom one, here.'

127

Pushing himself through, he dropped to the floor and stayed down while his eyes adjusted to the dark.

* * *

Matt had been sitting there for a while. The whisky had worn off some time ago but he'd replaced it with lager and he had some whiz in his pocket that he'd bought in town.

'Vicki didn't want us on the gear so I laid off it, but she can fuck off now,' he thought as he surveyed the scene. The place was virtually in darkness, which was just how he liked it when he was half-pissed, but he could see the creeping figure quite clearly.

'Plenty carrots when I was younger,' he thought. *'Plenty veg off me mam, she fucking forced it down us.'*

Then, feeling the wrap of whiz in his pocket and knowing how it would affect him, he smiled. *'I'll just do what I've got to do, neck this then get meself down the Stag's, I think.'*

Staring at the figure in the corner he moved slowly towards it, right arm outstretched.

Rob had sat tight for a few minutes with his head down, controlling his breathing so he made no sound he just waited and listened. Nothing. The house was definitely empty. Slowly standing he stretched his legs to allow his blood to circulate again, he knew from bitter experience that trying to do an unexpected runner with cramp was a fucking nightmare.

Then, when he was sure that he was ready, he started to make his way to the door.

'They mustn't have moved all their gear in yet, this room's empty. I heard the music though so they must have some decent stuff in here somewhere. No one can live without the essentials; telly and DVD player and that.'

Creeping slowly to the door he grasped the handle gently and inched it backwards, hoping it wasn't one of them typical Byker doors that squealed if you looked at it. Even though he was certain that there was no one about he didn't like to take chances. After all, as the Ghostboy he had a certain reputation for getting in and out unseen and it was this as much as the money and Falcus that drove him on. Looking out in the dark passageway, he congratulated himself on his professionalism; he hadn't made a sound.

'There could be a fucking dog in here and it wouldn't know about me. I'm the fucking Ghostboy, I am.'

Looking first in the main bedroom and then the third, smallest one, he was puzzled, nothing in them at all.

'What the fuck kind of family is this? I bet they're Pakis and downstairs is full of fucking mattresses. Fuck's sake. I might as well go now; there'll be nowt to nick.'

Stopping on the landing while he thought it through, he decided his best course of action would be to look straight downstairs and not waste time in the bathroom to his right. If the living room didn't have a telly or anything then he'd just fuck off. However, what he didn't know was that if he'd looked in the bathroom then he would have noticed that there were no taps on the bath or sinks and that the boiler cupboard didn't actually house a boiler; these were all long since looted after Spugger had flown the nest.

The combination of this and the obvious lack of furnishings and living accessories would have rung alarm bells in his young but very streetwise head and he may just have had the good sense to have fled the scene. But he didn't. Instead, he went downstairs in the dark.

As he descended the stairs, Ghostboy had a clear view of the dining room and could clearly see a table and a small tape machine by the window.

'Fuck it. I'll take that if there's nowt else. Might be worth twenty quid.'

Leaving that for the moment, he stepped off the bottom stair and headed left into the darkened living room. There was absolutely *nothing* in there. Fuck all.

Except.

Ghostboy could make out some kind of graffiti on the wall. Moving closer he could see it was like a big slash mark or something. Then, as his mind was slowly forming the concept that it was actually a letter of the alphabet, the tape machine started up:

Some kind of eighties heavy rock blasted out of the tinny speakers and scared the fuck out of him. Bolting for the door, he brushed past a figure in the dark and started shouting as he reached the handle.

"HELP, *HELP*. A FUCKING NUTTER'S GOT ME. HELP... *HELP!*"

The noise on the tape simply increased, drowning him out:

Then a thumping on the wall from a neighbour.

"Keep the fucking noise down man, I'm on shifts."

Rob, pumping the double-locked handle furiously, could feel the futility of his gesture as physically as he could feel the piss running down his jeans and the tears down his cheeks. This was the bloke everyone was talking about, he had smashed up Beany and his lass – properly smashed them up – and he'd battered that mugger and fat Colly as well. Now it was his turn.

"HELP US, MAN," he banged on the wall. "FUCKING HELP US, THE FUCKER'S A NUTTE—"

A gloved hand covered his mouth and he saw two staring eyes through a balaclava before a headbutt broke his nose.

Doing something about It

Looking down at her sleeping son Vicki felt a tear dribble from her eye. He looked so innocent and pure while he was asleep, not like when he was awake and had to mix with the scum that infested their estate; there were no frowns or lines on his young face. She stroked his head gently; careful not to mess up the hair he took so much care of these days.

"When you were a little lad," she whispered, "you loved your head rubbed when you were going to sleep. That's a long time ago, Son, eh?"

He was getting discharged tomorrow and the main thing was that he had survived and was okay. That's what Matt would have said anyway; thinking of him increased the volume of tears to a light shower.

'I'm sorry for taking it out on you Matt,' she thought. *'I really am. Once Nick's home and safe I'll really try to make it up with you.'*

She was kicking herself for pushing him away and felt the pain of their split like an amputee felt a limb that was no longer there.

"It's true," she whispered again, but this time to no one in particular. "You don't know what you've got until it's gone."

For some reason this made her think of Nick's waster dad, comparing him to Matt was like trying to match chalk and cheese. Where Matt would approach any situation with logic, reason and a bit of consideration she remembered Dave as a hothead, intent on improving his reputation and above all keeping his image as a 'bit of a lad'.

She remembered when she had just come home from hospital in a taxi after having Nick and found the house in darkness. In her youthful insistence that what she and Dave had was true love she had just ignored this and gone to make herself a cup of coffee and discovered there was none left in the house. When he'd eventually staggered in, he'd told her there was no housekeeping money for coffee, oblivious to the fact that he'd been out drinking for three days, buying everyone else's beer and 'wetting the baby's head'. Wanker.

She wanted better than this for Nick. Fuck it, she wanted better for herself, for Matt, for *everyone*.

'Bastards robbing their own, pensioners beaten up and killed for pennies and people locked up for defending themselves. This country's a mess.'

Maybe The Special had the right idea; at least he was doing something about it.

Old Hands

When Rob came round he was tied up and couldn't see. His mouth was really dry but the amount of piss that soaked his jeans mean that he probably wasn't dehydrated. He carefully and quietly stretched his legs and feet as best he could to ascertain whether his legs were tied. They were. Then, keeping his breathing quiet as he had practiced, he listened for sounds of movement in the house. Nothing, no sound at all.

'He's gone,' he thought. *'The cunt's given us a clout, put one of them calling cards on me body somewhere and probably rang the bizzies.'*

KNOCK
 KNOCK

'Here we go. I recognise that knock; here's the bizzies now, neighbours probably complained about the noise or something. Fuck it, I've been nicked loads of times, I'm too young to be locked up so they cannit do owt anyway. Belter, I've beaten the vigilante. Call that a hiding? Beany must be as soft as shite if he ended up in hospital.'

Feeling quite chipper, he planned his next moves.

'I'll be held for a few hours, I'll say I came in here cos I heard a noise and I was curious. Then, when I get out, I'm gonna do Latif's shop, I think. I sold him some burglar lights a month ago but I know they don't work very well. Yeah... I'll do him and sort Falcus out for this month with the cash. Job's a good un.'

KNOCK-KNOCK

"THIS IS THE POLICE, IS THERE ANYONE IN THERE?"

Opening his mouth to shout, Rob's jubilation was short lived as a ball of material was rammed into it, almost choking him and the sticky feel of Sellotape was wound round and round his head to keep it in. As the knocking stopped, he could feel the piss running down his leg again and then his blindfold was ripped off and he looked straight into the eyes of the vigilante.

He was holding a finger over his lips in a shushing gesture and holding his face just inches from Rob's. After a couple of seconds of this, he seemed satisfied that the copper had gone and he dragged him to his feet and leant him against the wall. Rob decided it was time to end this charade; the man obviously didn't know who he was dealing with.

"Mmmmm... mmmmm," he tried to speak, shaking his head furiously.

The vigilante had his head tilted to one side as if he was considering this development, like people didn't normally try to talk their way out of it and then he straightened up and walked

133

towards Rob, producing a knife from nowhere and holding it in front of him.

"Mmmm, *mmmmm*," Rob was panicking now, "MMMMMMMMMMmmm."

The vigilante held the knife against Rob's throat and then calmly cut through the tape over his mouth before using his left hand to make the shushing gesture again.

Rob nodded to show he understood. At the end of the day they were both professional men; both old hands at this game and it was a simple case of letting him know that he had moved onto someone else's patch and he would leave it alone. Simple as that.

The vigilante held the knife to his throat as he removed the gag from Rob's mouth and then nodded to tell him it was okay to speak.

"Listen mate," he whispered at him. "You've dropped a bollock here. I work for Falcus and, at this moment, you are treading on his toes and he won't be best pleased. Now if you fuck off quickly and leave me alone, I'll let it go and you'll keep your face. Now, what do you say?"

Rob could feel himself growing in stature. This bloke had went very quiet during his speech and it was obvious he was shitting it at the mention of Falcus's name, so he thought it was time he exerted himself over his attacker.

"Listen, pal," he said, voice a bit harsher and louder. "Stop fucking about now. Untie me and then fuck off or I'll be speaking to my good friend Mr Falcus and you'll be in deep shit. Understand?"

Rob never saw the right hook that broke his jaw but he certainly felt it. As he crashed to the floor and saw the bloke's left boot approaching his face rapidly he realised that quoting Falcus's name might not have been the best thing to do.

'That's taught that little reprobate. You should never spoil the rod in my opinion. There are those who might feel I've went a little too far, but the amount of misery this child has caused over the years,

without redress, has been immense. Maybe now they'll start to realise that they must respect the law. Maybe now the criminals will comprehend that it's not just the police after them. Maybe, just maybe, society can still be made safe.'

The balaclaved man moved towards the bathroom door, taking one last look back at the figure in the bath. In the darkness, the only thing that stood out was the white business card that was stapled to the burglars head and some of his dislodged teeth on the floor.

The boy's comatose body was covered in letter Vs... letter Vs that were carved into his skin with a dexterity that would have pleased a tattooist. They were so neat, even the big ones, that they looked like tiny zippers. The blood dripping from his body would add to the scene in the morning and would make a horrific sight for both police and criminals alike.

'If I've achieved nothing else, then at least that boy will remember not to break the law every time he looks in the mirror for the rest of his life.'

Smiling at the thought, he left as silently as he had entered.

The Three Amigos

"Aye man, Jackie, man. So, what I'm saying is, that film earlier, *Silver Hammer* or whatever it was called, it was shite in context with this day and age. But, at the time of its conception and production, it was fucking marvellously ahead of its time."

Matt knew he was rambling and also knew that he was talking so fast and so single-mindedly that no one else could get a word in. He didn't want them to though. He was aware that the wrap of whiz he'd necked before entering the Stag's had impacted on him and that as he'd not done any for a while it would hit him like a fucking train. And it had.

"I'm telling you, Jackie. When I was sitting watching it earlier I got a real feeling of being in the film; the black and white imagery, the moody setting and the tense atmosphere all contributed to a top movie in its day. I sat there watching it in the dark an' all, man. Fucking class when that burglar gets his head stoved in by the law. Heh-heh... that taught the fucker."

Then, moving towards his new best mate and putting his arm around him, Matt whispered conspiratorially, "Fucking scum round here man, Jackie. Some of them cunts deserve a good hiding. Take that Ghostboy twat for instance; he needs punching the fuck out, he does. Can't say nowt though, can we, one of Falcus's boys, isn't he? He wants to be careful though. There'll come a time when his boss doesn't need him no more and it'll be open season on the little prick then."

The man known as Jackie just nodded ambiguously; he'd only met Matt an hour ago and had ended up drinking with him through a combination of financial hardship and alcohol dependence and therefore wasn't prepared to get into trouble with nutters like Falcus because of him, but at the same time he didn't want to stop the free pints coming his way courtesy of this drunken, drugged-up mess.

"Two more pints mate," Matt said to the barman, taking Jackie's nod as a sign of agreement, "Am off to the bog."

The barman watched him stumble jerkily towards the toilet and sighed to himself; another heed the ball full of amphetamines and being systematically removed of his wages by the local old soak.

Putting the pints on the bar, he smiled at Jackie. "Who's getting these then, Jack?" he chuckled, not even expecting a response.

There were times when he quite enjoyed working here, loads of different characters, always entertaining and sometimes a bit of violence, which he didn't have to sort out. The wages weren't brilliant but as they were cash in hand he wasn't that worried; he supplemented them through fiddling the till and reasoned that if he was working at night he couldn't be out spending money, could he?

The place was typical Byker, though. When he came to see the manager about the job he'd walked past a mountain of gold and electricals in the lounge and was simply asked one question: "Do you want to be on the books or off?"

He'd replied, "Off."

"Right then. I pay three-fifty an hour fiddle or five-fifty an hour official. You'll be on three-fifty. Can you work tonight?"

And that was it. He'd become the latest in along line of Stag's Head barmen. It certainly beat some of his past jobs, particularly the month he'd spent washing traffic cones in a scruffy quarry-cum-builder's yard. That too had been a fiddle job and he'd taken it only so he could afford some spending money to go on holiday with his brother to Tenerife.

The irony hadn't been lost on him that for a month he'd been outside, mainly in the rain, washing traffic cones that would then be placed outside, mainly in the rain. It wasn't all glamour, though. Every now and then he'd be sent to the quarry side of the yard to fill up those little sandbags that held down the 'men at work' signs in the wind. Putting two scoops of wet sand into hundreds of those horrible, filthy bags and then breaking your back loading them onto the wagon for that night certainly made you appreciate the salubrious surroundings of a council estate public house.

Smiling to himself, he plunged another glass into the washer and considered how this evening's entertainment would end.

'This can go one of three ways,' he thought. *'The young lad will realise he's bought all the drink all night, get angry and start kicking off. Jackie will decide he's had enough free booze, get rapidly sick of matey boy's company and tell him to fuck off or the boss will come back pissed from wherever he's been and buy both their*

137

drink until the early hours when one of the triumvirate will start fighting with the other two.'

Putting the half clean glass back on the shelf, he glanced back at Jackie who was drunkenly mumbling to himself and then at the second cash register under the bar, the one that was used for non-official transactions and the one he regularly dipped when the landlord wasn't about.

'Whatever happens, I'll be getting paid to watch it. Ha-ha.'

Jackie contemplated the fresh pint in front of him. How had it come to this? He hadn't always been an old pisshead propping up a succession of shitty bars and being mocked by the scum that frequented them. There was a time in his life when he'd had respect, when he'd been a face around town but no one knew about that now. They all lived in their own worlds now, walking the streets with headphones in their ears to avoid speaking to anyone and staying inside the house and conversing with like-minded souls on their computers rather than mixing with real people in the outside world.

'All hail the communication age and the wonders of modern technology,' he thought. *'Mobile phones, the internet, email and all kinds of pagers and things. There's never been as many ways to talk to people and everyone ignores each other. Fucking ironic.'*

He gulped his pint, still greedy for the taste despite the volume consumed thus far that night. Remembering far off nights in The Oxford dance hall with Robbo; his mind's eye racing ahead and backwards all at the same time as a flurry of images burst into his befuddled head leaving him happy but sad, warm but bitter. Robbo and him chatting up birds, his first girlfriend and his first kiss, him and Robbo fighting them two lads behind the chip shop at the top of Shields Road, that's a Chinese now, and the respect that winning accorded them, Robbo dying and the fury and rage that engulfed him and then Doreen, he could never forget Doreen.

Looking at himself in the mirror behind the bar he knew, without a shadow of a doubt, that it was Doreen that had put him here.

Special

From being a respectable, professional soldier with a career and a pension... to this: the town drunk, shabby, unhygienic and a laughing stock. Even from this side of the bar he could see the tears forming in his eyes and he loathed himself even more; this once proud man, former fighter for Queen and country now wallowing in self-pity.

He looked back at the toilet door; this had gone on long enough. Begging drink off strangers, listening to their shite and putting up with wankers...

Now was the time to put his life back on track. He could walk out now before the gobshite came back and start cleaning himself up. All he had to do was turn around and walk. He was going to do it. He could hear Robbo screaming at him from heaven to do it. To walk tall. To hold his head up again. To be the man he once was. He straightened his back and pushed himself off the bar... In one second he'd be rotated one hundred and eighty degrees and be ready to start his life again... this was the turning point.

"Here, Jackie. Get this down you. On the house, mate. Before your new pal comes back." The barman handed him a double whisky and Jackie's hands, on automatic pilot, had it to his mouth before his brain could resist.

As he slumped back against the bar, he fancied he could see another tear forming in his eye. These bastards wouldn't let him change, they were all in it together, keeping him full of the drink and stopping him from leaving. It was this place and he knew it, he just had to get out of here and there would be no temptation, no one throwing drink down his neck. He just had to get out of here; once he finished his drink he would simply leave... no matter what anyone gave him. Yes that was it; he would definitely start his new life after this drink. *Definitely*.

Games Night

The Hare and Hounds was busier now. Wednesday was Darts Night and the two teams were just assembling in the bar, the banter had already started.

"Fucking hell, Largey. Have you been on a diet?"

"No."

"Nah, I didn't think so either, you fat twat!"

"Did your lass get you them darts, Tadger?"

"Aye, for me birthday. Why do you ask?"

"Well, I heard the rumour she was into little pricks. Suppose it's true now, isn't it?"

Normal council estate humour resounded around the pub. Despite the abuse, the two teams knew each other well and this was going to be a friendly game. Falcus and Crowbar were having a game of pool and, when the Axel F ringtone started loudly, everyone in the bar looked up and held their breath. It was always bad news when anyone rang Falcus these days. He opened the phone and, holding it to his ear, he headed for the door, those nearest to him and sufficiently interested may have noted a frown cross his face to be instantly replaced by a blank expression just before he snapped the phone shut and returned to the bar. Ever the professional, he didn't let what he had just heard show on his face. Instead, he picked up his pool cue and took his shot, body on autopilot while his head was a whirl of questions:

'Ghostboy, trapped and slashed up, left in a bath unconscious. Same as the last lot as well; a fucking card stapled to his head. I might be a paranoid fucker, but I haven't heard of this bloke doing anyone that doesn't work for me. No reports or rumours of him working the West End, just here, just my little patch. Vigilante?

Special

Fuck off, someone's moving in. This is a bastard challenge and I've been too slow to work it out. Who, though?'

Smashing the white ball hard against the nest of its spotty and stripey brothers on the cushion, he enjoyed the satisfying cracking sound and the clunk of two of his number going down the pockets.

'These last few weeks has cost me a fair bit of money already. I can't allow it to go on. I can't get any advice either, fucking Crowbar and Terry are as thick as mince and I'm not trusting any fucker else from here on in.'

Belting another ball into the top pocket with controlled aggression, Falcus plotted his next move.

'Double into the middle, plant at the bottom then fire the black fucker home. Job done. Then I need to be getting some snouts out to find out who's fucking at it.'

Winking at Crowbar in an exaggerated, wind-up fashion, Falcus cleared the table of spots and then he sighted the black ball at the other end and lashed it home; the white ball bouncing off every cushion such was the fury of the shot then coming to land perfectly inside the D. An excellent clear up. No one would ever know how pissed off he was about that phone call and thus would never see any chink in his armour. He was proud of his poker face.

Crowbar surveyed the table nervously as Falcus headed to the bar to celebrate his victory, that phone call had obviously pissed him right off judging by the way he had switched from stripes to spots mid-game without noticing. He, however, had no intention of telling him and claiming the game. That just wouldn't be sensible.

You ain't so Bad

Matt had no idea how long he'd had his head resting against the wall of the toilet, could've been seconds, could've been hours. The thump of the jukebox suggested that the pub was still open and feeling the notes in his pocket meant that he hadn't been robbed, so no one else had been in here. Taking all that into account he decided it must have been a very short length of time that had elapsed while he waited for his massive drug piss to finally finish.

Moving over to the cracked sink and the – miraculously for this place – intact mirror, he took a very good look at himself.

'Ten years of pissing and drugging it up,' he thought, *'and I'm still a good-looking bastard.'*

Giving his hands a splash and then rubbing his head while they were still wet was nice, he'd learnt this trick years ago when he'd taken his first pill. His mind travelling back to Walkers nightclub in the nineties and his very first ecstasy tablet.

'Fuck me, man. I just danced and danced and danced. I cuddled every fucker. I talked to everyone in the club, even the fucking bouncers. It was class.'

It seemed the whole world was on one then; clubs were nice places to be and people just talked normally without agenda. Then the gangsters moved in. Once there was money involved, then the quality of the gear went downhill rapidly followed by prices. Once a twenty-five quid pill had you jumping around all night, now you could buy them for three fifty and they lasted about an hour.

'The fucking tabloids were the best though; they properly showed themselves up, them cunts. Big front page headlines on ecstasy and how it was dead addictive and killed people, then they'd print pictures of acid tabs next to the article with the smiley faces on. Thick fuckers, no wonder concerned parents didn't have a clue.'

Smiling to himself at the memory, he rubbed his hands through his hair again and had one last look before moving out to tell his new mate some other vital stuff he'd remembered.

The jukebox was blaring Van Morrison when Matt came out of the bog, a sly look at the clock on the wall confirmed he'd been in there ten minutes; not the end of the world. His new mate Jackie was dancing round the bar and shouting something about Doreen and Robbo. It seemed important to him whatever he was saying.

"DOREEN," he shouted, "DOREEN, WHY DID YOU DO IT? WHY... *WHY*?"

This Doreen had obviously fucked him over in some way, Matt thought, as he started necking his pint in an effort to catch up.

"ROBBO, WHY DID YOU HAVE TO GO, WHAT DID YOU EVER DO WRONG?" Jackie was pulling at his hair as the song finished, obviously a bit distressed.

Matt looked over at the barman quizzically; he just shrugged and smirked. Horrible bastard.

Jackie was tugging at Matt now and, while sympathetic to whatever was upsetting the old alchy, he still wasn't keen on being manhandled and slobbered on.

"WHY DID SHE HAVE TO SLEEP WITH HIM? YOU TELL ME THAT, SON. HE WAS A SEEDY, HORRIBLE MAN, BUT SHE SLEPT WITH HIM AND CONCEIVED HIS CHILD."

"No need to shout at me, Jackie, I'm just here. What you on about?" Matt gently but firmly shook himself loose of Jackie's grip.

"DOREEN, SHE WAS MY WOMAN. SHE SLEPT WITH A BLOKE SHE USED TO KNOW WHEN WE WERE ENGAGED. EVEN GOT PREGNANT WITH HIS KID."

"Stop fucking shouting at me, Jackie." Matt was pissed off now. Sad story right enough, but fuck me they were only yards away from each other, his big piss-up was starting to take a downward turn.

"I'm sorry, son," he said, tears in his eyes as he grabbed at

143

Matt's arm again. "I got the pictures in the post when I was serving in Northern Ireland. She was naked and posing with this... thing inside her. I was livid, confused and numb all at the same time."

Matt felt a bit guilty about getting arsey with him, but he still didn't want the bloke grabbing at his arm.

"Then, half an hour later I was out on patrol with my unit when we chased some twats into a pub who'd been throwing bricks at us. I remember it like yesterday. The jukebox was playing Van Morrison and the bar was empty. No staff, no customers, nothing, it was an obvious trap but I was still fuming about Doreen. The little fuckers had dived through a window at the far end and I chased after them, I just wanted to batter someone, to let it all out. Robbo chased me; realising the place was going to go up but he couldn't catch me. I dived through the window just as the place was blasted to bits. I survived and got pensioned off, Robbo was killed instantly. We could only bury bits of him. I never saw Doreen again after that either. I didn't want to."

Matt felt shit. The bloke had probably wanted to tell someone this for fucking years, and his heart went out to him.

"Yeh well, Jackie... That's all very well, but moaning about it now won't bring him back or stop her being a slag, will it? Stop whining and get on with your fucking life, man. You're bringing the atmosphere of the place down."

Matt stared in amazement at the barman as he finished his rant; the cunt was smirking as Jackie broke down in tears. He'd taken fucking pleasure in destroying the poor old bastard. Without realising what he was doing Matt grabbed the fucker's collar and dragged him headfirst over the bar through the stack of glasses waiting to be washed.

"What fucking *atmosphere*, you heartless fucking bastard? There's only us three in this shitehole now, are you worried that a busload of footballers might turn up at any minute, seduced by the lure of overpriced, water filled lager and seventies décor?" He shouted. "Scum like you doing down an old soldier like that, pricks like you boil my piss."

The whiz was coursing through his veins once more and he felt invincible, noble even; defending the honour of an upstanding old soldier who'd fallen on hard times. The barman's blows just bounced off him to no effect as he picked his punches. The youthful boxing lessons came in handy as he ducked and weaved, jabbing the increasingly desperate barman to death. It was like being in a film, he saw the punches before they came, dodged them, then countered like Bruce Lee.

When the barman had collapsed to the floor bruised and bloodied, Matt felt that a classic quote was in order, just to let the man know he had been beaten by a defender of old style morals. Pointing to his fallen victim and with a head full of films to choose from, he stated clearly and with conviction, "You ain't so bad."

Then he walked over to check that Jackie was alright thinking to himself, 'Rocky Three? Fucking-Rocky-Three? That was fucking shite.'

What's the score, John?

Gladys looked down at her grandson. He looked so small in the hospital bed, hooked up to all kinds of wires and machines. His face so innocent and untroubled by life in that bed. She was the only family he really had. His father – her only son – was in prison and was going to be there for quite some time and his mother, well, leaving aside her profession which would be understandable and forgivable if she did it to put food on the table rather than the drugs and drink she purchased for herself. No, his mother's interest in Robert could be summed up by the fact her son was in a coma in intensive care and she hadn't bothered coming to see him, preferring instead to see her regular 'clients' knowing that Gladys would be there and would never give up on her grandson. As soon as she'd heard the news, she phoned Vi to tell her she wouldn't be in to work the next day and to sort it out for her, then she'd raced up to the hospital.

He'd never had a family life, not like the generations before him. He'd never have one now and he'd never know what it was like to be secure and looked after.

'That,' she thought, as the tears streamed down her cheeks, *'is the real tragedy.'*

* * *

The flashing blue light outside the pub window hit the mirror behind the bar and reflected onto the ceiling, giving the place a surreal, half disco-like look.

'Might've been handy a few hours ago when I was buzzing me nut off that, like,' mused Matt. *'Could've put on the classics and had a little dance.'*

He was sat in a chair by the now switched off jukebox while the coppers established what had happened. The barman he had clouted was sat opposite him giving his statement and hamming up his injuries for all he was worth.

"I don't know why he attacked me, officer. He had been bothering old Jackie all night and shouting about criminals and scum and how they all needed fucking... sorry *sorting* out."

'Slimy, grassing prick,' thought Matt. *'I bet he got fucking bullied at school.'*

"Then, when I was cheering Jackie up as he was a bit distressed about something, the nutter just attacked me. He dragged me over the bar and set about me." The barman's voice dropped to a stage whisper, "Between you and me, officer, I think he's on drugs. He spent an awful long time in the toilet earlier as well."

Matt was in the shit and he knew it. Luckily, he'd taken all of his gear, meaning they couldn't find any on him but they'd probably test him down at the station and harass the fuck out of him, personal issue or not. The assault charge would be more serious though; he could even get jail for it once the poxy twat over there started claiming for all sorts from the Criminal Injuries Board.

Sighing, he slumped back into his chair. He'd only just got his fucking job back and now he was almost certainly out again, along with a criminal record and some form of sentence. Poverty beckoned.

And then salvation walked through the door in the form of Special Constable Latimer.

"What have you done, Mathew?"

Matt's heart jumped. Alright, him and Latimer didn't get on that well, but he wouldn't let that sleazy barman twat get one of his staff sent down, would he?

"Alright, John. I had a few too many pints and the barman started abusing the old fella over there so I gave him a slap. It was nowt really, but he's playing it up for the compensation, isn't he?"

The supervisor-cum-copper looked over at the barman and nodded.

"He obviously thinks he's trying to get a part on a soap, judging by his overacting. Leave it with me."

Latimer approached the officer taking the barman's statement and pulled him to one side, asking for a quiet word.

"What's the score, John?" the copper asked him.

"Well," replied Latimer, with his back to Matt. "You know that burglar getting done over earlier? Matey boy over there might well be worth questioning about it, obviously violent and apparently shouting about burglars needing a good hiding. What do you think?"

The senior officer gave him the nod and Latimer smiled broadly as he approached Matt.

'Revenge is a dish best served cold, Johnny boy. You learnt well.'

"Mathew Blake, you have the right to remain silent..."

THURSDAY

Stick to Business

Vicki was having a shite day; Gladys hadn't turned up at work and no replacement could be got as no one wanted to work his or her day off. The big delivery had just arrived, ready to go on the shelves and in the freezers for the weekend free-for-all and she was on her own. The driver was friendly enough and very patient with her while she checked it all off; luckily for her it was his last drop and he was heading back to the main warehouse in Wales after this, so he was happy enough to go for a cup of tea while she struggled through. It was also freezing in the back next to the cold store, as you would expect in a frozen food shop, and she was shivering through her regulation thin jumper.

'If I'd known Gladys wasn't here today, I'd have worn the bloody big thick one but I thought I'd be on tills today and it gets too hot out there. Sod's Law, I suppose.'

She'd slept in that morning, spilled milk everywhere when trying to sort some breakfast out in a hurry and then had to get Nick from hospital. On top of all this, that copper had been lurking outside her house when she'd come flying out with exactly four and a half minutes to get to work and in no mood to chat. He hadn't said what he wanted, just waved at her as she'd shouted about being in a hurry and not having time to stop. It obviously wasn't that official or important as he hadn't stopped her and insisted on speaking, just let her go on her way.

Picking out a damaged box of fish fingers from the bottom of the pallet broke her line of thought. Matt always loved fish finger sandwiches.

'White bread, plenty butter and red sauce, pet.' She remembered his preferences exactly and more than a little wistfully.

'He'd better ring soon,' she thought. *'Being in a huff's alright but he needs to grow up. And anyway, I'd hate to have to ring him first.'*

Turning her attention back to the job in hand she realised that she'd finally finished checking off the delivery and, with her mind shouting hurray and her body doing mental somersaults, she headed for the driver who was by now back in his cab. Reaching up and pulling open the door she handed him his paperwork and gave him a cheery goodbye, hoping against hope that some other poor bastard got this shit job next week before slamming the cab door shut again.

As she headed toward the back doors of the store and her long-awaited first break of the day, something caught the corner of her eye and she turned to see the copper, Latimer, right in her face again.

'What does this creepy twat actually want?' she sighed inwardly to herself hoping it wouldn't take long. Her first cigarette of the day suddenly being snatched cruelly from her reach and disappearing over the horizon.

"Can I help you, officer?" she asked, in what she hoped was a tone that conveyed displeasure at his interruption of her day... but just subservient enough to get away with whatever else Nick may have done.

He smiled at her, not a nice smile; it made her a little bit uncomfortable, to be honest, like he was hiding something.

"You certainly could help me, Miss Hughes. No doubt about that, but let's stick to business for now. Ha-ha." His familiarity left her feeling slightly creeped out and she was instantly on guard.

"No, seriously," he said, having laughed at his own joke just a little too long. "I just wanted to check that young Nick was okay after his ordeal at the hands of the burglar."

'Maybe I've misjudged him,' thought Vicki, relaxing again. *'He's weird, but just concerned and doing his job. I'm always jumping to conclusions about people; I should give him a chance. Maybe he's not comfortable round women, so he acts like that. Probably went to public school or something, all boys and that. Anyway, it's very nice of him to ask.'*

"He's fine now, thanks. He just needs a bit of rest then he'll be back to causing havoc."

There was a pause... a long pause... and Vicki thought to herself, *'isn't this the bit where you say that you were just checking and you'll be off now?'*

Instead he just looked her up and down, his eyes taking in her body from head to toe and Vicki started to feel uncomfortable again. Just when she thought that she was going to have to be rude, he extended his hand to her and despite herself, she shook it, her skin recoiling in protest at coming into contact with this man's sweaty palm.

"If I can do anything for you in the future; anything at all, Miss Hughes... you only have to ask."

"Erm, thank you, officer. I really have to go now. I'm needed in store."

As Vicki headed for the tearoom she made a mental note to ring Matt herself, regardless of how they'd left things, and tell him just what a fucking letch his boss was.

Call me Guv

Barney poked his head surreptitiously above his desk, which wasn't easy from his sitting position on the floor just underneath it. No one could see him from the window if they happened to walk past, which was good. He didn't want a lack of confidence in him during his first big case, and so he was looking back over his university notes on the quiet in order to refresh his memory. There was something about these crimes that had him convinced it was someone in authority, but his boss hadn't seemed to share his enthusiasm for this theory, and he wanted to check he wasn't imagining the psychological pointers he thought he recognised.

"It's definitely in there," he mumbled to no one in particular. "A large amount of evidence of Finkelstein's theory is inherent in these crimes. The rebellion against the impotence of position added to the desire to rectify things overrides all reasonable mental opposition and ignores human morality in order to achieve the subject's desired state of affairs and then maintain their imagined status quo."

"What the fuck are you talking about, Barney? And why on earth are you under your desk?"

Suzie's entry took Barney by surprise, making him jump.

"Ow, I've banged my bloody head now."

Rubbing his now sore cranium and emerging from under the desk, he was confronted by a grinning Suzie who handed him a cup of coffee.

"You should call me Guv, not Barney. After all, I am your senior officer on this investigation."

Suzie just kept grinning and gave him a quick V sign before replying, "A: Barney is a lovely name and suits you down to the ground and B: we are not driving around the grim shitehole that is London in a seventies Capri so no, I will not call you *Guv*. However, you can have a cup of coffee, Sir."

Barney just kept rubbing his head; he was trying hard to get the image of her calling him Guv in the bedroom out of his mind but succeeded only in blushing hard and sitting down before his discomfort became apparent.

"Have you got the file on Mr Falcus detailing his past misdemeanours for me, Ms Holmes?" he said in semi-serious senior officer tones.

"Why yes, Sir" replied Suzie, performing a mock curtsey before him. "Would you have any other tasks for this lowly police service wench?"

'Any other tasks at all,' she thought. *'I'll do anything you want, Barney boy. Just ask.'* He was blushing again though and she knew he wouldn't take this conversation much further. She was right.

"Just keep on top of everyone for me while I go through these reports on Falcus. Make sure that the forensic boys are progressing all the evidence and not slacking. And Susie..."

"Yes, Boss?" she replied, he couldn't have finally got the courage up could he?

"You couldn't get me a cheese sandwich from the canteen, could you?"

"No bother" she replied, a little disappointed.

Looking back at the file on his desk, Barney sighed, took a deep breath and then opened the flap.

NORTUMBERLAND POLICE AUTHORITY
PRIVATE AND CONFIDENTIAL

SUBJECT: ALEXANDER FALCUS
DATE: 02/03/88
CHARGE: ASSAULT

ARRESTING OFFICER: PC LOGAN
TIME OF ARREST: 17:25

PARTICULARS OF ARREST:
I was called to attend an incident at Dobson Amusements on Shields Road in Byker after being told

of an altercation there whilst on my beat. On arrival at the amusements, I witnessed Mr Alex Falcus holding down the manager of the amusement arcade, Mr Frederick Finlay, and repeatedly banging his head off the ground. Before I could intervene, he also punched to the ground an assistant, Mrs Rita Runcorn, who had tried to help her manager. Mr Falcus resisted arrest strongly and had to be subdued physically. Both Mr Finlay and Mrs Runcorn had to attend hospital for their injuries, Mrs Runcorn's resulting in treatment for a broken nose.

NORTHUMBERLAND POLICE AUTHORITY
PRIVATE AND CONFIDENTIAL

SUBJECT: ALEXANDER FALCUS
DATE: 05/08/88
CHARGE: CRIMINAL DAMAGE

ARRESTING OFFICER: PC KNOTTS
TIME OF ARREST: 19:44

PARTICULARS OF ARREST:
Following an anonymous call from a member of the public, I attended Raby Street, Byker where I witnessed Mr Alex Falcus attacking a Ford Sierra with a sledgehammer. After challenging him, he desisted from damaging the car any further, commenting only that 'this bastard knows who done me dad'. The owner of the car, Mr N. Reeder did not come out of his house until after the incident, but once outside kept shouting, "I know nowt. I honestly don't know who did it. Me car was nicked and I've just got it back off the bizzies."

Special

There didn't seem to be anything on Mr Falcus after that. Maybe he'd turned over a new leaf then... or more likely he'd got others to do his dirty work in order to keep his hands blood-free. His father's death had obviously hit him hard though, and he'd been convinced it was murder going by these reports.

Knock

   Knock

"Cheese and onion okay, Barney?" Suzie had stuck her head round the door.

"That's lovely. Thanks, Suzie. What do you know about Falcus's father? More importantly... his death?"

"I wasn't around here then but I remember reading about it in the local papers. It was a hit and run, I think. The driver was never caught. There was a bit of a spread about it in one of the nationals as well with him doing that prison officer in."

"Doing what prison officer in?"

"Didn't you know? He killed a prison officer while inside in the late seventies. He served an extended term for it and was knocked over not long after coming out. Falcus went mental for a bit, trying to find out who it was. I don't think he ever did though, and no one was ever charged for it."

Barney's brow furrowed and his eyes narrowed to slits in his head. He may have been looking at this the wrong way round.

"Suzie, a couple more favours and I promise that's it for today. Firstly... could you get me the personnel files on the former PCs Logan and Knotts, plus any info we've got on what they're doing now, and secondly... could you dig out anything we've got on Mr Falcus senior? Thanks."

With that he sipped his coffee and made himself comfortable; this was going to be a long shift.

Andy Rivers

Winning is Everything

John Latimer was at his proper job now; he'd only worn the uniform to see Miss Hughes so she didn't think him too familiar. Luckily, his shift was on lates this week so he'd had time to get home and change without being spotted by any on duty officers. The service frowned upon specials who used their uniforms for their own ends and John knew that this would be considered for his own ends.

It was only temporary though, all this sneaking around and being covert. Soon they would be able to bring their relationship out in to the open and he could start to mould them into a proper family unit; the kind that his father would have been proud of. The more he thought about it, the more he realised it was all falling into place at the right time. Blake was presently in the cells being interrogated over the spate of vigilantism that had engulfed the area just recently, which meant that as far as Vicki was concerned, he'd be out of sight and out of mind. His boss, the useless ginger one, had applied for a promotion to become an area manager down South, based in the giant council estate that was Milton Keynes, leaving a vacancy that was surely stitched on for him.

He had approached the Human Resources Department as soon as he'd started work that day to report that Blake wouldn't be in work and his involvement in his arrest. They were concerned that it would look as if Latimer was victimising someone who he'd already tried to sack, but what could they do or say against the law of the land? As a police officer he'd had to arrest a perpetrator of a crime and that is what Blake now was, particularly if they could stick the vigilante thing to him. He'd played it well with HR telling them that he felt it would be better if someone else dealt with Blake's termination when he was eventually, if ever, released from custody.

They'd agreed that it would be seen more sympathetically in favour of the company at any possible tribunal if Latimer was not the man to sack Blake and, as he pointed out to the woman, he can hardly put a good shift in if he's not at work, can he?

'Mind you, I was quoting the law of the land and police procedure at them, but I bet a pound to a pinch of shit that he'll go squealing about his human rights to some bloody European court and get a big lump sum for it. After all, they run this country now, don't they? My father would turn in his grave if he knew his once great country was being run from Brussels by an assortment of spics, dagos and garlic-munching cowards. Even the businesses here now are bloody foreign; water companies owned abroad, Chinese investment escalating rapidly and the Scottish mafia sitting in parliament.'

Sitting back in his chair, he looked down at the multitude of clocking in cards spread across his desk.

'Not here, though. This may be a German company, but in this depot, on this shift, I'm in charge. All those people depend on me,' he thought. 'To a man they are unskilled, dense and compliant and they rely on me to keep a roof over their heads and food on their table. Yes, they moan when they have to work an extra hour overtime to get the goods on the lorry and yes they pretend to dislike me, but deep down they know they need me and that if I didn't look after the business as I do then they would be out of work.'

He picked up Matt Blake's unused card and smiled then threw it across the room into the bin before getting out his wallet and removing a black and white photo and holding it up to the light.

"As far as these numpties are concerned, I am their God, Dad. I control their lives and I have the power to change them if I deem it necessary. I've come a long way since that frightened, orphaned little boy and I know I've made you proud of me. I did what I had to do, Dad. I know you know."

A small tear seeped from the corner of his left eye and Latimer felt a sense of deep nostalgia; memories of his childhood slid into his mind's eye for a second or two and were then replaced by another memory as if on a presentation slide: at the beach with his dad poking at crabs in rock pools, riding a carousel at the travelling fair on the town moor, his dad wearing a cowboy hat, Christmas morning and opening his stocking, the smell of cooking turkey pervading the house. Then the memories changed, attending his dad's funeral, being placed with the Latimer family and the bullying and teasing that followed because he was different, because he had morals. Doreen as well; he remembered her walk, the way her skirt clung to her legs hinting at the shape, the way she pouted when she couldn't get her own way in class and the way she unbuttoned her blouse at the top to allow you a tantalising glimpse of what might be. He also remembered the day at the cinema again when she and his stepbrother had conspired to humiliate and embarrass him, to help ostracise him further from the small community he had been dumped in. Oh, yes, Doreen... she wasn't the first and she won't be the last, but they all learn the lesson eventually. You don't mess with John Latimer.

He'd grown up a bit by the time she got her comeuppance; a young man, he'd been doing his apprenticeship at the Swan Hunter yard in Wallsend. Life was good then, he had a few mates, not close but at least they were mates. He'd moved into his own flat on the High Street and had been solvent enough to buy a few of life's luxuries for himself including his pride and joy, the latest Polaroid camera.

He'd heard on the grapevine that Doreen, who'd dumped his by now alcoholic elder stepbrother some time ago, was engaged to a soldier. John himself had seen a few girls by now and knew the routine, drink, bit of chat and a few compliments then round the back of the dance hall to see what was on offer. Even though he'd broken his duck he still felt a burning rage every time Doreen's name was mentioned and he knew he still had to gain revenge for the horrible trick she'd played on him. He'd been talking to some people who knew her at various dances over the months and had gained a picture of her and how much she loved this squaddie who was apparently going to marry her once he came back from sorting out the little quarrel over in Ireland. He knew this only gave him a window of a few months at most as he couldn't take on a member of Her Majesty's armed forces. His father would have disapproved of that, particularly as the man in question had done nothing to him. No, he had to deal with Doreen now while he was out of the picture.

His chance arose on a Friday night. He'd been in town at The Oxford dancehall and had noticed Doreen out with her usual crew. One of her friends was going out with a chap, Dennis, that John vaguely knew from work and he'd said hello to earlier. The more John watched them, it became apparent that Doreen was playing gooseberry to this chap and his girlfriend, a situation that John knew from experience would be winding up Dennis as he saw the precious little weekend time he was allowed to spend with his girlfriend being wasted on chaperoning someone else. As Dennis headed to the bar, John made his move and nudged his elbow in the crush.

"Alright, Den. How's it going?" he asked cheerfully.

"Oh not bad, mate," Dennis had replied before turning his attention to the barman. "A pint of Exhibition, a half of mild and a Gin Fizz, please."

"Gin Fizz? Your lass is going upmarket, isn't she?"

"It's not for our lass, John. It's for that Doreen, her mate. Not only have I got to put up with her hanging round us like a bad smell all weekend, but she's bloody bankrupting me as well. That's five of these I've bought her now."

"Five, Den! She'll be drunk."

"She's pretty much there now, John," and then a light came on in his head just as Latimer knew it would. "You don't fancy taking her off my hands, mate, do you? I'll owe you one if you keep her

159

occupied for the rest of the night, make sure she gets home alright and that. Go on, mate."

John did his best to look like he was thinking about it when in reality it was too good a chance to miss.

"Oh, all right then," he said. "But you do owe me a favour now, you realise that?"

"Smashing, I'll tell our lass we're dancing when I get back and you can bowl in and sweep the drunken Doreen off her feet for the rest of the night."

Latimer smiled as he remembered exactly how he'd gone about isolating Doreen from everyone else, he'd simply went over to her with a free drink when Dennis was on the dance floor and she was his. Then after plying her with gin all night she could barely stand and he made his move.

"Time to go home, Doreen," he'd said to her in front of as many witnesses as he could before smiling ruefully at them while they tutted and disapproved at her swaying, drunken figure. She'd clung to him while they boarded the bus and John had rolled his eyes at the driver who'd cheerfully asked if she'd had a bit too much. Then, before she'd known what was happening, they were back in his flat and her clothes were off.

Latimer shivered with pleasure as he recalled how he'd first had her while she clung to the bed to stop herself from being sick, then came the coup de grace; his treasured instamatic, the camera he'd purchased for this very purpose came into its own. After pouring more drink down Doreen to keep her in the confused state he required, he'd produced some sex toys procured through mail order.

"That's it, love. Now lie back and think of England. It won't hurt for long. That's it."

He'd taken photos of her naked, legs splayed and dildos inserted, photos of her playing with herself, photos of her playing with him, ever careful not to get his head on any pictures as he didn't want a mad squaddie after him, and he'd made sure that the photos went across the sea to her fiancée. Not long after that she stopped wearing her engagement ring but that wasn't even the best part. Doreen disappeared some time later. Rumour had it that she was pregnant and had been sent away by her outraged parents; no one knew that she'd turned up at his flat, had asked him for help, asked him to do the decent thing.

Latimer knew though, he also knew that after laughing at her he had uttered one word "freak" and then sent her on her way, slamming his door in her face. He'd never seen her again, the shame she'd brought on her family had seen to that, and that meant that he had won.

'Winning is everything, Johnny boy.'

No one would ever mess with John Latimer again.

FRIDAY

As Paranoid as Fuck

Matt was shitting it; his body shook against his wishes as he sat in the plastic chair that had held numerous detainees at Clifford Street Police Station over the years. The chairs opposite him were empty awaiting the arrival of his interrogators and this wasn't helping his fear, something was wrong and he wasn't convinced that he wasn't going to get at least a couple of punches. The attitude of his captors, from the desk sergeant booking him in the night before through the various coppers that had looked in on him during his incarceration had left him with an uneasy feeling that there was something more to this than met the eye.

'Fuck's sake, I had a drunken fight. No more than that. The bloke wasn't really hurt, nowt was damaged or nicked and I didn't even have any drugs left on me. What the *fuck* is going on?'

This copper in the room now was a prime example, he'd taken Matt his breakfast that morning, a full fry-up, all the trimmings: toast, fried bread, tomatoes, everything really. Now Matt wasn't an expert on being nicked but he knew you didn't get this type of treatment off the fuckers.

'The eggs were full yolkers, not smashed or nowt. No greasy handprints on the plate where they've fucked about and, as far as I could tell, no spit on it either. It's like they don't really want to be nicking me, like I've done something they approve of. Maybe the bastard was one of them nonces that they aren't allowed to tell you about, maybe they'll just make a show of nicking me and then quietly let me go.'

He put his head in his hands, more to stop it shaking than anything else. He knew he was just suffering the after effects of the whiz from last night and that was making him as paranoid as fuck as well as making his body suffer.

'I'm just kidding myself here; that breakfast wasn't that good really, was it? They must do it for everybody these days, human rights and that. They must do.'

Rubbing his aching head, he wondered how long it would be before the interviewers turned up. If they were quick he could make it into work on time.

'Fucking Hell,' he thought, looking at the clock on the wall as it struck him that he was still on a final written warning. *'Work. I've got to get there; I'll get finished if I don't make it in. Fuck.'*

* * *

John Latimer left the operations meeting with a smile on his face. Blake was buggered now, without a shadow of a doubt. He had known that the Human Resource woman would be initially reluctant to take on board anything he suggested as he obviously had 'previous' with Blake, so he'd taken the opposite approach.

"It should be nothing to do with me whatever you decide," he'd said looking grim. "After all, I arrested him in the first place and it was me that gave him a disciplinary hearing not so long ago."

Both Atkinson, his boss, and the HR woman had nodded at that so he'd gone for the feint, knowing that the ginger biscuit would automatically think the opposite to him.

"I would actually be loath to lose him as he's a good, reliable worker. I think we should give him a chance; it's not the end of the world if he doesn't make it in today, it'll only be a problem if he's gone for longer."

The HR woman, pleasantly surprised at his reasonable stance, had smiled and nodded and, as expected, Atkinson had gone into one about appearing weak in front of the staff and people getting an inch and taking a mile.

The meeting had finished with them agreeing that Blake had the weekend to sort his life out and get back to work. If he wasn't there on Monday then he was getting the chop. It was also agreed that Atkinson and the HR woman would perform the deed, leaving no blood – metaphorically speaking – on Latimer's hands.

'Yes,' he thought as he headed back to his office. *'That call from the station this morning was extremely handy. I know they're not letting him out until Monday, so that's him gone and officially it's nothing to do with me. This might call for a little celebration; I'll have to ring Reg and see if he fancies a drink over the weekend.'*

Policemen and Pirates

Pascoe had put off answering the phone for as long as he could, he'd virtually completed the online Sudoko game he'd been stuck on for weeks and didn't want to stop, but eventually he'd had to concede defeat as whoever was on the other end of the line was not about to go away.

"Pascoe... *What?*"

The voice on the other end of the line was unmistakeably that of his superior officer, the all-knowing and all-seeing, Chief Superintendent De Montford; the man who held his career in the palm of his hand. Pascoe immediately regretted his impatient tone of voice and set about retrieving the situation.

"Ah, good afternoon, Sir. You've just caught me on my way to interview a prime suspect in the vigilante case."

De Montford's voice, or indeed face, rarely gave away his

thoughts but Pascoe, through numerous staged contact with him at the lodge, where he was 'just passing, fancy seeing you here, Sir' and also in his professional capacity, had learnt to read the faint alterations in octaves and knew that what he'd said had caught the attention of the senior man.

"Yes, Sir. A local man. Works in a warehouse. His girlfriend was burgled by the most recent victim and her son was hospitalised. We picked the man up after a violent incident in a local pub last night."

Pascoe could tell De Montford was most definitely interested now; this could be a flagship case for him if he handled it right and made sure the light of glory shone brightest on him.

"I said to Netherstone he was barking up the wrong tree," he said pointedly.

De Montford's pause at the other end let him know that it was his choice whether to continue this new line of conversation and stain Netherstone's reputation forever. Pascoe didn't hesitate.

"Well yes, Sir. I think it's time you knew just how incompetent that boy was. I mean I've tried to help him and tried to shield him but he's not up to it. He's convinced it's an authority figure committing these crimes and won't listen to anyone else. I know his father was an excellent officer, Sir... but, with all due respect, Netherstone is *not* his father."

As the phone went down at the other end, Pascoe sat back in his chair and contemplated his puzzle with a great feeling of satisfaction. Not only had he advanced his own prospects without breaking too much of a sweat, but he'd also struck a lethal blow at the career of the son of a man he hated. Excellent.

Barney looked the suspect up and down as he strode into the interview room. This man was the closest they had come to having a lead, but even so the evidence against him was sketchy to say the least.

"Mr Blake, my name is Barney Netherstone and this is my

colleague, WPC Holmes. We are here to interview you in relation to a number of crimes that have been committed recently in the East of Newcastle. Do you understand?"

Blake shook his head, confusion in his eyes. Barney remembered him as the chap who had scared off the vigilante when he'd attacked the mugger. Suzie slid a piece of paper under his eyes.

THAT'S NOT OUR MAN – THAT'S THE GOOD
LOOKING BLOKE WHO SCARED HIM OFF
WHEN LOZZO O'BRIEN WAS BEATEN UP!

A brief feeling of jealousy and rage enveloped Barney as he read the words 'good' and 'looking' in Suzie's note and he couldn't help himself.

"There have been a number of serious assaults committed in this area recently and, whether the recipients of these assaults deserved it or not, is not for us to decide. No one can take the law into their own hands, as I believe you were guilty of last night, and get away with it. Vigilantism, for want of a better name, is unlawful and as such we bring the full weight of the law to bear on those responsible."

There was a brief blaze of fire in Blake's eyes.

"Yeh, you always go for the easy option, don't you? God forbid you might catch these bastards in the first place and put them away. As long as you fuckers are alright in your little safe ivory towers we can all be beaten, robbed and raped and live our lives in fear."

Barney looked straight at him, unblinking.

"Well, now that we know your opinions on the matter we can continue with the interview... So, Mr Blake, you were on the scene when the mugger was beaten up quite severely and you have no alibi for the sickening assault on a child burglar that occurred when you say you were 'in town'. What exactly were you doing in town, Mr Blake?"

The confusion in Blake's eyes was replaced by fear as the implications of what was being said and what his little outburst may have just cost him sank into his brain.

"I-I was just in a couple of bars."

"Which bars, Mr Blake?"

"Ehm... the Fish Bar and the Black Garter over by the Green Market before coming back to Byker."

Barney felt a nudge beside him as Suzie added to the piece of paper she shown him earlier.

THAT'S NOT OUR MAN – THAT'S THE GOOD LOOKING BLOKE WHO SCARED HIM OFF WHEN LOZZO O'BRIEN WAS BEATEN UP! **CAN'T YOU READ? IT'S NOT HIM!!!!**

THE BLACK GARTER AND THE FISH BAR ARE SHITEHOLES FREQUENTED MAINLY BY MARKET WORKERS, ALKYS AND THE OCCASIONAL PUSHER. HE'S EITHER GOT A DRINK PROBLEM OR HE WAS BUYING GEAR OR BOTH. NEITHER MAKES HIM A VIGILANTE!!!

She'd written it in red, which probably meant she was pissed off at him, but he had to follow every lead and he knew something she didn't.

"We'll check those bars, Mr Blake and, if you're telling us absolutely everything, then you have nothing to fear. Are you telling us everything, Mr Blake? Who were you with?"

"I was on my own. Honestly, I just went for a couple of pints after work. I've just split up with my bird and wanted to get out of Byker and clear my head a bit."

Barney didn't look at Suzie because if she had smiled when Blake had said he finished with his girlfriend then he'd have charged him there and then.

"Your girlfriend was the only one who witnessed the alleged assault by someone in a balaclava on the mugger, Mr Blake.

Therefore, if she's now your ex-girlfriend, then she'd have no reason to protect you, would she? We'll definitively be having a word with her." Blake was either a good actor or he genuinely did disturb the vigilante in action that night as his expression did not betray one ounce of guilt.

"Anything else you want to tell us, Mr Blake? Anything at all? Honesty tends to work in your favour if things go to court," Suzie butted in.

"Well," he replied looking worried. "I bought some gear in town. Just a wrap of whiz for my own use. I'm not a pusher and it's the first I've bought in years. I was just upset."

"Where and who off?" Suzie again, Barney, having pushed the man a little more aggressively than he normally would was now strangely quiet.

"In the Garter. I've never met the bloke before," he replied again before adding quickly, "and I doubt I'd be able to recognise him again because I was pissed. Honest, there'd be no point in me identifying him at all."

Barney leaned forward, signalling that he was re-entering the fray, putting his elbows on the table. He agreed with Suzie that this wasn't their man but he did have to clear something up.

"We have a problem here, Mr Blake. If you're not the vigilante, then how come your fingerprints and therefore presumably your DNA are all over the business card attached to the latest victim's head?"

The confusion came back into Blake's eyes as Barney sat back.

"I really don't know, officer," he replied with what appeared to be sincerity.

"We can't let you go yet then. Not until we've tested the other cards and interviewed all concerned," Barney said simply, before nodding at the attending officer. "Take him back to cell two."

The card was a definite lead, he was sure of it.

* * *

Special

John Latimer took a step back from the mirror in the hall and eyed his reflection appreciatively. His hair was neat and tidy, short but not shaven. His shirt was freshly pressed and looked crisp against his wiry frame. His police issue trousers had starched creases down the front that ensured he never looked shabby and his clip-on tie had been manipulated so much that it looked for all the world like it was in a Windsor Knot. He was ready.

Well, he was ready *physically* at least; mentally he had to build up to this. He was going to visit Vicki again and ask her out.

This was why he'd put on his uniform again, even though he wasn't strictly supposed to, as he wasn't on police duty tonight. Latimer knew though that women couldn't resist a man in uniform, he knew as well that all they really wanted was a strong man to control them and to raise their offspring in a disciplined manner. Some of them didn't realise that's what they wanted, but he knew that underneath all of the modern bluster and bravado that they did.

'After all,' he thought, *'every little girl loves her daddy and then spends the rest of her life subconsciously looking for a replacement.'*

That's the card he was going to play with Vicki tonight; he'd pretend that he was there as there were concerns about the gang her son hung round with. After all, they were doing drugs, were they not? They were vandalising local amenities and causing distress to elderly residents.

"Surely as a concerned and responsible parent you would like to steer your son away from this path, Miss Hughes. What's that, you don't think you can on your own and you need a strong man to help you; someone rugged yet caring, someone disciplined yet humorous? I think I know someone like that, Miss Hughes. What are you doing, Miss Hughes? I'm a police officer. What's that you're saying? You need me? You *want* me? This is most improper, Miss Hughes; you should pull my zip back up and take your hand out of my trousers. Why, Miss Hughes... you could get me sacked."

169

BONG

　　　BONG

The clock striking midday halted his monologue and he looked around, feeling guilty at his arousal. Looking back at the mirror, he caught a brief glimpse of his own reflection before his face adopted its natural frown. He looked almost contented; a state of mind enhanced by the bulge in his trousers and the thought of Vicki Hughes performing fellatio on him.

Then the radio alarm kicked in; he liked it set at midday, a throwback to his dad's old shift pattern and belief that it was better to be early than late.

> "Go call the vigilante
> He'll turn this place upside down
> Go call the vigilante
> He don't need kids around"

> "Hold on there's a new wave coming
> Feels like it's arriving tonight
> There's no more hiding or running
> Everything's gonna be alright"

Latimer smiled to himself; this was about the only station he could tolerate these days and he, particularly in the present climate, enjoyed that song. Then as if something previously unthought-of of had struck him, he checked his watch.

"Bloody thing's a minute slow," he said frowning again.

Heading to the television, he switched it on and put the screen straight to Ceefax – you could always rely on the BBC to do things correctly – and then using the time on screen as his guide, he proceeded to reset every clock in the house.

Special

Shirley

Matt heaved a big sigh of relief as he pushed open the main door of the police station. They'd told him not to go anywhere in a hurry in case they needed him for further questioning but, to all intents and purposes, he was in the clear for the vigilante thing. He'd also accepted a formal caution for both the assault on the barman and admitting buying a small amount of a banned substance. *Accepted it?* He'd nearly snatched their fucking hands off. It turns out that the snidey barman was a bit of a petty thief and was well known to the law for various things over the years so they weren't actually too bothered about him getting a slap. Lucky as fuck, really. He sat down outside the station and tried to piece together the events of the last few hours; his mind was fucking whirring like an out of control Kenwood mixer.

'Still a bit of whiz in the system, I think,' he thought to himself, recalling his time in the interview room with that lady copper and the southern one. *'Fucking spit of Boris Johnson an' all he was, now I come to think of it.'*

Thinking about the heart stopping, tortured minutes when he was alone in the room waiting for them, that second time as they got the results of the tests off the other cards. It had been weird, he knew that he wasn't this vigilante fucker and that, apart from smacking the barman, he was innocent but he still felt guilty cos the bloke had said his dabs were on the card that had been stapled to the boy's head.

'Probably still coming down hard off the gear then,' he thought, knowing that it made you feel guilty and dirty about almost everything. *'That's the payoff as well. You don't do it for ages so the buzz is immense, just like the first time, but you've forgotten what it's like when you hit the floor the next day and it's worse than if you were at it regular.'*

They'd come back in the room looking grim, those same two bizzies, fucking Dempsey and Makepeace mark two, and he'd nearly shit himself, expecting bad news. He could just see the rest of his life being spent sharing a cell with some big fucker who wore a wig after lights out and made you call him Shirley. The little negative voices in his head that always showed themselves in times of stress were screaming at him:

'You shouldn't have had a go about them being soft on real criminals, you're going to be fitted up now you stupid, stupid twat, when will you learn to wind your fucking neck in you prick?'

He'd believed them as well, truly believed this was it and he was going down for something he hadn't done. He'd end up in the same wing as Eggy and Gonch, the world's most inept criminals, and his status as one of life's proper losers would be confirmed. All his old teachers would nod and say to themselves, "Told you he was destined to be a failure." He'd have lived down to every expectation of himself that he'd ever heard expressed in his direction and had spent his life striving to avoid. Fucking heartbreaking.

Then the copper spoke.

"Mr Blake, having run some preliminary tests on all of our evidence so far, it is apparent that your fingerprints and DNA are on some of the cards. Now, personally speaking, I don't think you're the man we want, but I do think that you hold some information or clue to his identity and you're not leaving here until we get it."

Matt's heart had jumped. In his cell in his mind's eye he could see a little tunnel appear marked 'escape route' and he was diving in head first just as Shirley was approaching the door shouting "Coo-ee, pet."

"Mr Blake, please pay attention, this is serious. How did the card get your fingerprints on?"

Matt gulped; he didn't have a fucking clue. This was obviously a bad thing because, back in the cell, he was stuck in the tunnel with his bottom half sticking up in the air just as Shirley entered and said "Oh, look... someone's left me a present."

"I really don't know, officer," he said quietly.

"Right then, let's go through it all again. Where do you work and what do you do?"

"German Wizard. It's a white goods distribution depot at the back of Shields Road. I'm a warehouse operative, well I'm probably not anymore cos I was on a final written warning before I didn't turn in today."

"And what was that for?"

"Oh, they thought I was nicking stationery," Matt replied resignedly, not noticing the look on both Barney and Suzie's faces.

"Stationery?" they replied in unison.

"Aye," said Matt, starting to catch up rapidly. "Fuck me... aye, there's a chamber in there that we rent out to a stationery firm. It's mainly card and paper and that."

"So, were you in there and have you touched the card?"

Matt sighed again; he was about to admit to another crime to these bizzies as well as the drugs. They were gonna throw away the key here.

"Aye, I used to nick reams of A4 paper and sell them to Eddie Venables for his shop on Headlam Street. People are mad for cheap paper now they've all got computers and my wages are shite, to be honest. I suppose I'm just talking myself into more trouble here, am I?"

Barney and Suzie looked at each other and smiled before turning back to Matt who had returned to his mental cell and could feel Shirley pulling his prison issue jeans down.

"No, Mr Blake," Barney replied. "I don't give a monkey's how much paper you've nicked over the years, but I need to know... did you ever steal card for the shop?"

"No, just paper. More of a market for it, apparently."

"So – and make sure you think hard now – how would the card have your prints on it?"

"It all comes in on pallets with the card on top holding the paper down. I have to move the card to get the paper and then replace the card the way it was to avoid suspicion."

Barney looked ecstatic and slid a pen and a bit of paper over to Matt.

"Write down your company's name and address on there and everyone you can think of that would have access to that chamber where the card is kept. *Then* we'll look at getting you out of here."

That was precisely forty-five minutes ago and now he was outside sitting on a bench, dialling Tonka's number to find out if he still had a job. Regardless of whether he'd been sacked or not, he still felt well chuffed at somehow managing to snatch victory from the jaws of defeat. Just as Shirley's hands had been on his arse, the tunnel had expanded and he'd slipped away, the frustrated shouting from above mingling with his own enthusiastic cheering.

'Good old Boris coming up trumps like that... fucking close, mind.'

Exactly what she Needs

Vicki was knackered; she'd spent the majority of her precious day off doing all of the cleaning jobs she used to spread across the week when she was unemployed. So far today she had cleaned the kitchen, dusted everywhere, Hoovered the entire house, cleaned the bathroom until the taps sparkled, wiped down all the walls and sills, replaced toilet paper and light bulbs and touched up the odd bit of paint here and there. She knew that it would be easy to let these things slide now she was working, but was determined not to become like some of the other mothers on this estate with their convenience TV dinners, lack of self-respect and reliance on state money. She wasn't content to live in a shitehole either and the thought of being compared to these fat shell-suited, foul-mouthed bitches kept her going.

'Not much left to do now anyway,' she thought, *'a little bit of shopping and empty the bins. I should have time for a cup of tea and a read of the paper later.'*

* * *

John Latimer removed the face from his car stereo, applied the crook lock and then got out of the car and set the alarm. After all, you couldn't be too careful in an area like this. Making a pretence of looking back into the car he checked his reflection, looking back at him was the face of a straight, honest and reliable man.

"Oh, yes," he said to himself. "I'm exactly what she needs."

Taking a moment longer to straighten his tie, he then turned and headed towards Vicki's house. Noting that the light was on in the kitchen he pushed the gate open, the squeal of the hinges masking the very audible, to him anyway, beating of his heart.

'Bloody Hell,' he thought, *'the last time I was this nervous around a woman was when I went to the pictures with Doreen Walkinshaw. I hope it turns out better than that.'*

The door opened just as he got there, his hand already raised to knock on the frosted glass. Vicki was obviously throwing the rubbish out as her impetus pushed a bulging bin bag straight into him, knocking him off balance and leaving a mark on his shirt.

"Oh, sorry," she said, sounding anything but. "I didn't see you there. You shouldn't go creeping up on people."

"That's okay, Miss Hughes," he replied, regaining his feet and

175

trying desperately to keep the irritation he felt at her clumsy ignorance out of his voice.

'There'll be plenty of time for training her properly when we're married'.

He checked his shirt; there was a nasty brown stain there now. It smelt like stale tea and felt wet on his chest.

'She must throw hot tea bags straight into the bin without letting them dry out and harden first. There's a lot of room for improvement here Johnny, definitely.'

"Aha, ehmm... don't you leave your teabags out to dry first before binning them, Miss Hughes?"

"No," she replied looking nonplussed. "Why would I?"

"Well," he continued, less nervous now they were talking about housekeeping and he was on safe ground. "If you put them straight in the bin when hot and wet, not only does the steam make mildew forming condensation inside your bin, the bag itself can burn through the liner if they come into contact while it's still hot resulting in..."

He looked down at his shirt, she'd realise how much she had to learn and how much he could teach her now.

"Fascinating."

He looked back up, surprised at the sarcasm of her tone; she wasn't even looking at him, just wiping down the kitchen worktops.

"Also," he said, "you shouldn't use what is obviously your dishcloth to wipe down worktops that have been used to prepare food and may contain traces of raw meat. You should use a separate cloth and some anti-bacterial agent to be on the safe side."

She was glaring at him now; he couldn't understand why, this was valuable advice.

"What is it you actually want, officer?"

Ah, the time had come; Latimer had practiced this and was ready with his plan of attack. Firstly: exaggerate the danger young Nick was in of going to prison and messing his life up, secondly, promise to look out for him. Then the third point: declare undying love, catch swooning woman, listen to her declaring undying love back, have cup of tea and biscuit... best china.

"Well, Miss Hughes... there's a couple of things: firstly, young Nick."

"What about him?"

"Well, as you know, he's hanging round with a bad crowd and it isn't good for him. Now I know he's not a *bad lad* but if he keeps following them around he'll..."

"What do you mean *bad crowd?* They're fine. All they do is hang round the park and drink a bit; they don't steal or mug people, just make a bit of noise. He's known Stimp and Bridey since he was two-years-old. I've known their parents the same length of time and they're nice people. In fact, they all did a sponsored swim at school last year and raised nearly two grand for the British Legion to send some old soldiers over to France for Remembrance Sunday."

"I'm just saying, Miss Hughes, that he's been arrested now for drugs and the like and he really shouldn't be hanging round with them if he wants to keep out of further trouble."

'This is harder than I thought it would be,' Latimer thought to himself. *'Still, the mention of drugs ought to concentrate her mind a bit.'*

"*Drugs?!* Bollocks, they had a bit of smoke. All it does is make you mellow. Jesus, they weren't on crack and running round with axes, were they? A smoke and a bottle of cider in the park... hardly Britain's Most Wanted, is it?" Vicki was obviously unimpressed with his scare tactics.

'Cheeky fucking slag. Who does she think she's talking to? Put her right, Johnny.'

"Well, we can agree to disagree on that one; drugs are drugs as far as I'm concerned but anyway, all I'm saying, Miss Hughes, is that Nick is at a crossroads in his life now and needs some direction and guidance. A strong male role model would help him enormously at this time of his life."

She'd stopped answering back and looked thoughtful at this; Latimer saw his chance and went for it.

"And as such, I'd like to offer my services..."

Vicki just looked far away so, taking this as a good sign, Latimer moved closer and put his arm around her. "Miss Hughes... Vicki... I know there's something between us. I've felt it since the day you first came to the station. We could be good together and I'd be good for Nick. What do you say?"

Her left breast was touching his chest and, as she turned to face him, her right followed suit, this stirred passions deep within him that had lain dormant for quite some time. He knew that life wouldn't be the same from here on in and wondered whether she would drag him upstairs straight away or wait a few days before consummating their relationship.

"You're having a fucking laugh, right?"

His reverie was rudely interrupted by her sarcastic question. The shocked expression on her face told him that this maybe wasn't going to go as smoothly as he thought.

"*You?* You think I would want anything to do with *you?* The very thought of touching you makes me sick. Let me make this quite plain, officer: I do not like you and do not want anything to do with you. Unless you have to speak to me in a professional capacity then I do not wish for you to speak to me. I would rather fuck George Galloway than see you naked. Do you understand what I'm saying?"

Latimer couldn't believe she was speaking to him like this. He was stunned, and before he knew what he was doing he had muttered a cowed "Yes, Miss Hughes," and was being ushered out of the door.

"Good," she replied. "Now FUCK OFF."

Latimer headed back to the car, face red as his cheeks burned with embarrassment and his blood started to boil at this patently unfair treatment from a common slag.

'The fucking bitch, fucking fucking fucking bitch bitch bitch. Can't open the car door; get it open, Johnny, fucking get in there bastard key. Fucking slag, opens her legs for everyone but not us, fucking bitch OPEN THE FUCKING DOOR, JOHNNY.'

The car door eventually opened, now with a nasty scratch near the lock, and he got in.

'You're too good for her anyway, Son. I'd turn in my grave if you slept with that whore. Fucking bitch, fucking bitch, fucking bitch. Her son better not step out of line again, fucking slag.'

Getting a Result

Nick had been going stir crazy in the house for the last few days and was pleased his mam had finally seen sense and let him out. His senses tingled at all the things he'd been denied lately: the cold wind on his face, his eyes adjusting to the twilight, the sound of the city early on Friday evening, cars and people all hurrying this way and that. It felt good to be out again, he liked that his mam worried about him, but she had to realise that he was a man now and could look after himself; he'd grown up around here so it's not like he was a mug, was it? Yes, he'd had his jaw broke by that Ghostboy wanker but that was a one-off and wouldn't happen again. And anyway, he had a bit of security these days. Fingering the lock knife in his pocket, he smiled. Anybody who wanted to fuck with him now had to realise that he was bringing the equaliser into battle with him, particularly since his mam had given Matt the elbow. He liked Matt and hoped he came back at some point but, until then, he had to face up to his responsibilities, after all, he was the man of the house now.

Anyway, he was out and off to the park to see his mates. Stimp had rung him and said he'd see him there, Nick couldn't wait, hopefully Becky would be there as well and they could carry on where they'd left off before his jaw was busted. She was definitely up for it; he knew she was and he couldn't wait.

'Virginity might be getting trendy again in America but not in Newcastle, not on this fucking estate it's not.'

At fifteen he knew he should have done it by now. All his mates claimed to have, but he had his doubts over some of them fuckers; Bridey and Callum were both a pair of lying bastards for a start, maybe Dobba had though, he was a bit of a smoothie with the ladies. Nick'd had his opportunities in the past, but turned them down through a combination of fear and general disgust at the fat slappers who were offering it. Becky though, she was different and he was sure they'd be getting it on sometime soon... hopefully tonight. Patting his pocket again he turned up his collar against the wind and headed down the fast darkening road towards the park.

* * *

Barney was getting excited; they were getting somewhere now. He'd taken the list of names that Blake had given him and was steadily working his way through them; background, criminal record, employer's disciplinary records and parents' backgrounds... that kind of thing. He'd also discovered that the card used was of a very high quality and only produced by one firm in Britain and that they only had two storage facilities, one in Milton Keynes and the other in Newcastle. So, either someone is travelling up here from down South to assault local criminals or the person responsible works at German Wizard.

One name above all others had stood out to him when he perused the list, John Latimer. He knew that he was a Special Constable based at this very station and, as a supervisor at the warehouse; he would presumably have access to all chambers and storage areas. While this was only a hunch, the clincher for Barney had been the fact that Latimer had arrested Blake on suspicion of being the vigilante in the first place.

'Classic behaviour: seek to disseminate misinformation, cast doubt on leads and fit someone else up.'

Barney looked around the deserted offices; Friday night in Geordieland was a big one, this was evidenced by everyone grabbing their coats and getting down to the pub as soon the big hand hit five. Suzie had even disappeared with only a quick goodbye, she probably had a date or something, couldn't blame her. The nightshift had come in and gone out again, ready to police the streets of the party city and gain the chancellor as much in fines as they could, leaving only Barney and his hunch about Latimer.

Picking up the phone he stole one more quick glance around the room; it was probably best he did this without anyone else knowing, he especially didn't want Pascoe finding out until he was sure of the facts. He dialled the number and listened to it ringing for some time, obviously the National Adoption people didn't hang around on a Friday either. He was just about to replace the handset and start composing an e-mail when a voice appeared at the other end of the line and asked him what he wanted.

"Ah, good evening. Barney Netherstone here, from Northumberland Police. I require some information on a boy who was adopted some years ago. I would like to know what his birth name was and, if possible, the reasons behind his adoption. Authorisation? Yes Superintendent Pascoe of Clifford Street Station has authorised this request."

Barney gulped hoping they didn't check with Pascoe, at least not until he'd got some evidence to back his theory up.

"What's that? The boys adopted name? Latimer, John Latimer."

Andy Rivers

The Nightmare Scenario

The rest of the gang had turned up eventually and Nick had started to feel more comfortable. Arriving at the park first hadn't been a good idea, particularly when he'd gone to sit in the little cubby hole underneath the kiddies slide and he'd noticed a huge V spray painted over it. Luckily, Stimp had shown up virtually straight after he did and hadn't given him the chance to fuck off home, then a little while later Becky had put in an appearance looking absolutely gorgeous and there was no way he was doing off now. Everyone had been a bit nervous about the V but they'd all put on a show for each other especially the lads.

"You look like you're going to cry there, Dobba boy. Shall I give your mam a ring and get her down to hold your hand?"

"Fuck off, Bridey. We all know you shit yourself when you go on the ghost train, so don't pretend to be hard now."

Then Callum had pulled out some smoke and they'd clubbed together for a few bottles of cider before congregating in the seats under the slide to tell ghost stories and prove how not scared they all were. Nick thought this was a great idea, particularly as Becky was next to him and squeezing his hand every time a spooky story was told. Some of them were utter shite and weren't frightening at all so Nick reckoned she was doing it just to hold his hand.

'Right then,' he thought, *'this'll scare the fuck out of her and she'll be begging me to take her home.'*

"Reet... my turn," he said, looking round at the expectant faces in the enclosure. Switching his phone on so it illuminated the underside of his face, *Blair Witch* style, he started to tell his story.

"This is more of an urban myth than an old-fashioned ghost story and I don't know if it's true or not. You decide."

Looking around again he could feel Becky cuddling right into him and he could see the expectant faces of his mates as they put down bottles and finished off joints.

"There was a lass I heard about a few years ago, Daisy her name was, and she was coming home from town on the metro. She was only the same age as us but her parents were much stricter, they wouldn't have let her do owt like this. Her dad was a bit of a cunt by all accounts and she had to be in before it was dark."

Nick knew how to tell a story; it was a skill that he had inherited from his prick of a father and as such it both entranced and abhorred him in equal measure. He knew though, that to mix in truth with fiction, to blend the everyday with the fantastic could only make a story all the more enthralling as people related to the aspects they recognised and their minds made a link with that which they didn't.

"Anyway, she'd been shopping, lost track of the time and was late coming home and she knew it; the darkness outside the train windows screamed it at her. Her dad had specifically said to be home by eight and it was gone ten past now and she still had to go another five stops before the walk home from the metro station. She knew her mam would understand when she showed her the shoes she'd bought but her dad wouldn't."

Looking round at the group he drew them into his tale with matey complicity. "Eh, lads and lasses? We've all heard wor dads kick off with wor mams."

He affected a deep, outraged voice. "*What?* You had to look around every shop and then go back to the very first one to buy the shoes you first tried on at half nine this morning? Fuck's sake."

They were all nodding and smiling. He had them.

"So, Daisy's on the metro and she's feeling a bit pissed off with herself cos she knows she'll be grounded just as the school disco comes up and she'll miss her chance to show off her new shoes and get it on with that hunky sixth form fucker – the one who looks a bit like me – so it's all been a bit of a self-defeating exercise, really. She's not really taking much notice of what's going on, so when the train pulls into the next station and stops, it brings her back to earth with a bump. It cheers her up a bit cos now there's only four stops to go, but typically, she takes her phone out and sees she forgot to charge it the night before and can't even ring ahead with an excuse. Feeling the useless phone in her hand just underlines her sense of helplessness and she scans the carriage for anyone she might know on the off-chance they would let her make a call on theirs.

"And was there anyone on that carriage she knew? Was there fuck. Not one soul. Three girls her own age had shuffled on at the other end of the carriage but they were scummy charva types and she didn't know people like that. Most people had got off at this station and it was Byker next, she knew it took a while to get there cos of going over Byker Bridge so she sat back, resigned to her fate. Still, only four stops now so she wouldn't be that late, hopefully."

"Then, for some reason, she looked up and casually glanced back up the carriage again and noticed the three girls were standing against the doors of the train, which was strange really as there was loads of seats. Two of them were staring at her and she felt a little bit nervous about it as she wasn't really a fighter, what with her parents being so protective. Luckily for her she knew a little bit about psychology from various science lessons at her private school, so she decided to present a confident appearance and make herself a 'hard target'. Looking the girls up and down in apparent disdain she noticed that the two who were staring at her were supporting the middle girl who looked off her nut on drugs or glue or something."

Looking back around the group Nick noted a few pinched-looking faces and said, "I mean, someone high as a kite on the metro? Not an uncommon occurrence is it, eh?"

Only Stimp replied, the rest were hanging on his every word. "They're fucking vampires Nick, aren't they? They are, aren't they?"

Nick just smiled at him and continued. "Daisy kept staring back at them and noticed every time the train swayed and rolled the middle girl went with it, being held up by the others. For their part, they looked quite fierce and had obviously been at the glue as well as they weren't quite there, mumbling to each other under their breaths all the time and just ignoring their, obviously comatose, mate in the middle. When she could hold the stare no more she looked away, she would have liked to have studied them a bit more closely but she didn't want to antagonise them and risk a kicking or worse. The dark rings around their eyes and blotchy skin were obviously by-products of hanging round with the 'shock your parents crowd' that infest Old Eldon Square. You know the ones; they strive to be different but end up looking all the same. Anyway, the scabs and sores around their mouths and nostrils indicated to Suzie that some heavy solvent abuse was happening and she didn't want anything to do with people like that.

"So putting them out of her mind in order not to stare at them anymore, she thought ahead to the oncoming argument with her dad and how best to approach it. She thought it was probably best to stay calm and apologetic, it might be worth inventing a transport problem but the pedantic bastard would probably check. 'No,' she thought, 'I'll just tell the truth and apologise.'"

Dobba broke in, "You mean she stopped keeping an eye on the bastards? They could just sneak up on her." He sounded shocked, "Is she fucking daft or what, this lass?"

Nick smiled again, giving nothing away, and then continued. "The train pulled into Byker station and Daisy quickly scanned the platform again hoping someone she knew was there but no one at all was getting on and, to her dismay, she saw that everyone bar her and the girls had gotten off. She was a bit scared now and quickly weighed that up against getting off herself, knowing that she didn't have enough money for a bus ticket and her dad would go mental if she spent an hour walking home from there.

"The decision was made for her as the doors closed and the train started to move into the tunnel. Risking a quick glance at the weirdos up the carriage sent a shiver up her spine; they were both staring straight at her now and their mumbling to each other was getting louder. Their friend in the middle had her head back and it was rocking violently as the train sped through the long, dark tunnel. Daisy looked away in fear; there was something about these girls that wasn't right. She didn't believe in ghouls and ghosties but there was malevolence and a touch of evil about them that scared her.

"She clenched her fists, ready to fight if she had to, but hoping against hope that it wouldn't come to that. The train let out a hoot as it hit a bend in the tunnel and she stole another glance up the train; of course, they were still looking at her and whispering to each other. One of them was slapping the girl in the middle round the head, obviously bringing her round so they could attack Suzie mob-handed. She was scared now. Her breath was coming in short, sharp gasps and her legs were shaking."

Becky's hand was clutching his hand tightly now and her other hand was squeezing his arse like it was a stress toy, her head burrowed into his chest and her fantastic tits dangled, excruciatingly, an inch above his knob.

"Controlling her breathing through deep gulps, Daisy calmed herself. These were just your average Burberry clad Muppets; they weren't vampires or monsters and they wouldn't do anything if she appeared confident. When she was composed she looked round again, ready to stare them out and show them she was no pushover. Unfortunately for her, the comatose friend was now lying down on a seat and the two girls were walking slowly towards her.

"Their movements were shaky but measured and they were grimacing at her. Daisy tried to stand but couldn't, fear engulfed her and froze her to the spot. She felt sick, she was shaking, she wanted to go to the toilet but all she could do was stare at these freaks approaching her. Then she noticed one of them had a screw-driver in her hand and she felt the urine trickling down her leg."

"Fucking hell," exclaimed Stimp. "The poor cow. This is brilliant, what happened?"

"Well," said Nick, shining his mobile round at each on of their anxious faces. "I'm not sure I should tell you, you might never get the metro again."

"Ooooh just tell us man, Nick," said Becky while simultaneously burying her head back in his chest as if to protect herself from whatever it is he was going to say.

"Okay then, if you're sure…" He smiled back at them, the light back under his face and his eyes widening just to unnerve them further.

"I bet they're vampires. I bet they're fucking vampires," Stimp jumped while the rest told him to, 'Ssshhh.'

"The lasses were about five feet away from Daisy just as the train pulled into the station. Luckily there was an inspector on the platform and, because he was there, they backed off from her muttering under their breath and continuing to stare. Daisy jumped straight up and the inspector grabbed her as she headed for the door.

"She tried to tell him that she had a ticket and what had just happened, but he ignored her and just kept saying she would be prosecuted if she couldn't produce a valid pass. Daisy was proper confused cos she was waving her ticket at him, but he ignored her and kept saying, 'You must come with me, young lady.'

"Then something strange happened. When they were both off the train and the door warning was sounding he whispered to her from one side of his mouth, 'Just act like I've caught you until the train pulls away.'

"Daisy was so confused and frightened now that she didn't care about her dad anymore and just did as he said. As the train pulled away she noticed that the girl who had been comatose on the seat had fallen off onto the floor but her two friends were ignoring her and just staring at them out of the window.

"Daisy looked back at the inspector and said, 'They're nutters. Their friend is high on something and they were about to attack me.'"

Nick looked slowly around at them, his mates, hanging off his every word, their faces willing him to frighten them but begging him not to. And he continued.

"The inspector looked down at her, he was so nervous that sweat was dripping off his furrowed brow and said to her, 'We know, it's all on CCTV. The police are waiting for them at the next station, but we didn't think you'd get that far so we had to get you off the train without arousing their suspicion.'

"He paused again then went for it: 'Their friend isn't high, she's dead.'"

"Aaaaagggghhh, Nick... you bastard... that's horrible."

The sighs and gasps of his mates was music to his ears as they decided that was definitely the best story of the night. Becky, pulling him towards her and kissing him, was better again though.

"Will you walk me home Nick, I'm far too scared to go on my own now."

"Fucking right I will," he said, before moving in for another snog.

Just before their lips touched they were interrupted by a scream. Nick looked past Becky's head and smiled saying, "Fucking hell Bev, me story wasn't that scary."

Her face was white, even in the dark. Her eyes stared straight past his shoulder to the space behind the slide. Nick slowly turned his head to face whatever it was, fear rising in his chest as he hoped against hope it wasn't two charva lasses holding up a third and muttering to themselves. What he saw was marginally less frightening but still as scary as fuck... five yards away from them was a bloke in a balaclava holding a baseball bat.

Special

The next few minutes were bedlam; Nick pushed Becky away from the bloke and shouted "RUN", before making off himself dragging her along. The bloke with the bat had caught Bridey and had smashed him to the ground, booting him in the head for good measure as he lay unmoving. Kaz and Callum were too slow off the mark, their blood full of cannabis and their bellies full of cider. They were savagely beaten as they tried to get up from the swings.

The time it took him to do this gave Nick and Becky the chance to escape, at the gate of the park Nick looked back and saw his three friends prone and lifeless as the attacker dropped what looked like business cards on them. Nick felt in his pocket for the knife as the bloke turned his head to him, it felt small and insignificant and no match for a baseball bat. He wasn't hanging round to see any more, dragging a shocked and hysterical Becky with him he headed for home; they weren't stopping until they were in the door.

SATURDAY

A Regional Chip

Barney watched the lorry ahead that had been holding everyone up for the last ten miles move back into the slow lane of the dual carriageway.

'Bloody lorry drivers do that on purpose. Go to overtake one of their mates for a laugh knowing that they're only doing about a mile an hour more than them resulting in a slow rolling blockage of the whole bloody carriageway. They only do it to wind people up.'

The delay had given him the chance to survey some of the scenery on the A19 as this was the first time he had traversed it in daylight. Unfortunately, he had been going through Middlesbrough at the time and his view had been that of the dark, menacing, chemical works and the kind of heavy industry that belonged in a previous era. For the first time since his move up here he'd felt quite pleased at his choice of workplace; Newcastle was very northern and still strange to him, but at least it wasn't bloody Middlesbrough.

Turning his attention away from the rapidly growing, albeit adopted, regional rivalry inside him, he thought instead of the progress being made on his first ever case. If he was honest with himself he'd admit that this was why he was going to visit his parents, not because he missed them overly... but because he wanted to get his dad's advice and also to let them both know he was doing well.

'It's got to be Latimer,' he thought to himself as, finally free of obstruction, he eased the motor into fifth and put his toe down.

'He must, at the very least, be involved in some way. He

190

has access to the card; he has access to the names and aliases of known criminals in the area as well as their movements and modus operandi. He is obviously considered above suspicion by my boss and probably everyone else by virtue of being a copper, not just any copper either – one who gives up his free time and risks his neck for nothing. I can see the logic in their reasoning but, in my opinion, that makes him more suspect... anyone who does this job for nothing is clearly mentally unhinged and therefore more than capable of cutting up petty offenders to prove some kind of point.'

Then, braking heavily at the appearance of an imminent speed camera, his thoughts turned to Pascoe.

'I really should have passed on the information about Latimer to Pascoe and let him make the call whether to bring him in or not, but I can't face him blowing up at me again. I can't discuss the case with Dad either because Pascoe will just go up the wall if he finds out I'm going outside the station again. I can ask Dad about Pascoe though and his opinion on the man. He's bound to know him, and then I can speak to Pascoe on Monday about Latimer. I'll just have to cross my fingers that nothing happens until then.'

His course of action determined, Barney moved into the outside lane, the speed camera a yellow dot in his rear view mirror and the M1 at Leeds fast approaching.

'I can't believe there's no bloody motorway this far North either. A dual carriageway the only way into Newcastle once you get past Leeds? That must add about half an hour onto every journey outside of the region, sometimes even I can understand why they have a chip on their shoulders about the decision makers being based hundreds of miles away. Fucking Cockneys!'

Andy Rivers

Men of Action

John Latimer carefully grasped the nose hair in between the tweezer legs and then yanked. He winced in pain and then checked the results of his handiwork in the bathroom mirror.

'Old age won't take me without a fight,' he thought to himself, splashing freezing cold water onto the reddening area around his now sore nostrils. Then, satisfied that no more hairs were protruding from his nasal passages, he went back into the bedroom to get dressed. Pulling on a freshly ironed shirt, he thought back to the debacle in Vicki Hughes's house last night.

'The stupid bitch didn't know when she was being done a favour, Johnny. How often does a tu'ppeny ha'penny slag like that get offered a future with a man like you? How many chances does a bottom-of-the-heap and falling, no prospects, dregs of society bint need before she takes one?'

Selecting a new tie from his large holder he moved towards the full-length mirror and placed it around his collar.

'I think you're maybe being a bit harsh on her,' he thought, fiddling with the knot. *'I don't, Johnny. I think she's a fucking ungrateful whore and you should put her in the picture as soon as possible.'*

He weighed up the evidence; she was indeed ungrateful but, at the same time, she was probably still upset about her son being attacked and her house burgled. In fact she was probably even a bit upset about breaking up with that idiot Blake. Latimer was a man of action, decisive and bold, but not without compassion. He decided to give her one last chance. After all... he was a grown up, logical, reasonable man and she was, after all, a little behind him in the evolutionary scale so he had to make allowances. Yes, he would do it today, strike while the iron's hot. She would probably be feeling bad about the way she had treated him and would want to make amends.

"Excellent! That's settled, then," he said to his reflection. Then he frowned and stooped forward towards the mirror. Something was wrong, but what? The knot in his tie was perfect, his shirt was immaculately ironed and his trousers had creases sharper than Tony Hancock. What was it?

Then smiling almost in resignation he headed back to the bathroom.

'It looks like old age is going to put up a fight as well,' he thought, turning sideways to the bathroom mirror and lifting the tweezers to his ear.

* * *

Matt was positively bouncing down Shields Road; he was in a great mood. Saturday mornings had this effect on him as a rule anyway, but after the trauma of being locked up all day yesterday with the expected outcome of many years' jail along with the obligatory male rape nightmare... he was definitely a lot happier today. As well as being as free as the proverbial bird he was also chuffed at the news he was keeping his job; a phone call to Miss Latif the HR woman that very morning had confirmed that, as long as he was in work on Monday, then yesterday would be treated as an authorised absence. The puzzling thing was that apparently Latimer had stuck up for him; from what he'd gathered over the phone he'd actually been quite reasonable about the whole thing and had stopped Atkinson from binning him.

'The fucker must be on Prozac or something,' he thought, feeling a little ashamed at the hard times he'd given the bloke in the past. *'Anyway, enough of that... let's go and do what a man has to do.'*

He'd done a lot of thinking during the boring hours he'd spent in the nick yesterday. He considered himself a witty and urbane chap but he was the first to admit when you've only yourself for company, then eventually you have to stop making jokes. His thoughts had veered from the bleak future he'd imagined for himself in a jail run by homosexual predators to the bright new day he'd dared dream about if only he could have got out of the mess he'd somehow stumbled into. Now he was out of that particular quagmire, he'd decided to pursue the radical thoughts that had crossed his mind in the cell and had continued plaguing him, despite his release.

'I'm thirty-years-old. I drink too much. I take drugs, which make me feel great for a while but shit for a lot longer. I live in a council flat. I have no savings. I live hand to mouth from a dead-end job that pays minimum wage but expects maximum effort. Over the years I've had a succession of one night stands that have sometimes turned into two or three month stands, but I've never had a proper, grown up relationship where I talk about things and do stuff for the other person. In short, I've never grown up and it's time I fucking did. My life needs to change and I'm the only one who can change it.'

Looking further up the road he could see Vicki just outside Iceland. He knew she wasn't working today and had guessed when she wasn't at home that she'd be exercising her staff discount perk and doing her shopping there. Just seeing her made his heart jump; that and the fear of what he was about to do.

'I have never felt anything for the women I've shagged. Actually, sometimes I've physically felt nothing as well but that's the whiz for you... but this girl... she has punched me clean in the heart and left a big fucking bruise. I think about her all the time, I miss her since we're not together anymore and, if the truth be known, I quite enjoyed being around Nick as well. It's taken thirty years, but I'm finally going to tell someone I love them.'

Then, gulping in air and fighting off panic, he started walking towards the woman he'd only recently realised he was in love with.

One hundred percent Detection Record

Barney looked around the spacious lounge of his parent's home; the walls were littered with photographs of him. The time he'd been made a prefect at school marked with a Kodak moment and hung up for all to see, the same when he'd been made house captain and in his final year head boy, all recorded for posterity and available for public viewing. He hadn't thought about them much before but now, not having seen his parents for a while and having mixed with people in the real world at last, he realised that the photos weren't about one-upmanship over the neighbours or the bridge club but they were a tangible indication of just how much his parents loved him. He'd never really missed home when he was a boy at boarding school, he'd actually had a great time with his friends and, contrary to popular opinion about such places, there was no buggery went on – well not unless you wanted it to – but his parents had obviously missed him when he was away and that was why they took so many photos.

"Probably a Catch-twenty-two for them really," he murmured to himself. "They wanted the best for me so sent me to the best school they could and, in return, they never really got to see me grow up."

He could hear his mum bustling about in the kitchen, his dad was in the shower after doing a bit of gardening but he knew Barney was here so he wouldn't be long. Since his retirement he loved to hear every bit of gossip about police life. A photograph on the sideboard caught Barney's eye; amongst the sea of pictures of their little boy his parents still had a reminder of the love they had for each other. It showed his mum in an evening dress and his dad in a black tie and tuxedo. They looked younger than Barney did now and his mother was very pretty back then.

'She still is now obviously, just in a different way,' he thought, guiltily looking round in case she'd somehow read his mind and had come to bollock him.

His dad was a big chap back then, not so small now either even though old age was catching him up, and Barney recalled him being scared of nothing and no one.

Picking up the photo he tried to cast his mind back. What was his earliest memory? They'd lived in this house all his life so it wouldn't be anything before moving in here, not for him anyway. He reckoned the first thing he could remember was tottering to the gate at the end of the big front garden and seeing a strange creature through the bars. That was the start of his detective career as, after trying to lick the creature which was tantalisingly out of reach, he'd decided he had to find out more about it as it hopped away. He'd gotten over the gate and followed it; he remembered it teasing him by always being one jump ahead of him all the way to the end of the road.

'Bloody mirrors my career so far, actually,' he smiled to himself. *'I haven't got near the vigilante yet. Still that's going to change next week.'*

His fledging Attenborough tendencies had come to an abrupt end when his mum had picked him up and dumped him back in the garden with a stern warning not to go outside again. Still, he'd found out that the strange creature was called a frog, so the end justified the means.

'One hundred percent detection record so far,' he thought. *'I can't let that slip.'*

"Barney! Welcome home, Son." His dad extended a manly right hand, caught his in a vice-like grip and pumped his arm furiously. The old man was definitely not past it yet.

"How's it going up in Geordieland?" He asked, sitting in his big chair and motioning Barney to do likewise on the sofa.

"Oh, I'm getting my feet under the table now I think, Pops. I've been struggling with a big case just lately but I'm closing in on the bad guy now."

"Oh yes..." his eyes sparkled and he leaned forward, "need any help from the old man?"

Barney sighed. He would love nothing better than to run it by his dad, but if it got back to Pascoe or he inadvertently let it slip then he'd be in for the high jump.

"No can do, Dad," he shook his head at his obviously disappointed father. "I'd get it right in the neck from my boss, Superintendent Pascoe."

"Oh," his dad looked disconsolate for a moment and then "Pascoe?"

"Yes," said Barney, "Do you know him?"

"Do I *know him?*" His dad snorted, "Is he late forties, first name Colin?"

Barney was intrigued. It seemed strange to find out that your parents had had some sort of life before you but it made sense, after all he'd retired six or seven years ago after a thirty-year career that had seen him seconded to many regions and investigations so he'd obviously know a lot of higher ranking and longer serving officers.

"Yes, he's about that age and I think his first name may well be Colin. Why?"

"Well, Son, unless he's had a radical change in attitude, demeanour and moral fibre then your boss is a coward, charlatan and a backbiting sneak of the highest order."

Barney was amazed, he didn't particularly like Pascoe but, at the end of the day, he was a high-ranking police officer in the service of Her Majesty. His dad shouldn't really be talking about him like this and he was about to tell him so. His dad looked round to the kitchen conspiratorially and then back at Barney.

"Do you see that photo on the sideboard there, me and your

mother some years back at a force do? Well that was when I first came across Pascoe."

His dad, satisfied that his mother wasn't going to come in and hear any of this, shifted in his seat until he was comfortable and then began.

"It was a Long Service Awards ball for the South Eastern region as it was then. All senior officers and local politicians; I was head detective with the now defunct Anglian force, but I was looking for a move to the Met. I'd heard whispers of a new crew being formed, the CID, so I'd gone to this party with your mother, then my fiancé, with the intention of making my motives known and talking to some of the right people. You'd call it networking now. After all, I had an excellent arrest and conviction record and quite fancied making my mark down in the smoke."

He paused, took a sip of his wine and sneaked another look at the kitchen. Barney was transfixed; he'd never heard any of this before and any loyalty he felt to his boss, albeit only because of his position, was put to one side as he listened.

"Anyway, we had a good dinner. The table consisted of some good company, all good solid professional coppers who had risen through the ranks and I was making headway in getting myself known outside of the Anglian region. Unfortunately, on the next table was a very young, fresh faced police constable who, in all honesty, shouldn't really have been there. It transpired that his uncle was a junior minister in Whitehall and had pulled some strings to get him in there, presumably with the same intentions as I, to further his career. He'd had an awful lot to drink by the time dinner was over and had taken to pestering some of the ladies..."

Barney could already see what was coming; he knew his dad didn't mess about even now where matters of dignity and decorum were concerned. Back when he was young he wouldn't have hesitated to set someone straight.

"When he bothered your mother she told him she was with

her fiancé and to leave her alone. I heard all of this as I was only a matter of yards away, talking to my boss and his oppo from the Met. The next thing we all heard was your mother telling him to get his hand off her breast and we all turned as one to see this young scrote groping your mother.

"You can imagine my fury, the woman I loved and was going to marry being accosted by this idiot. My jacket was off and I had him outside in two shakes. I gave him a damn good thrashing, observed by a number of the officers present to ensure fair play, and everyone agreed that I had followed the gentleman's course of action and had taught this popinjay a lesson that might just do him some good in the long run."

Barney sighed silently. This might explain Pascoe's aggressive attitude towards him.

"Apparently, he was off work for two weeks," his dad continued, smiling at the memory of his glory days, "and then tried to make a complaint about me. This was quickly and quietly quashed and, as far as I'm aware, he was told just how lucky he was that I hadn't killed him. Unfortunately, his uncle didn't see it that way and I was officially informed a month later that my transfer to the Met wouldn't be going through as it was felt that I was unsuited to a more cosmopolitan environment. I was told unofficially by my boss, who had been in touch with his opposite number, that it was nothing personal but he had been told that he wasn't to employ me or else."

"Bloody politicians!" Barney said, outraged at his dad's treatment.

"Yes," nodded his father. "It didn't end there, though. I got implicated in a corruption ring not long after that and was suspended, along with a few others, for a month while we were investigated. Obviously, we were all cleared and all charges dropped but the chap who'd blown the whistle, a certain Police Constable Pascoe, found himself shunned by everyone in the force. I heard he was transferred up North quite swiftly, albeit after a bit of a kicking outside his police quarters one night, and I never heard about him again. To be honest, Son, it wasn't the end of the world that I never got the transfer to the Met; I got to raise my family here in this lovely village where I know everybody instead of dirty, violent London. It was probably a blessing in disguise, really. It looks like young Pascoe must have learnt to think before he acted and wound his neck back in a little to have got up the ladder in the end."

Barney agreed that it may have been a hidden blessing but couldn't now hold any loyalty to the man who had groped his mum and blocked his dad's career.

"About this case, Dad..."

All her Fucking Lives

John Latimer didn't walk anywhere; he strode like a victorious general traversing no man's land after a particularly bloody battle. He ate up the distance like a sports car on an empty motorway; in short, when he had to get from point A to point B he did *not* mess about. Today though, something stopped him from marching right up to Vicki when he saw her leaving Iceland with her shopping. His body was shouting at him to get on with it, relishing the sensation of walking fast with a destination in mind, but his mind told him to stall, the copper's instinct told him something was wrong and to watch and wait. He didn't have to wait long.

Unable to believe his eyes, he saw Vicki hand the majority of her bags to a smiling Nick as the unmistakeably loutish figure of Matt Blake handed her a bunch of flowers and they hugged and kissed in full view of everyone.

Special

'What? He's in a police cell. She's meant to be with you, John; you were giving her one last chance. The slag is kissing him in public. Fucking, fucking, fucking slag. Why doesn't she just suck his cock here and now? Every one can see she's a slag anyway, what would it matter? She's obviously got no pride to lose; fucking whore.'

So, Blake was out and had obviously wormed his way back in with the slag.

"That's all of her fucking lives used up now," he heard himself murmur. Did he just swear in public?

He could feel the blood rushing to his brain and he felt a little sick. Leaning against a wall with his eyes closed helped a little as he started to get dizzy. He noticed he was also clenching and unclenching his fists with rapid regularity.

'They're not in my class; neither of them. I'll simply walk away and leave them to their squalid little lives.'

'They're fucking laughing at you, John. They've cooked it up between them. That slag and the fucking layabout junkie are taking the piss out of you. You can't let them get away with it.'

'I'm not doing anything silly. I could get into trouble and neither of them are worth it. I'm not doing it again'

'I wouldn't let them laugh at me, John. Not a slag and a junkie. Did I teach you nothing, boy? Fear is control, control is power. I wouldn't be scared to do something about it. Are you scared, John, you fucking queer?'

"I'm not a fucking queer!"

He opened his eyes to see two old ladies looking at him.

"All right, son?" one asked.

"Yes," he replied, then whispered. "I'm a copper. I'm

201

undercover." Putting his finger against his lips he then said, "Ssshh..."

The ladies looked at him and then walked away. He heard one of them saying, "This road's full of them now, Gladys. We'll have to move."

'I'm not going to do anything silly. I've told you already I've worked too hard to get where I am.'

The sweat was running freely down his face and the pain in his head was becoming unbearable.

'Can't you hear me? They. Are. Fucking. Laughing. At. YOU. Do something about it, you spineless article. NOW. I SAID FUCKING NOW, BOY.'

Latimer caught Vicki about ten yards from her house, young Nick was already at the door fiddling with the key and the bags. She turned as he came up behind her. He had every intention of just telling her what he thought of her but the sight of the flowers in her hand and the sneer that appeared on her face when she saw him made his blood boil.

'Taking the fucking piss out of you.'

He grabbed at the flowers, succeeding in beheading a number of them as she tried to pull the bunch back.

"You've been stringing me along, you fucking slag," he growled at her.

'Good boy. Fear is control, control is power.'

"Just fuck off, you freak, or I'll call the law."

He smiled at her, "I *am* the fucking law around here, bitch. And you need to learn your place."

'Do it, Johnny. Do it now.'

She ran to the house where Nick had the door open but he grabbed her coat as she tried to get in, dragging her back and then slapping her hard across the face before pushing her back onto the kitchen floor.

"You can't just tease men, let them think they're getting a sample of the goods and then withdraw the offer. It doesn't work like that, love, so I'll be having my order now if that's alright, slag." He stood over her and started to undo his zipper, the erection trying to poke its way through his Y-fronts making it slightly more difficult than it needed to be.

Nick came flying into the kitchen with a frozen chicken and tried to hit him with it but Latimer ducked it and gave Nick a right hook to the jaw, leaving him on the floor next to his mum.

"From what I can gather, young man, you were lucky to avoid worse than this last night, so you'd better just stay where you are if you don't want your jaw broken again."

He looked down at Vicki; she was terrified. Good. His dad was right: slags only understand one language. He knew that now and wouldn't need this lesson repeating. He'd been too soft with her, should have just told her that she was his and that was that. Still, he considered... better late than never.

Turning his attention to Nick, he said, "I suggest you go to your room, young man. Your mother and me are going to be busy for the next hour."

"Why's that then, Mr Latimer? What will you be doing for a whole hour?"

Latimer jumped... Blake was behind him. He'd forgotten to lock the door. He swung round and saw Blake along with the next-door neighbour. Trying not to show he was shaken by this unexpected intervention and to regain the upper hand he said, "Take two of you does it, Blake? You not man enough to take me on your own?"

If he was expecting the other man to flare up and risk re-arrest then it didn't work as Blake said coolly, "No, I just wanted a witness to your assault and attempted rape. I suggest you fuck off now before I call the police and I'll be expecting to be called into your office on Monday to discuss my promotion and substantial pay rise.

If you're seen round here again, we'll be at Clifford Street before you zip your trousers back up. Understand, you *weird cunt?*"

Latimer glowed red, his rapidly subsiding erection made zipping his trousers back up a lot easier and, with a last glare at Vicki, he pushed his way past Blake and headed down the street.

'You fucking idiot, boy,' echoed round his head.

SUNDAY

The Life of Stanley

Ben Stanley didn't have many problems in his life. He hadn't worked since leaving school twenty-five years ago, preferring to live off the state and supplement his benefits with the cash in hand he received from Axel Falcus in return for stealing cars for him. His house boasted the latest in state-of-the-art games machines, televisions and DVD recorders and his overweight, spoilt children drowned in a sea of bling every time they left the house. His wife, bless her, loved him with a passion for keeping her in the manner to which she was certainly now accustomed and made damn sure that his every need was met. Yes, life for Ben Stanley was good and he'd never really had to break a sweat to make it so.

Take today for instance: he and his newest partner, trainee wide boy, Sam the Spanner, needed a decentish motor to reach their target for the week and had been given a tip by Falcus himself about an unlocked Saab right outside his local. A job that would be a piece of piss and take them about fifteen minutes from start to finish; the finish, as far as he was concerned, being the exact minute they drove it through the garage doors and the ringers took possession.

He fucking loved Sunday drinking better than any other day of the week. The crack and banter with the football team when they turned up after their match with the usual black eyes and broken teeth; the jovial atmosphere in the boozer as everyone tried to forget that Monday was just around the corner and pissed it up at a steady rate, fucking ace it was.

Luckily, as this was going to be a quick job, it meant he'd still spend the afternoon in the pub playing cards and reading the papers like normal until the match came on. And then afterwards he'd go home for a big cooked dinner before crashing out on his leather Ikea settee.

'Aye, life's not bad at all really,' he thought, before his attention turned to his boss's state of mind. Falcus had been getting a bit twitchy about this vigilante fucker and wanted the motor nicking straight away before it was discovered and snatched from him.

John wasn't too concerned about the vigilante personally, mainly because his new protégé, the Spanner, was the only son of the mighty Crowbar. Everyone on this estate knew this and you'd have to be properly fucking mental to want to have him coming after you.

"Shall I use the popper, Stan?" Spanner asked him, as they looked the motor up and down.

John sighed. He could see that the doors were unlocked, so surely young Sam could as well; this could be the longest apprenticeship in history. The lad loved being called 'The Spanner', assuming it was a generic term of affection and respect related to his dad's moniker. John however, as the person who'd bestowed the nickname upon him, knew the real reason he'd gotten it because he was, in effect, a tool that was useful for one job and one job only, breaking things open. Well, that and he was as thick as fuck.

"No, son. We'll open the door and get in like we own it. I'll pretend to fuck about with the keys while I pull the wires out and you scan the glove box and the CD rack. Right?"

"Okay, Stan. You're the boss."

John, observing further the boy's amateur efforts at looking casual and visualising a stretch at Her Majesty's pleasure further down the line as the result of this useless young twat's incompetence, had changed his mind; maybe even his uncluttered life had some stress in it after all.

A Headstart

One minute past twelve. Falcus lifted his pint after checking his phone; no messages yet. It was a bit early for him to be drinking, really. He'd normally still be getting ready at this time on a Sunday, but he wanted to be in the boozer when the motor got nicked so he could be nearby if needed but suitably detached from the crime itself. He didn't actually want to get pissed as he had the court case with the boy tomorrow and didn't want to be smelling of drink when he paid the bail. The law had been sniffing round the garage lately as well, but they had nothing. So, while being in here was a handy alibi, it was also an opportunity to kill two birds with one stone, taunt the bizzies and let them know he ran this estate not fucking them. It might just send a message to this vigilante cunt as well; Axel F runs from no man and is scared of *nothing*.

Three minutes past twelve: they should be in it and ready to go about now.

He caught the barman's eye and gave him a nod then looked round the bar; just the smattering of pensioners, dropouts and yesterday's giro day millionaires he'd expected, they all liked to get a head start on the day's drinkathon. The football lads and the trainee gangsters would all be up at the Stag's or on Shields Road before heading back here to finish off the day or continue into the night. Looking them all up and down so they could testify he was definitely there he turned back to the bar, his attention now focused on the plates that adorned it. He loved a bit of cheese and crackers on a Sunday morning. His stomach groaned with the memory of the fry up he'd had a couple of hours ago, the acid still struggling to break down and digest Mrs F's legendary, artery-clogging, heart-stopper of a breakfast. Even so he was having some cheese; filling his mouth with Mr Ritz and Mrs Morrison's finest combination, he savoured the tastes and texture of the two combined. Then, appetite sated for the moment, he leant back against the bar with his pint in his hand satisfied and content, things were getting back on track. The temporary interruption to his cash flow was about to become a memory. Fucking good thing an' all.

Seven minutes past twelve: the phone rang and he jumped slightly, not expecting it.

'That's a bit quick, they can't be at the garage yet.'

"Yeh?"

"Axel? It's Stan."

"Problem?" He never gave fuck all away on the phone. *Never.* That was rule number one.

"No, mate," laughed Stan. "Quite the opposite."

Falcus was confused now. Had that divvy been on the glue? What was he on about?

"Axel, you still there?"

"Yeh, what you on about?"

"This ehmm... shed you asked me to paint."

'Good lad, Stan. You know the game. Experience always counts.'

"Yeh. What about it? You found the paint alright?"

"Oh aye," the fucker was still laughing away and he could hear young Spanner chortling in the background as well.   "Well, we found some goods in it that you might like to keep rather than throw away."

"What kind of goods?" Falcus wasn't happy now.

"Business cards," John said. "Business cards with a big red V on them and something about cleaning up the streets. I think we've painted the wrong shed by mistake, Mr F, and have inadvertently coloured the outside receptacle of some kind of civic refuse operative. I imagine he'll be furious if he doesn't like the finish. What do you think?"

'Fuck me; it's only the vigilante's car. They've nicked his

fucking car!' The excitement rose in Falcus, like mercury in a ther-mometer, until his cautious, criminal's instinct kicked in.

"Have you moved the paint to our shed yet?"

"Just doing it as we speak, Sir. Just thought you'd like to know..."

Falcus could sense something wrong here. His brain was trying to tell him something as Stanley's voice droned on in the background. A decent motor, abandoned and unlocked in front of his local, filled with Vigilante cards? This was a set up.

"Stan, leave the shed right away. Just get out of the fucki—"

BOOM

The explosion was loud enough to shatter the windows of the pub and shower it with debris. This didn't shake the hardened alkys who carried on drinking not wanting to waste the beer they'd paid for. However, Falcus didn't fancy his pint anymore; he'd always liked it with a head but not one attached to the still open eyes of someone he'd known most of his life. One of the ale-sodden old lushes started wailing and this seemed to kick-start the general panic and rush for the doors. Falcus waited until the bar was almost empty before he allowed the nausea to pass his lips; even in shock he was in control, no one would know that this vigilante cunt was affecting him, no one.

Taking one last look back at the head of Ben Stanley as it stared at him balefully, he couldn't shake the thought off his mind that the bloke had died as he had lived; simply detached from all of life's little problems.

Andy Rivers

The Country's Fallen Apart

Barney had left his parents' house early that morning in order to get back and prepare for the coming week. This was going to be a big one for him as, after talking with his dad, he'd decided to arrest John Latimer at some point in the next couple of days and get warrants to search both his home and place of employment. He'd seen a different side to his dad last night as they'd burned the midnight oil together interspersing work with nostalgia. His image of his father was always that of a strict, fierce, morally upstanding man while his mother had been the caregiver and more loving of the two and he'd been happy with that. Two different shaped pegs for two different shaped holes, but the lines had blurred last night, actually a *lot* had blurred given the amount of port and brandy they'd put away.

His dad was a product of his times it seemed; his clearly defined role had been as breadwinner and protector as he had seen his own father do in a time of austerity for many, but he had also longed to put his arm around his boy sometimes and tell him he loved him; a fact he'd drunkenly admitted last night and one which they'd skirted around this morning in as English a manner as possible.

It had all left Barney feeling rather strange; both happy and sad at the same time: sad that he'd missed out on lots of things with his dad as a boy, but happy that he was a very loved and wanted child both then and now.

Nosing the car into the Tyne Tunnel, he reflected on their conversation last night. His dad was of the opinion that yes it *did* sound like they had a very strong case against this Latimer fellow, but it would be silly to assume it was him at this stage. The chances are he's connected in some way, but it's not necessarily him.

The thing that surprised Barney most though was his dad's

attitude to the vigilante. He had expected a tirade of abuse aimed at the man for taking the law into his own hands, but instead got a weary shrug of the shoulders.

"You see, Barney," his dad had said. "I can understand the man's logic. The politicians have given up. They don't have to fear crime of any sort in their big well-protected houses. They don't leave their big secure cars to get the tube or the bus at night, do they? They only fear rape if they're on Hampstead Heath in the early hours and even then some of the buggers would pay for it anyway. The rest of the country though... we see criminals getting away scot free with everything, murderers and rapists are freed after half their sentences to kill and assault again, burglars are very rarely convicted and even then their sentence is measured in months and is halved almost immediately. Muggings, assaults and criminal damage go largely unreported by the general public as the police can't do a lot about it anymore and if you dare to fight back in your own home when you discover an intruder, well, you're more likely to go to prison than he is. The country's fallen apart, Barney. It really has."

Throwing his money into the toll collection point on the Newcastle side of the tunnel, Barney reflected just how much their relationship had changed as he had found himself arguing away with his dad about change and reform and had even made him concede a few points. Yes, they truly were equals now and long may it continue.

His thoughts were interrupted by the shrill tones of his mobile and, as he hadn't yet mastered the technology behind hands-free kits, he pulled over to answer.

"Netherstone... Where's that...? Right, see you there."

An explosion outside the local pub of a certain Mr Falcus, killing two known car thieves and showering the immediate area with business cards belonging to the vigilante himself. This may or may not be another lead but it most definitely was a statement of intent. the vigilante had just upped the stakes.

Barney attached his flashing blue light just as a concerned tunnel security man came over to his stationery vehicle, giving him a wave he sped off towards this latest crime scene.

A Policewoman's Lot

WPC Suzie Holmes was not impressed with the way her weekend had panned out at all; the fact that she had been rostered for duty due to staff shortages when her status as a member of Barney's vigilante investigation team should have made her exempt was the main reason. The other was that Barney had simply disappeared and this could only mean he had a girlfriend on the go.

'Some short-skirted Bigg Market slapper got her claws into him,' she had thought bitterly that morning after her tenth failed attempt to get him to answer his door while she was 'just passing'.

However, her attention had been diverted away from her failing love life at about ten past twelve when an explosion had been reported outside the Hare and Hounds down Raby Street in Byker. Unfortunately for her, she'd been quick off the mark; her schoolgirl competitive streak was still very much a driving force and she'd been the first copper there. This, in police terms, made her the first responder and fucked her day up entirely.

She was now responsible for, and in no particular order of priority, securing the scene and ensuring witnesses did not leave the area before being identified and interviewed, which was difficult as they were all attempting to get off out of the way and claim they saw and heard nothing. She had to ensure all evidence was preserved, which was also going to be damn nigh impossible as bits of car, bodies and those fucking business cards were all over the street and the pub. As well as all of that, she also had to record field notes and first impressions and finally ensure the safety of the general public by keeping them back, particularly if there was more than one bomb. She decided to do this first.

"EVERYBODY BACK. THE AREA IS NOT YET SAFE. PLEASE STEP BACK AND MOVE AWAY FROM THE AREA. NOT YOU, MR FALCUS."

Other officers were arriving on the scene now, which was handy. She instructed two of them to set up an exclusion zone and tape it off. Then she pointed out the initial position and wreckage of the car to the photographer so he could crack on and designated five officers as evidence recorders and started them off sifting and bagging the scorched area. Pointing out the people she recognised as definitely leaving the pub to another couple of PCs and instructing them to get names, addresses and statements, she moved over to the recently arrived bomb disposal team as they prepared to search the area in case of any more explosive devices.

"What do you know?" The soldier demanded.

'Time was money with these boys,' Suzie thought. *'Very professional.'*

"Just that a car blew up outside the pub. Two dead; they were in the car when it happened. Some injuries in the pub, mainly from flying glass, not serious though."

"Okay," the young sergeant responded. "I'm gonna need you to clear the houses and get everyone back another hundred feet or so. This may take a while."

Suzie gave instructions to another passing officer, reflecting that being first on the scene wasn't actually that bad as she didn't have to do any of the shit jobs like moving people away from the *EastEnders* omnibus. She watched the bomb disposal boys taking the piss out of each other as they suited up, just young lads really, and not scared of death at all. She'd seen a photo passed round the station once taken from the internet, it showed one of them defusing a land mine in some foreign country, the tension etched on his face and the pain in his legs as he squatted over it, deliberating which wire to pull, beads of sweat captured brilliantly by the photographer as they ran down his nose. The photo also showed one of his mates behind him with a blown up crisp packet, poised and ready to pop it right in his ears and scare the shit out of him.

'Fucking nutters the lot of them,' she thought as she smiled and turned away.

A car pulled up and her heart jumped, the excitement of the job had died down a little after the initial flurry of adrenalin, but now it was flowing freely through her veins again as Barney jumped out of the car and rushed over looking concerned.

"Suzie, what happened? Are you alright?"

"Fine. A car was blown up outside the pub. It appears to be the work of our newest law enforcer, rather than any international terror group, judging by the cascade of business cards that floated down afterwards."

Barney looked around; they were everywhere. He looked back at Suzie, she looked knackered but gorgeous.

"Did you get called in to attend this on your day off?" he asked her.

"No," she replied. "I was rota'd on this weekend. Bit of an overtime ban from Pascoe and they needed me."

Barney was furious but also a bit chuffed. Furious because WPC Holmes was part of his team and shouldn't be exhausting herself on other business when he needed her fresh. A bit chuffed because it meant she hadn't been out with a boyfriend like he'd first thought. He'd be bringing this up with Pascoe as well when he saw him about Latimer.

"Right, then," he said. "first things first... we'll need a number plate check on the car. I presume there's a number plate left to check? And then I'll need your field notes, sorry."

Suzie sighed, she'd planned a hot bath, a curry and some telly tonight but now she was going to be spending most of it typing. "We're working on the number plate now. A bit of it survived. I'll have the notes on your desk first thing tomorrow, Barney. If that's okay?"

She was toying with the idea of inviting him round to hers to help her with the notes and go over this latest event when he stopped her mid-thought by striding off towards the evidence gatherers. Looking back, he shouted, "No problem Suzie, I'll be busy all night with this stuff anyway and then we're in court in the morning, remember? So tomorrow afternoon would be fine, really."

Then swivelling and grabbing the first available body he pointed at the cards littering the bushes and pavements and said, "Make sure you get every single one of those, please. They're very important."

Suzie realised the moment had gone and walked the other way. Now wasn't really the time anyway.

Moving up a Gear

Falcus was in an ambulance. He wasn't really hurt, but thought he'd better play the game with the filth infesting the place and asking questions. They'd taken his name and address and had put a copper in the ambulance with him and two other unfortunates who'd caught a bit of flying glass. Standard practice to make sure no witnesses got 'lost' between hospitals and crime scenes; he knew that. His wife had come steaming up the street while they were putting him in the ambulance, but he'd fucked her off; he didn't want the slack-jawed cow shouting the odds about anything in front of the bizzies. He knew this was the vigilante making a big point to him;

he also knew that this was now a fucking war between them for control of these streets and he didn't want any distractions from his idiot family while he thought on what to do. He had the boy's court case tomorrow for dipping that copper and then he'd put everyone on full alert to find this bastard.

'Motivation won't be a problem anyway,' he thought, observing a grieving, mental Crowbar being held down by five burly coppers through the ambulance doors as it pulled away. *'In fact, it'll be harder to stop Crowbar killing the prick with his bare hands before I get to talk to him.'*

Stonewalling all attempts by the wily old PC that accompanied them to get him into a conversation, he nevertheless was smiling inside.

'In killing young Spanner that fucker may well have just made his first mistake,' he thought.

Barney was back in the office; he had a mountain of evidence to go over and couldn't wait to get stuck in. Despite it being a Sunday he already had a number of forensic reports to hand. These were based on various bits of evidence from the crime scene; a big incident like this tended to remove professional barriers and two deaths helped concentrate the minds of everyone concerned in the, what was now, very public quest for answers.

The registration plate had been narrowed down to suggested numbers and individually checked on the DVLA computer; each result had been eliminated until only one remained: a car was reported stolen two days ago and had been taken from Heaton Road, only a few miles from Byker, and the kind of area where a Saab wouldn't look out of place. Although far too obvious to be the actual vigilante's car Barney had gotten excited anyway and had checked out the owner who turned out to be a sixty-year-old retired science teacher; a miss Rachael Redgrave. Barney had visited her on the pretext of breaking the news about her car and giving her a crime number in order to claim the insurance back. His real motive was just to check out the area as he didn't know it well and to have a look around her house. Maybe she was related to Latimer or had taught him.

He'd been disappointed to find nothing unusual at all; Miss Redgrave was a spinster and had no relatives. Her house was very clean and tidy and there was a distinct lack of photos of old classes or favourites, suggesting she'd never really bonded with any of her pupils enough for them to commit any crimes for her. Other than the car, she'd never been a victim of crime and therefore had no motives for vigilantism herself, not that she'd have been physically able anyway. In fact, the only possible incident of any interest had been that she'd locked her keys in the car the other day and one of her neighbours had to get them out for her; a copper, she reckoned. Might be worth checking out who lived up here as apparently he'd suggested leaving a spare set somewhere handy like in the bin shed. Keep that one on the back burner anyway.

Taking his leave, Barney had noted a big pub on the corner of the road and, feeling his tummy rumble, had wandered in and enjoyed a very decent roast. He'd also read some adverts for a Sunday night quiz and quite fancied having a few pints and seeing if he could join a team but had resignedly gone back to work instead.

'Still,' he thought, reflecting that it wasn't a wasted journey, *'it's always an option for another time. It could make a great first date.'*

MONADY

Making lives better

John Latimer put the phone down. He had an impressive one hundred percent attendance record at German Wizard and his ringing in sick for the week could not be questioned by anyone, least of all the ginger imbecile that he had just spoken to. He wasn't sick; he never was. His healthy lifestyle saw to that. He didn't even have a hangover after the quiz last night.

'Bloody should have, though,' he smiled to himself. *'Winning the quiz is enough for me, but Reg insists on spending the beer tokens.'*

"John, we work hard through the week trying, in our own different ways, to make lives better for the community. We're entitled to some rest and recuperation at the weekend. It helps to charge up our batteries for the next week's struggles."

That was his friend's weekly speech, which usually came at about nine o'clock when he'd had a few pints inside him. John himself rarely drank, but Reg always implored him to at least show willing, particularly if they won first prize in the quiz as they did last night.

No, he wasn't sick, but he couldn't face Blake at work today, not after yesterday's incident. He'd spent all last night discussing it with Reg, whose advice had been to simply forget about her and to transfer Blake to a better paid job within the company, reasoning that any woman as morally deficient as her would get her just desserts eventually. He'd have a week off anyway to think on his next move and to frustrate any attempt to blackmail him.

Special

'Could do with the rest anyway, John. Eh? All this Sheriff Latimer palaver must be taking it out of you.'

Nodding and agreeing with himself he moved over to the toaster, fastidiously placing a large tray underneath it and then turning it upside down. Approximately three crumbs fell from it onto the tray and he smiled. Grasping his miniature dust buster he quickly vacuumed them up. The benefits of cleaning his toaster every single day of its working life, regardless of whether he'd used it or not, meant that he'd never get ants.

'That slag could do with some housekeeping lessons from you, John. Definitely.'

'I'm forgetting about her, she was no good for me anyway. I'm moving on.'

"That's right," he reiterated out loud. "She wasn't in my class and I'm better off without her."

Even though he knew that was true and that she was a no good common whore, he still felt a burning rage at her dismissal of him. He also knew that he'd end up doing something about it. This was the closest to how he'd felt all those years ago back on Shields Road.

'No,' he thought again, standing in front of the mirror and looking himself straight in the eye. *'That's wrong. She doesn't compare to that man. No matter what she did to me, I couldn't hate her as I did him.'*

'Johnny, she still fucked you over. You were still made to look a fool by a slag. You've never let it go unpunished before, so why do it now? What do you think I would have done?'

Latimer considered this; he'd acted stupidly yesterday and would now have to pay the consequences when he saw Blake again. Hopefully, he'd have persuaded Vicki not to make a complaint in the hope of getting more money at work and, by ringing in sick, John had stalled him while he thought things through.

He would fall back onto his police instincts; that was the best way. Observe and act... yes, that would do it. Grabbing his coat, he headed out of the door and turned left out of his gate. Shields Road was a ten-minute walk from here and the North East wind might just clear the noise in his head.

* * *

Barney swished the cold water around the basin and then plunged his head in it.

"Ooohhhh, my God," he gasped.

Feeling better for doing it he then dropped his flannel in and started using it to splash his face. These late nights were all very well, but didn't help too much when you had a court appointment first thing.

'I need to be wide awake today,' he thought. *'Mainly because there'll be intimidation going on if the episode in the chip shop was anything to go by, but also because I'll be spending the morning with Susie and I'd hate to say anything stupid again.'*

His heart lifting at the thought of seeing her, despite how scared he was at the prospect of giving evidence against a Falcus family member and everything that went with it, he started to get dressed. He'd visited courts before as part of his degree course and had even starred in mock prosecutions at university so he had some idea of the process and the argument that would follow, but this was the *real thing.*

'I suppose it's like a football team practicing penalties on the training ground before a big match and then having to do them for real in front of the crowd... mocking you and baying for your blood, knowing that the whole thing rests on you.'

Exhaling silently in an effort to calm his panic before it set in properly he thought about giving Susie a ring, but decided against it. She was a tough northern girl and wouldn't think much of a southern softie like him bricking himself at the thought of what was essentially part of his job and he wanted her to like him. He very much wanted her to like him.

Buttoning his suit, he opened the door, his mind flicking back to his previous football analogy; the prospect of certain elements of the crowd baying for his blood wasn't that remote at this particular trial. Gulping silently, he pulled the door shut and headed for the car park.

Tattie Lugs and the Lazy Bitch

"And Crowbar, I'm serious... that bastard is alive when you bring him back here."

Crowbar just stared at him and Falcus felt a shudder up his back. That was one evil stare. He almost felt sorry for the vigilante bloke. *Almost.*

"Listen, it's just so I can find out what the score is in case there's anything more to this fucker attacking me. After I know everything, you can have him. Just don't get caught and banged up. And remember, the other thing you need to do sometime this week... make sure you use those cards we swiped from the bushes as well. Alright?"

The lumbering hulk grunted back at him and headed for the door, taking Falcus's five best men with him. This was the type of manhunt that the law could never hope to mount. Crowbar had methods that would never stand up in court, particularly now with what was left of his son lying in a funeral parlour, but this particular fugitive would be lucky to see the outside world again once apprehended, never mind a courtroom. Before he died though, Falcus would have the pleasure of pointing out how he'd used him to get a foothold onto the lucrative drugs market. A simple bit of deception would mask a corporate murder and avoid a costly turf war. Happy days.

Now with that little task assigned, he could concentrate on the day's other events; his son's impending trial and probable slap on the wrist.

"Terry, are you ready yet? Terry... TERRY."

'Has that prick got tatties growing in his fucking lugs?'

"Aye, Dad. I'm ready now." His only son emerged at the top of the stairs.

Falcus looked him up and down; the boy was in court today for trying to rob a police officer. He's got previous convictions for theft and robbery with violence but had thus far, thanks to his old dad's intervention, managed to avoid incarceration. You'd think he'd take his predicament a bit more seriously.

"Why the *fuck* aren't you wearing your suit?"

"It's not comfortable, Dad. And the shoes hurt me feet. I'll just go like this, it'll be alright."

Falcus fought hard to control his rising temper at the fucking idiot stood in front of him. He was a sorry sight. From the dirty trainers through the Toon Army tracksuit, all the way to the bits of toilet paper stuck to his bleeding face and shaving foam piled up over his ears, he looked a complete *twat*.

Breathing deeply, Falcus felt the anger subside. He was half tempted to let the dozy plank go to court like that and get hammered by the judge, but knew he'd never hear the end of it from his mother. He also needed a bit of extra protection while Crowbar was otherwise engaged, so he bit his tongue and gently ushered the boy back upstairs to change.

* * *

'She hasn't moved from that sofa in an hour, the lazy bitch. She's smoked three cigarettes and had two cups of something hot-looking in that time. Shoved a big sandwich down her lying throat in double quick time as well. I bet the route down her throat's been well-worn by now though, the fucking whore.'

Special

John Latimer shifted his weight from his right leg to his left; careful not to disturb the bush he was hiding in too much. The last thing he wanted was some nosey, Neighbourhood Watch type ringing his colleagues at the station. It had been raining this morning and drips of water from the overhead leaves were rolling down his face as he sat there impassively. He'd always loved observation; loved the feeling of watching someone without them knowing you were there. All those scrotes and scum incriminating themselves because they thought they were alone and safe. He had walked to the shop at the bottom of the street and, on the pretext of looking at magazines, had observed the comings and goings outside her house before working out the best observation point. Once he'd done that it was simply a case of deciding on a point of entry into the bushes and creeping up them until he was almost opposite her back window, affording him a good view into the house.

'I really don't know what I ever saw in her. She's a mess. Wandering around the house in her dressing gown at this hour. No pride. No backbone. Symptomatic of the mess this country has become.'

'Johnny, that's not the fucking point. You should have been the one to do the dumping, not that slag.'

Latimer couldn't argue with that and thought about moving off; his inquisitiveness about her movements satisfied for the time being. He was just about to leave when Vicki got off the sofa and headed upstairs. He thought for a moment she was going back to bed when he saw her shape appear at the frosted glass of the bathroom window. A few seconds later steam started coming out of the boiler flue and then she appeared back downstairs, her dressing gown hanging open, exposing her cheap underwear when she bent over the coffee table and picked up a magazine.

'She's obviously having a bath. I'll hang on a bit longer just in case anything happens I need to know.'

Maybe Judges should be getting it up the Arse

"I was approaching Shields Road from the Byker Metro Station cut through, when I witnessed the defendant cross the road suddenly and for no apparent reason. Finding this behaviour suspicious, I continued to observe the defendant from my position ten yards behind him. I then witnessed him deliberately bump into Mr Netherstone whilst simultaneously putting a hand into his jacket pocket. I shouted at the defendant to stop and he looked around at me and made a move that suggested he was going to run, so I restrained him using my handcuffs. I then conducted a quick weapon search of the defendant in order to make the situation as safe as possible. This search actually turned up Mr Netherstone's wallet. I then read the defendant his rights and arrested him for theft."

"I see, WPC Holmes. And after reading the defendant his rights did he comment at all?"

"He did, Sir. He laughed and shouted that Mr Netherstone wouldn't testify against him if he knew what was good for him. I then informed the defendant that Mr Netherstone was in fact a police officer and that he certainly would be testifying and his demeanour changed somewhat. He then said..."

Suzie paused, pretending to read her pocket book she sneaked a quick look at the judge; he looked fucking furious. *Brilliant*.

"A copper? I've dipped a fucking copper? Shit, me dad'll go mental. Can we not buy a way out of this?"

The judge had a face like thunder. Suzie knew this one; if we still had capital punishment he would be a hanging judge without a doubt. Falcus junior was definitely in trouble, particularly as the judiciary were becoming a bit sensitive about public criticism of their perceived softness with habitual offenders. That business with the immigrants being released instead of deported wasn't exactly anything to do with them per se, but as it was reported on the same tabloid pages as loads of cases about violent criminals re-offending while on bail, it didn't spare them from public criticism.

'Mind you, a lot of those bastards have gone out and raped and murdered, so maybe the judges should be getting it up the arse. After all, that's the risk they're exposing us all to when they fall for these bastards' sob stories and listen to the bleeding heart social workers' recommendations.'

As Suzie stepped down from the dock, she was certain Terry Falcus was going down and smiled to herself in triumph.

"What are you laughing at, Filth?" a voice hissed at her side.

Turning she looked straight in the eyes of Falcus senior. It wasn't as frightening as she expected it would be. He was the type of high-profile hard man that she imagined would command a Kray-style aura. She thought it would be like looking into the eyes of a lion; a deep pool of black malevolence that screamed pure evil, but instead all she could see was protruding nasal hair and a tinge of red around his tiny pupils. This was obviously his hard man stare, but Suzie was not in the slightest bit impressed.

"I'm laughing because your boy is going down, Falcus. And if you don't watch yourself, you'll be next."

She knew he was struggling to contain his fury; he went white, his fists clenched and his head bobbed. He obviously wasn't used to being spoken to like this, so Suzie smiled again, trying to push him over the edge. If he took a swing here in court then he'd get a week for contempt. Falcus held himself in check though, he wasn't stupid, and she knew that now as well. Best not to underestimate him. Dismissing him with a sneering smile, she turned back towards the door just as Barney walked in, called as the final witness, and Falcus turned his attention to him.

"If my boy goes down, so do you, Ginger," he hissed at him out of earshot of the judge.

Barney blanched and gulped, and Suzie squeezed his hand supportively then looked back at Falcus and laughed again.

"Hey, Falcus," she said making a phone to ear motion with her other hand. "The future's shite, the future's porridge. Ha-ha."

Falcus sat back. His boy was going down, no doubt about it. He knew she was trying to wind him up as well; make him do something daft in court. She thought she'd won, but the little exchange he'd just witnessed between them meant he knew how to teach these two cheeky fuckers a lesson about pain and loss. They'd learn not to fuck about with Axel Falcus ever again.

Two years, seven minutes and twenty-five Seconds

John Latimer removed the digital camera from its case; as with all his possessions, this too was immaculately clean. He could see his reflection in its shiny metallic body and the thought of going back into the bushes and getting any mud on it filled him with discomfort. Making a quick fire decision to stay in the car, he got out his atlas and buried his head in it; looking to all the world like he was lost, he held it up as if using the light from the windscreen. Unbeknown to the general public, there was a transparent flap cut into one corner of the atlas that afforded it a clear view of whichever way it was pointing and allowed him to take surreptitious pictures of his various targets.

Speaking of which, this particular target had, in the time he'd gone home, had his lunch, did a bit of cleaning and collected his camera, managed to drag her lazy, fat arse off the sofa and get dressed.

'Well, John. She must be expecting a client or something, the fucking whore. What are you going to do to get back at her?'

226

Special

John just smiled to himself, the camera clicked and whirred and Vicki's image filled the screen in a variety of positions in the kitchen. After seven minutes and twenty-five seconds his watch beeped at him. That was the signal to put down the atlas, scratch his head and start the car. Reg had once shown him a report commissioned by the Police Associations of Great Britain that had stated that eight minutes was the point at which concerned citizens would confront a suspicious character or call the police. While John didn't think there'd be any concerned citizens in a ghetto like this, he didn't want to arouse any suspicions or have anyone remember him for any reason, so seven minutes twenty-five was more than enough time.

Having one more look at the atlas and then shaking his head theatrically, he put the car into gear and moved off. She'd keep.

* * *

"And so, Mr Falcus. Taking into account your previous appearances before the court and the promises you have made to change your ways, the nature of your criminal record and the circumstances surrounding this particular case, including your comments after your arrest, I have to inform you that the only viable sentence will be a custodial one. Do you have anything to say before sentence is passed?"

Axel Falcus stared into his son's back from across the courtroom, willing him to say sorry and look remorseful. A reduced sentence would save him a lot of earache at home.

"Do what you like, I don't give a fuck. I'm Terry Falcus and you're getting it, you ginger bastard. Me dad'll make sure of that."

Falcus cringed inside; outwardly the poker face never moved and he made a conscious effort not to look in the direction of the copper responsible for this.

'How can that stupid prick be my son? Not only has he just extended his own sentence, but he's made it a lot more difficult for me to get that cunt without being implicated now. She must have

been shagging a fucking spastic or something while I was inside all them years ago, must have been.

"I'm sure you don't care, Mr Falcus. People like you never do until the door closes and then you start bleating about human rights. Well, now it's time for the general public to have their human rights upheld, they deserve to be protected from criminals such as you and that is what I shall do. You will be imprisoned for two years and will also pay the costs associated with this case. Take him down."

"Two years... two fucking years? For a fucking wallet... Dad... Dad... *Dad*."

Falcus could feel his teeth grinding themselves into powder as he struggled to maintain his neutral expression. Two big fuckers who looked like they were enjoying it dragged his son from the dock and it was all he could do not to leap the barrier and get stuck into them.

'No, priorities first. The boy's gone for at least a year now. I'll make the calls tonight; make sure he's well looked after. That's all I can do.'

Looking across at the smiling faces of the two coppers who'd given evidence as they congratulated each other, he changed his mind and headed outside reaching for his mobile phone.

'Maybe that's not all I can do.'

"Crowbar, owt happening?"

Falcus was aware that he wouldn't normally discuss business with Crowbar over the phone, but needs must at present, and he tried to keep the conversation as light as possible.

"Well, keep looking mate... we all want this particular problem solved. Listen, I've got to see someone tomorrow about some fixtures and fittings I want to buy for some of the pubs in the area. I won't need you there, though. The bloke's helpful when it comes to heavy lifting and is a very good business acquaintance, so you keep on with the headhunting."

Crowbar grunted a couple of times, which was his way on the

phone, as he himself knew that he was thick and didn't want to incriminate himself either; the problem with this was that you never knew if he understood or not. Falcus tried to make it crystal clear when he next needed his presence.

"After I've sorted out the business with the sales rep, I'll be turning my attention to something else. Terry got unavoidably detained for two years today, so I might need to make sure everything relating to that is dealt with at our end. I'll give you a ring if there's anything you can bring to the table for that particular meeting. Ok?"

Another grunt meant that Crowbar thought he understood. Falcus snapped the phone shut and strode off to where he'd left the car, unaware of the two men taking his picture repeatedly from the car parked across the street.

Making your Mark

'Must be prepared for this. It's time to make my mark. I've been ignored for too long, but now they'll see... now they'll know.

'I handle the weapon, sleek and black. Only a small thing, but containing enough power for my purposes. There are just too many scum in the world for one man to contain but when I do this, when I've liberated these people, when my actions become known then I'll have followers... acolytes. Once I have them I can sit back as they wreak havoc on the criminal community. I'll be like a scorpion, biding my time as everything goes on around me, my initial role forgotten, then BANG; I'll strike at the main players and remove them from the picture. This is just the beginning. I must be strong. I must complete the job I started and send a message.

Andy Rivers

'It's time now. Where's my balaclava?'

* * *

Axel Falcus pushed his egg around the plate half-heartedly with a half slice of fried bread. He wasn't hungry, but had to show willing otherwise the volume of earache he was currently being spared due to last night's incident would simply start again as his wife's anxiety over her first-born son's incarceration would override her fear of him and incrementally increase until his fucking head exploded. She'd started the minute he'd got back last night.

"Where is he? Where's my baby?"

"He's in prison – two years."

"Two years? *TWO FUCKING YEARS?* You said you'd sort it. You said he'd be okay."

"He'd have been okay if he hadn't abused the fucking judge. But because he's a stupid, spoilt bastard he thought he could just do what he wanted and the result was two years. He'll be out in twelve months anyway and I'll make sure he's alright in there."

"Oh you're blaming me, are you? Just for spoiling him a bit when he was younger. Just for giving him and his sisters all the things I never had. It's my fault, is it? Call yourself a man? You let your only son go to jail for two years instead of dealing with the bastards responsible..."

And so it had went, on and on... and on. All fucking night. Well not quite all night; after about three hours of constant nagging and whining, Falcus had snapped and smacked her in that huge fucking mouth of hers. That seemed to do the trick.

'Surprised I didn't lose my fucking hand in there, like.'

It wasn't the first time he'd hit her, but it was the first time he'd felt a bit guilty about it, reasoning that she was probably upset about her first-born child going inside. Still, it did shut her up and she still wasn't speaking to him so that gave him a bit of space to think about things.

He had that big meeting today with his newest supplier. He'd been cultivating this bloke for months. He was a new face on the scene, which would normally be a bit suspect, but Falcus knew where he lived, what pubs he drank in and what company he kept. He made sure that this bloke knew he had checked him out and that if he fucked him over then he could be found. He considered the bloke trustworthy and had heard he was reliable, but it was always best to make sure. He also knew that this particular character could supply him with regular batches of high-grade smack, Charlie and ecstasy. The profits would be enormous and would enable him to move out of this petty shite his father had started all those years ago; the loan sharking, the protection and the thieving. He was moving into the big league and the main players had better watch out because he was coming through.

It was probably a blessing in disguise that Terry had got some bird, as it kept him out of the way when this was going on, stopped him from fucking anything up. He stood up, half of his breakfast still on the plate, and she took it away wordlessly. He smiled as he headed for the bathroom; things were falling into place, the only cloud was this vigilante fucker but Crowbar would have smashed his way round the estate by now and be right on that cunt's trail. Once that little problem was dealt with then the sky was the limit.

Stereotypical Hoodlums

Crowbar eyed the door; normally he'd burst right through, but this wasn't your average door. This one was high up in the Byker wall, a little bit along from the lift, and belonged to Micky 'Muzza' Murray.

The gentleman himself presented no great problem or

nervousness to Crowbar, he worked as a low-level drug dealer for a bloke named Patterson, who himself was simply a middleman for one of the main men in Newcastle. If, however, Crowbar interrupted Muzza's work enough to annoy the aforementioned top banana, then he could expect a visit from gentlemen with a similar job description to his own and Falcus didn't have enough clout to avert that scenario. There was also an added complication that Patterson, who was actually doing a short stretch at Her Majesty's pleasure for importing offensive weapons, was a close friend of the Reeves brothers who, while having nothing to do with the drugs trade themselves, were quite a formidable pair of fuckers to go up against, as the now dearly departed Vincent Merry found out not that long ago.

None of this, however, was what was stopping Crowbar kicking that door in and questioning Muzza as to his knowledge of this vigilante bastard. Even before his son's death, he had not been one to worry about ruffling feathers or the consequences of his actions, reasoning that he'd deal with things as they happened and not before. And since Sam was blown up he'd become, if anything, even more single-minded. No, the reason he wasn't kicking the door in was because he knew this was, in effect, a smackhead's lair and would have security measures that stopped the place being turned over from people very like himself.

So, weighing up the situation, he decided that making subtlety his first course of action was the order of the day here and gently knocked on the door. The other lads were out of sight back by the lift, so Murray didn't get spooked and refuse to answer. Crowbar could hear the faint sound of footsteps and a spy hole being flicked open.

"Muzza, it's Crowbar. You in?"

"Aye, mate. How's it going? Don't often see you up here. You wanting sorted out?"

Crowbar kept his temper in check. This cheeky little fucker

assumed that he wanted drugs. Did he not realise that this mighty body was a fucking temple? Does he not understand the training and dedication that went into maintaining this physique? Does the prick think that all the work he put into these biceps over the years means nowt and he'd destroy it for a bag of smack? Biting his lip, he decided it was a good thing he'd asked him anyway as he'd been meaning to stock up on his steroids and had forgot until now.

"Nah, mate. Just a chat? Have you got five minutes?"

"A chat? What about, like?"

The bloke was suspicious already, this wasn't good.

"Just want a bit of info, Muz. About this vigilante cunt. I know you know stuff that goes on. Open the door, mate, and we'll have a cup of tea."

"I'm not allowed to open the door, Crowbar. I don't know nowt about the vigilante either. I know he killed your lad and that, but I can't help you. Sorry."

Crowbar sighed; this subtlety bollocks was fucking overrated in his opinion. He was a busy man and didn't have time for this shite; time for plan B. Without another word he walked back to the lift and got the chainsaw.

"You brought the grinder for the iron bars behind the door as well, didn't you?"

A quick nod confirmed it and they headed back to Muzza's. In ten minutes they'd be in and, in fifteen minutes, they'd know everything this fucker knew. In fifteen minutes and thirty seconds he'd be dead. Crowbar had good reason to kill the drug-dealing little prick and felt in his pocket for the insurance policy against any comebacks.

* * *

'He's coming in now; I can pick him out a mile off. Stereotypical hoodlum; all gold chains and sovereign rings. His neck and knuckles just a collage of Indian Ink and Durham

artwork, complemented by the obligatory borstal spot; as worn by the most stylish old school hard man. These idiots remind me of the goths that infest Eldon Square at the weekends; they all proclaim their individuality by looking exactly the same. They're all desperate to be different but achieve the exact opposite and end up being clones of each other, all as unremarkable as the rest. They're like the talentless idiots on that Big Brother programme, their egos all screaming out 'look at me, please look at me' when together they make such a cacophony of noise that they end up blending their voices into one loud drone that makes you ignore them all together, thus subverting their own aims.

This is another one typical of his breed, he growls at the woman behind the counter as he orders his fry-up, haggles over the exact make up of his super seven; adamant he wants black pudding instead of tomatoes; another one who gets what he wants on the threat of violence. Sitting down with his paper and tea, he casually eyes everyone up in the café; they avert their eyes or lower their heads, studiously ignoring the gangster's glare and anxious to avoid bloodshed. I stare straight back at him, he holds my gaze for a few seconds before looking outside. I know that he wouldn't have given up so easily, so I follow his line of sight and see a car parked across Shields Road with two meatheads hanging out of it. Aaah... backup. The point at which both the police and serious criminals meet; neither can do anything without half a ton of cannon fodder to make them look tough.

I'm different, I do everything on my own, I blend in, do what I have to do and then slip away. I could take this man now if I so wished, the fact that he's already underestimated me means I could simply walk over there and split his head open before he knew what was happening. Not yet though, I have business today, important business that demands I play the game for the time being. I arrange my face into sorry fear, look back at him as he smirks at me and put my head down. I know this is enough for him; he thinks he's won this battle and, more importantly, his ego is satisfied now so the other customers and the woman behind the counter won't be bothered by him again.

Me... there was a time I would have burned with fury at this exchange; a time when I would have lain awake at night plotting how to get this man back. Not now. Now I know what I can do and I know what I'm going to do. I wait for a while, thinking on how to distract the muscle in the car, taking my time with my bacon sandwich and pretending to scan my paper until the second man comes in... the one I've been waiting for.'

"Axel, all right mate? What you having?"

'Then, when they are in conversation, I get up to leave. The man known as Axel glances my way and there is a flicker of recognition, but I'm a nobody to him. He no classes me mentally and has forgotten about me before I've opened the door. He's not the first to make that mistake and I'm sure he won't be the last. Fingering the weapon in my pocket, I step out on to Shields Road. Not long now.'

Local Radgies

Muzza's day had taken a turn for the worse. It had started off so well; young Nina had come round wanting some Es but with no money, so he'd taken a blow job off her as a deposit, given her a bag of fifty and sent her out to sell them for him. Then he'd checked the racing results on Teletext and found out he'd won a hundred and fifty quid at Kempton, add this to the fact that his new top-of -the-range telly and satellite dish, capable of picking up the Arab channel and thus getting him loads of free football, had been delivered this morning and he was up and running.

However things had quickly gone downhill since Crowbar and his crew had cut through his reinforced door and dragged him onto the balcony at the back of the flat. As he dangled one hundred feet up he decided that if he lived, he might consider moving away and out of his chosen profession. He was a handy boxer as a kid along with his mate Hammy, but they'd taken different paths in life since then. Hammy had gone on to win a bronze at the Greece Olympics and was now embarking on a professional career, endorsing all sorts of products and making a fortune as well as having a good time along the way. Crowbar, on the other hand, had gotten into drink, drugs and birds. His mantra at the time was *fuck getting up at five in the morning to go running when I could snuggle back under the quilt with whichever drug-addled council estate hood rat I happened to be fucking that week.*

It was amazing the way you could look at your life and the paths you'd mistakenly taken with any sort of clarity when you were facing certain death into some pensioner's back garden. Muzza couldn't help thinking that he'd made a bit of a mistake in not keeping up the boxing and an even bigger mistake in thinking he'd make a few quid from dealing and then get out. You never get out. Ever.

'What a crap way to go this'll be, dropped from the balcony of a poxy fucking council flat on an estate no one sensible wants to live on. I haven't even collected that fucking bet either. Some council bloke'll find that when they're clearing the flat out. Bollocks to that.'

"Crowbar. CROWBAR. I *have* heard something. It might be nowt, but it's all I know."

The blood was rushing to his head now and he felt sick. Crowbar didn't seem that worried though as, instead of hauling him back over the edge, he kept hold of his ankles and simply grunted.

"It'd better be fucking good, son... or the concrete all the way

Special

down there's gonna stink of drug dealer for weeks. Kna what I mean?"

"Listen, I've got a bird who buys off us, works as a civvy at Clifford Street. She's usually skint cos they pay shit wages and she's getting a big habit. I normally shag her for the gear, but sometimes I pump her for information as well as pleasure."

"You'd better stop waffling, son, and make it quick or there's ganna be blood spilt."

"No. *NO.* Keep hold, man. Honestly. She said that they've had one bloke in and let him go... Blake, his name was. But she said as well that the buzz round the office is that it's some fucker in authority. Some one with a bit of power. She said the card for the business things he leaves has come from that warehouse at the back of Iceland and they're going through the employee list now. That Blake geezer works there and so does that special that struts round the estate; that Latimer cunt. That's all I know Crowbar, honest."

Muzza could feel his heart smashing out of his chest as it desperately tried to fire blood round his upside down body. Crowbar said nowt and Muzza looked down again and gulped... that concrete looked fucking hard.

"That was all I wanted to know, Muzza. Why didn't we do this in the first place before I had to smash your door down?"

Muzza could feel the relief flooding back into his body. Crowbar didn't know about his boy running up a big tab before his demise. As long as he didn't say anything stupid, he'd be alright.

"I'm not allowed to let anyone in who might be from another firm; Big Tony's orders. You know how it is, mate." Mentioning Big Tony ought to help wind the fucker's neck back in anyway.

Crowbar was silent and then started to pull Muzza back up, when he was back on both feet they stood looking at each other on the balcony. Crowbar spoke first.

"Is Big Tony going to hear about this or will you just get the door fixed and tell him some radgies did it?"

237

After facing certain death at the hands of this lunatic, Muzza had every intention of telling his boss as soon as he could.

"Nah, mate. I'll tell him it was local dafties. No bother."

"Good lad," said Crowbar turning away and then turning back. "Oh, and that shit you were pumping into my boy? Did Tony know about that?"

Muzza felt his arse fall out of his trousers in the second it took Crowbar to draw back his fist and then he was falling. Images of his young life filled his head like a slideshow on a computer: him and Hammy having a scrap at school on their first day, the two of them playing football together in the street, him and Hammy boxing at the Reeves Gym that first time as skinny teenagers, both of them winning at the County tournaments, Hammy winning at the Olympics while he watched on the telly cheering wildly. Hammy would be the only one at his funeral as well, probably. He was most gutted though about not cashing that fucking bet.

"F...U...C...K...I..."

THUMP

A plain white business card with a striking red V on it floated down softly in the breeze and landed gently near his caved in head. Crowbar looked at the sky and nodded as if to say *that was for you, Son,* and then he turned on his heel and left.

A half gasp of Recognition

The two plainclothes police officers that had been tailing Axel Falcus and his drug-dealing associate for a number of weeks were dismayed to find that their back tyres had been slashed while they'd concentrated on the meeting in the café. Being resourceful types, they'd decided to simply follow the pair on foot to the drop, which they knew was going to be in a disused unit at the end of an industrial estate not far away. However, as they left their car, they were confronted by an angry mob accusing them of paedophilia and of cruising the area looking for stray children. The older and more experienced of the two, realising how suspect they looked in their dishevelled, unshaven and long haired state, sought to quell the fears of the crowd by reaching for his ID in order to prove their innocence.

As he was doing so, a voice from the back of the crowd shouted, "He's going for a blade. *Get him*. Our kids aren't safe from these bastards." And as the baying mob trampled the frightened officers underfoot, a figure slipped away from the back of the crowd. He'd taken out the backup and now it was time to deal with the real scum. As he rounded a corner towards the drop point he, pulled on his balaclava and felt for the weapon again.

* * *

Nisbett was getting a little edgy now. The smack was on an upturned crate in between him and Falcus, the money in a sports holdall on a crate next to it. His backup should have stormed in by now, lights flashing and sirens blaring. His secondment from the North Western branch of the Serious and Organised Crime Squad had gone well up to this point. This was his first job as the main man; he was the focal point of the investigation into this Falcus fucker.

Apparently, the bloke ran this whole estate and made people's lives a misery. Nisbett's brief had been to bring him down. When he'd arrived he drank in Byker, lived in a poxy council flat and hung round the local bookies, all the while hinting that he was a 'businessman' from Manchester. Eventually, the bait had been taken and a representative of Falcus, asking about his line of work, had approached him but he'd fucked him off. Displaying the arrogance of someone who was at the top of his chosen career path he'd got the message back that he didn't talk to minions and that he was a major proposition for the right man. Falcus had been cagey at first, but greed had propelled him to Nisbett's side and, before long, they'd got round to talking about money and drugs.

His backup team had photos and incriminating conversations of them anywhere and everywhere. Falcus had been careful at first but, as soon as he'd been sure of Nisbett, he'd dropped the caution and they had him on tape bragging about beatings, extortion and general thuggery. Enough to put him away, but not for the length of time he deserved so they had gone through with 'the deal'. Falcus had been so sure of Nisbett that he'd come on his own, confident that knowing where Nisbett's mother lived was enough insurance against any shenanigans. Nisbett however, knew that the 'mother' who had been watched by Falcus's heavies was in fact another officer from Manchester who, even as they spoke, was on her way back there out of harm's way and that any second now two of Tyneside's finest would smash through the door of this unit. Falcus would be looking at fifteen years and Nisbett would return back to Manchester with his Curriculum Vitae considerably enhanced and the prospect of promotion very real. Except the backup fuckers weren't here and it was just Nisbett and an anxious-to-get-away Falcus.

It's obvious that the dealer is nervous. He keeps rubbing his nose; a tell for sure that he's lying or ripping Falcus off in some way.

Special

Normally I would find it amusing that two scum were about to turn on each other, but this is my moment. I will not have another opportunity like this to get this man alone and the dealer; well... he's just a bonus, really.

Feeling for my weapon, I withdraw it from my pocket and move silently up to the two men, my rubber-soled feet making no sound at all. The dealer keeps looking at the door while taking an age to count his money and Falcus is starting to pick up on this and the alarm bells are ringing in his head, so he is looking at the dealer and the door while one hand stays in his pocket. Luckily, neither of them is bright enough to realise that any assailant might already have been in the building, particularly one holding a two thousand volt stun gun.

Falcus gets it first as he is obviously carrying a weapon. The look on his face is priceless as he receives more power than a dullard like him would ever know what to do with. The dealer is next; he is frozen to the floor as if this wasn't part of the plan. Even as he goes down, paralysed with electricity, he is looking at the door for possible salvation. Don't bother my man; your muscle is currently being strung from the nearest tree by a furious lynch mob. This is the thought that prompts me to action; I could look at Falcus's shocked and stupefied facial expression all day, but I must act quickly because even a posse of furious Byker mothers will eventually be overcome by professional thugs. Rummaging in his coat for his weapon as he tries unsuccessfully to move, I find the gun he was about to use on the dealer. In a magnificent stroke of poetic justice I find that he has also brought his axe; the one he uses to terrorise a whole community.

I flick the safety back on the gun and then, wasting no time, drag the two twitching but still compus mentus bodies into line and splay out their arms and legs. I fetch my nail gun and rest it on the floor by my feet, then remove a small pile of business cards and place them next to the nail gun. Finally, I remove my mask;

I want these evil bastards to know who I am. There's a half gasp of recognition from the dealer, he recognises me from the café… not so cocky now hard man, eh? It's not him I want to feel fear though, he is irrelevant. I glare at Falcus and there's nothing but smugness, like I won't dare to harm him if I know what's good for me. My first thought is that he doesn't recognise me at all, but then I realise it's because he does recognise me. In his eyes I am nothing. We have met numerous times in my official capacity and I have been unable to do anything with him, so he imagines this to be the case now also. He thinks I haven't the stomach to come over into his world. He is wrong.

The fury is rising in my veins. I am shaking with adrenalin. My hearing is flattened and there is nothing save the sound of my blood thundering through my ears. My sight has narrowed and I can see only Falcus. I raise the axe.'

CLANG

'The head strikes stone as I cut through his wrist first go. The dealer is panicking; his head able to move a little now he keeps glancing at the nail gun and then back at the axe. I look back at Falcus; his useless hand falls limp to the floor and the pain tries to manifest itself through a scream that his useless mouth can't deliver. His eyes though; they show it all, the smug expression has given way to shock and then pure fear as he also glances at the nail gun and then back up at me. He knows I won't stop there. I don't.'

The Perfect Cover

Barney's persistence had paid off and the phone call he'd just received left him sure that John Latimer was the vigilante. Latimer was not his birth name, it was Douglas; John Douglas. He was the only son of John and Eileen Douglas. Eileen had died during his birth and his father, who did not remarry, had solely brought up young John without any other female influence. Unfortunately, John senior – a well-respected prison officer – was murdered on duty during a prison riot in the late seventies when his son was twelve-years-old. The perpetrator of the crime was never officially caught due to lack of evidence, but it was common knowledge that it had been a prisoner named Sidney Falcus, father of the famous Axel, and he had been kept in prison on every little technicality and pretence in order to make him pay for his crime in some way.

Young John had been adopted by the Latimer family soon after and had, by all accounts, been a model child and pupil going on to become a respectable and worthwhile member of society; the type of person who pays his taxes and contributes to the moral fibre of the community by volunteering to help police, in his own time, for free.

'The man's got the perfect cover. If he was Irish he'd have been suspected of being a sleeper.'

These thoughts were interrupted by the phone ringing loudly and suddenly; the internal dial tone not often heard in this office shook him up immediately. It was probably Pascoe shouting about the check he'd made in his name.

"Netherstone."

"Barney, there's been an incident in Byker. You need to come to a crime scene," Suzie didn't sound her normal self.

"Okay where?"

"I'll come and get you. I've just got back from there. Be ready in five, and Barney... don't eat anything before we go."

Police Constable Steven Beech had initially been looking forward to getting back to the canteen and swapping war stories today. Whereas normally he'd be moaning about taking abuse off feral youths who all knew their rights or having to move on drunk and disorderlies, today he'd have a real tale to tell. He had been assisting in the dispersal of a mob that had attacked two plainclothes men thinking they were paedos on the prowl when the two detectives had rapidly co-opted him onto their drugs busting team in order to utilise his squad car. His excitement was palpable as they raced off to the drop where their undercover man was stalling Axel Falcus; a main player on the estate, and then drove straight through the closed doors of the warehouse into the deal area.

This is why I joined up; stuff like this. It's like fucking Dukes of Hazard crossed with Starsky and Hutch. Excellent.'

The two detectives jumped out of the car and raced across to two upturned crates that held both money and drugs. Pulling guns out of their pockets they swivelled round calling their colleague's name.

PC Beech smiled to himself, *'Fucking drama queens.'* Pulling out his torch, he shone into the dark corners one by one until something caught his eye. Relishing the fact that he, a mere uniformed plod, could get one over the glory boys in CID he went to investigate on his own. Pulling out his baton just in case, he concentrated on the flash he'd got when he moved his torch, it looked like it reflected off something.

'Probably a fucking rat or something.' If it was then it was getting a hiding with the baton; he fucking hated rats.

He got to within a foot of the place when the lights came on and he turned back around, the older detective had found the switch. He was about to shout them over when he noticed they were both looking at him anyway. Well, at him but past him if anything. With a sinking feeling, he turned slowly back to where they were looking and saw what it was that had caught the reflection of the torch.

The sightless eyes of Axel Falcus were staring back at him. He knew they were sightless as the head was no longer attached to the body; this was propped up against a wall a few yards away. The nail embedded in his skull, holding a business card in place, was what had reflected his torchlight. The expression on Falcus's face suggested he had died in pain, the fact that his hands and feet were nailed to the wall further along pretty much confirmed it. Beech threw up, turning away as he did so. By now the two detectives were by his side, cursing and promising retribution if their partner was not found soon. Something made Beech look up. As he'd tell the police shrink later on, he didn't know what but something made him look up. Detective Constable Nisbett was nailed to the ceiling, he had not been decapitated as Falcus had and appeared to have all of his hands and feet in the correct places, but he was most definitely dead. A business card nailed through his skull as well had seen to that. At that moment, just before he threw up again, PC Beech decided that the canteen maybe wouldn't be that good a place to tell this particular story.

A Good Lad

Barney had been unhappy after returning from the murder at the bottom of the Byker Wall. The dealer that had obviously been thrown to his death had died in quite gruesome fashion, but it didn't fit the modus operandi of the vigilante; a casually tossed business card had been lying a few feet away from the broken and shattered body and looked almost like an afterthought rather than the precision planning *he* usually displayed. This wasn't a vigilante job of that he was sure; probably just a copycat or even someone who'd seen an opportunity to get rid of a competitor without making too many waves.

However, this incident had been wiped completely from his mind when he'd attended the Falcus and Nisbett murder scene; that had obviously been the original vigilante and was a disturbing indication that he was stepping up the severity of the 'sentences' he passed on criminals. There had been evidence of some sort of stunning device being used and a quick check of the evidence store at the back of the station had thrown up the fact that one of the stun guns seized some weeks back had gone missing. The officer responsible for booking them in: one John Latimer. The vigilante had obviously been unaware that one of the people he had savagely and cold-bloodedly murdered was in fact an undercover officer on an operation and he had dealt with him as ruthlessly as he had disposed of Falcus. The crime scene in the warehouse had distressed Barney so much that without really thinking he had gone to Chief Superintendent De Montford directly from the evidence store. He knew he was breaking all the rules but, as Pascoe wouldn't listen to him and a good man had died as a result, he didn't really give a monkey's anymore. The Chief Super had listened intently to Barney's theory and evidence and had agreed that Latimer was definitely in the frame. He had also seemed deeply unhappy at Pascoe's intransigence where Barney's professional opinion was concerned and had then asked after his dad; another past acquaintance of the old fella. He was starting to realise that he really should have looked up these people before starting up here; his life would have been so much easier.

The net result though, bad etiquette or not, was that Barney was given the go-ahead to bring in Latimer and he quickly rounded up his team, along with a few willing uniforms. The whole station was enraged at the killing of a fellow officer and out for blood. In no time at all, two van loads of coppers were all set to head out to Latimer's house until a phone call from a concerned member of the public sent them into the top end of Byker. A suspicious character had been hanging round the bushes outside the house of one Vicki Hughes, girlfriend of Matt Blake; former chief suspect but exonerated once his evidence had moved Latimer up the rankings. It was now game on where Special Officer John Latimer was concerned.

Barney was in the canteen with Suzie when the word came back over the radio that they'd got him. A big cheer went up and then all eyes turned to him expectantly as he got up to prepare an interview room.

"Make sure you do that bastard, Barney."

"Remember, Barney: no technicalities, no excuses. Nail the fucker."

"He killed one of ours, Barney. Put that man down."

Barney would normally have blushed and stammered something about pressure as he slunk out of the room, but now he felt different. This was responsibility and he felt fine with it. The dead officer's family deserved justice and he was determined to give it to them. Looking at the assembled throng, he gave them a grim-faced nod and motioned Suzie to come with him.

As he exited he heard one man say, "He's a good lad, him. He'll do the business," and he felt good. Latimer was fucking getting it alright.

Before entering the interview room he stopped for a quick brief from the arresting officer, letting Latimer sweat for a minute or two.

"How did it go, Bob?"

Bob Forsyth, a big uniformed copper of twenty years standing just grinned.

"It was as you said, Barney. Suspicious character hanging

round the bushes outside that lass's house and we snatched him straight off the street. Obviously, he resisted arrest and had to be subdued."

Bob was definitely an old school lawman; the wild youths on the estate didn't even give him cheek. They could all quote their human rights at you, but he didn't bother too much with that nonsense; they all knew very well that Bob did home visits when he was off duty and usually at night when there was no witnesses. None of them were brave enough to want to take him on in a square go, so they kept on his good side. Barney shivered at the words 'resisted arrest and had to be subdued'. He knew exactly what that meant.

Giving Bob a wink and grabbing the door handle, he pushed it forward expecting a defiant and bloodied Latimer to look up. He was disappointed as a broken-nosed Matt Blake looked at him accusingly from across the interview table.

"What the fuck's going on here, then?" Blake looked really pissed off, not surprising really; smashed teeth were expensive to fix these days.

"Mr Blake, we're back here again," Barney was convinced it wasn't Blake but had to ask the questions to make sure. "Can you tell me why you were hanging around the bushes of Miss Hughes's house?"

Blake just glared at him, "I'm saying fuck all until a solicitor's brought in. You fuckers have assaulted me for no good reason."

Barney sighed inwardly; they didn't have time for this. Latimer was still at large and needed to be found quickly.

"Mr Blake," he snapped back aggressively, "I'm sorry for any injuries you may have sustained whilst being subdued, but apparently you resisted arrest and these things happen. Now, you may or may not know but we are now investigating the murder of two people earlier today. One of these people was a police officer, so you can understand why everyone's a little tense."

"Well, I'm sorry for the bloke and that but what the fuck has it got to do with—"

"Mr Blake, we don't have time for this. The murderer, who I'm fairly sure *isn't* you, is still at large and, until caught, everyone on that estate is in danger. Now please tell me... why were you loitering around the bushes?"

Matt looked sheepish and then started to blush.

"I-I-I..." he stammered, then clearing his throat, he looked Barney straight in the eye. "I was going to ask Vicki to marry me; I wanted to surprise her after work." He tailed off and looked at the desk. It all sounded a bit ridiculous when he said it out loud, but it had sounded so romantic in his head, proposing by streetlight.

Barney smiled sympathetically; despite his urgency in finding Latimer he still wanted to help the man out if he could. "What time does she finish?" he asked.

Blake shook his head slowly. "Too late mate, she'll be in the house now."

"We'll give you a lift back, then. It's the least we can do. You have to understand, though. This man needs catching before he kills again and you were in the wrong place at the wrong time. At least you know it wasn't him hanging round your girlfriend's house, she should be alright."

Barney felt quite bad about spoiling Blake's big moment but it had to be safety first when dealing with nutters. As they left the interview room Barney pulled Bob Forsyth to one side, "Bob, we need to get to Latimer's house and pick him up. Also get an All Points out on him in case he's not there."

Bob just shook his head and Barney felt a surge of indignation. Was this man refusing to take a direct order just because it came from a middle-class southerner? Bloody northern upstart.

"And why not, Mr Forsyth? tell me why you think we shouldn't do that in order to catch a dangerous criminal?"

"Because he's just reported to the station to start his shift."

Andy Rivers

Single Parent Teenage Lesbian Transsexuals

John Latimer knew that this day would come; he'd known in his heart that eventually he'd be facing his colleagues from the wrong side of the interview room. It wasn't shame or soiling his father's memory that tore at his soul though; he knew that his dad would have approved of his actions if anything... it was the disappointment that Reg would feel. His one mate in the world would be, at first, astonished and then deflated to see that he was a common criminal – no better than the ones he spent every Sunday night moaning about.

The officer facing him looked stern. It was the new one from down South, Netherstone. He didn't know much about him save for the fact he was one of a new breed; studied psychology as well as detection, scientific analysis alongside old fashioned door knocking. Latimer was an old fashioned kind of guy and preferred to work on instinct, but he had to concede that the new way must have its good points if they'd managed to catch him.

"So then, Mr Latimer. Where shall we start? Why don't you begin by telling me about the missing stun gun."

The stun gun? Oh, that? Jesus, he'd forgotten about that. It seemed so long ago; trivial compared to why they'd brought him in anyway, wasn't it? Still, it probably cleans up the figures, puts another tick in another box and hits another target. That's all police work was these days... massaging figures and media spin. If you want a good news story about ethnic minorities and problem teenagers getting their own football team sponsored by the law then we're your men. If, however, you want to report an intruder in your home threatening to rape or kill you, well, we might get round there on Thursday cos we're really busy so just try and keep out of harm's way. And whatever you do, don't hit him because we'll nick you for infringing his human rights to rob and assault you in your own home.

"The stun gun? I don't understand."

His interrogator just sighed dramatically. "Tell me where you got the stun gun from and why. We'll record it and then move on."

"I took it from the evidence store a while ago. There were a lot of them just sitting there after the mule had been sent down for bringing them in. No one seemed to be taking responsibility for disposing of them, so I borrowed one."

"*Borrowed*, Mr Latimer?"

"Well, okay... *took* then. I didn't plan on giving it back, but it wasn't even for me."

"What do you mean, it wasn't for you? Who else has used it, then?"

Latimer wasn't sure where this was going; no one had ever used the stun gun. It was purely for self-defence. This new copper didn't seem that bright.

"No one has used it. I gave it to my friend for self-defence as he was worried about walking the streets at night."

"Which friend was that, Mr Latimer?" The whole room had suddenly perked up and were staring at him.

"Reg Runcorn. He chairs the Residents' Committee in Byker and often has to walk home after dark. It's not the safest area, is it?"

The room suddenly burst into life as he said that; the posh one leapt from his chair and ran out of the room closely followed by everyone else. It was almost comical watching them try to squeeze out of the door at the same time. John wondered what was going on. Why were they so interested in Reg and the stun gun, rather than the real reason they'd brought him in?

After a puzzling minute alone, the southern copper came back in looking flushed and accompanied by a solitary uniformed PC who stood at the door.

"One question, John," he started. "You took your arrest very calmly, almost like you were expecting it. Why do you think you were nicked?"

John Latimer had prepared for this day; he was actually proud of what he was about to say. He sat up straight and looked Barney straight in the eye.

"Because I killed Sid Falcus; the man who killed my father."

'Ha, that's put him on the back foot; he didn't see that one coming, did he? Good old John, dependable, reliable John has actually done something in life. I've never been considered dynamic enough for promotion in my day job or proactive enough to become a full-time lawman, but have actually executed a career criminal and gotten away with it. I fooled both the police and the thuggish organisation of the dead man's son. I proved that I can 'think outside the box' and 'put all my trains in a straight line' and I didn't need some politically correct think-tank to hold my hand while I did it. They missed a trick when they'd spurned me; all of them. John Latimer is a force of nature.'

He smiled.

The man opposite him still looked a little shocked and then he leaned over to speak again.

"Did Reg Runcorn know about your father dying at the hands of Sid Falcus?"

Latimer couldn't understand why they kept asking about Reg, detracting from his moment of triumph, the moment he'd waited over fifteen years for. The whole world now knew that he, John Latimer, had killed Sid Falcus. The copper pressed him again and he snapped back.

"Obviously, he knew. I told him everything about myself. He's the only real friend I've ever had. I've told him all about the Falcus family and how that man took my childhood away from me. The only thing we haven't discussed was my killing of Sid Falcus. I didn't wish to incriminate Reg with this knowledge and so he thinks that it was a simple hit and run."

Barney looked thoughtful at this. "So your best friend in the world, who has possession of a stun gun, thinks that you have an unresolved grudge against the Falcus family when, in reality, you dealt with it yourself some years ago?"

"Well, yes, if you put it like that. I obviously had to play up to it sometimes in order to keep him from realising that it was really me that killed Falcus senior. I used to fake outrage whenever the name was mentioned and always told Reg about Falcus's criminal scams and acts. I even let him know who his accomplices and employees were, so he could warn his residents about them. That's how Reg thought I was getting back at them."

"And what about the card you were stealing from your employer? Where was that going?"

Latimer was shocked to the core. How could they possibly know about that?

"The... the card?"

"Yes, Mr Latimer. The card. You've been stealing it for some time, where has it gone?"

"Well, I've been giving it to Reg. He produces a community newsletter and it takes him such a long time to get the money back from the council. Obviously, he's at the back of the queue for such things behind single parent teenage lesbian transsexuals or something. It's an absolute bloody disgrace the way an honest community-minded individual such as—"

Barney held up a hand to stop Latimer's tirade.

"Just to make you aware, Mr Latimer. Your friend is being hunted, as we speak, in relation to a number of crimes committed over the last few weeks by someone calling himself the vigilante. He is also being sought urgently with regard to a double murder committed this morning on the aforementioned Mr Alex Falcus and an undercover policeman. Now stop rambling and tell me everything you know about Mr Runcorn."

Latimer went white. Reg *the vigilante?* It would make sense; he was always keen to know everything that was going on with this and that case, who was making his life hard on the beat and that kind of thing. Then a thought struck him and he looked back at Barney.

"He wanted to know where Vicki Hughes lived. I've had a... a thing with her and it ended. I took it rather badly as she was very offhand with me and I told Reg about it when we were at the quiz on Sunday. He said not to worry as they all got their comeuppance in the end."

For the second time that day Barney was swiftly up and out of his chair, bellowing orders as he went. Latimer sat back in his chair and contemplated the life an ex-copper would have in prison.

Definitely that Twat

'This is it; the final act before hibernation. A special one-off to help an old friend. I've achieved everything I set out to at the start of this and have made this community safer by far. The copy-cats have already started and they'll flourish for a while before they make mistakes and get caught, then the police, in a fanfare of trumpets, will claim to have arrested the vigilante. I'll wait a while longer before re-announcing myself, striking sporadically at whichever criminal thinks he is above the law of this land. I'll be a guerrilla lawman on the side of good and will strike fear into the hearts of the scum that think they can look down at us all. Before that though, there is one more immoral creature I have to set right.'

Special

Crowbar had waited for an hour outside the warehouse where the copper worked. He was on the verge of moving on when Matt Blake had come out with a load of other blokes. Reasoning that one of them was better than none he'd tailed him: firstly to the pawn shop on Shields Road then off up to the Stag's Head where the weird fucker had hung around outside one of the houses. He'd kept checking his watch and looked increasingly nervous, so Crowbar had took this as another sign that he was up to something. It looked like that snivelling little rat Muzza had been telling the truth after all, not that it would have kept him alive either way; Falcus wanted him out of the way and the vigilante thing was a present from God. Crowbar had also wanted Muzza dead, purely for being the bastard who punted that poison into his boy's bloodstream and so Falcus's orders had been well received by him as he now felt he was actually doing something to avenge Sam's death. Speaking of Falcus, he'd tried to check in with him a few times today but got nowhere.

'The fucker must still be socialising with his new mate from Manchester,' he thought, a little hurt that he was out of the loop. *'He thinks I don't know about his plans to be the new coke baron of Byker. Well, I'm not as fucking stupid as people think. I've tracked down this vigilante cunt before the bizzies, haven't I?'*

Crowbar looked over at Matt, hovering under a tree and trying to look like he was sending a text on his phone and smiled grimly to himself. *'I don't need a judge to convict the fucker either. I only need to prove it to myself then that bastard is mine whatever Falcus thinks. He's not living longer than today.'*

He watched him for another fifteen minutes, poncing around with his text messages, looking up and down the street, pretending to have conversations with the speaking clock and then finally kidding on he was tying his shoelaces. For Crowbar, this was the moment when he decided that this weedy little fucker was, if not the man himself, somehow involved with the vigilante fucker who had killed his boy. He started to make his move and had gotten within ten yards of the twat and was slowly sliding the duster onto his right fist when a police van screeched up ahead of him.

'Bollocks,' he thought, pocketing the duster and stepping back. *'What do these idiots want? I haven't done nowt yet.'*

Then watching in amazement he saw four burly coppers jump on Blake and give him some solid digs before throwing him into the van and screeching off again.

'Definitely that twat, fucking definitely,' he thought before heading back to where he'd left the car earlier. He'd wait outside the pig station all night in case they let him go then he'd make sure there was nothing left of him to charge.

Satisfied that he was sharper than Falcus could ever have thought possible, he put the keys in the ignition and started the engine. The movement that caught his eye in the driver's wing mirror caused him to kill it immediately. Maybe he wasn't as sharp as he thought he was, some cunt in a balaclava had just exited the bushes and went in someone's kitchen window.

Vicki lay back on the settee and gazed blankly at the telly. Life was definitely on the up. She was back with Matt and he'd told her he loved her and wanted to be with her forever; it was only a matter of time before he moved in. Nick had gotten his final school reports of the year and it screamed college followed by university followed by highly paid career. She was very proud of him. And her prospects? Well, her boss had told her unofficially that a new store's supervisor position was being created due to their rise in sales, Byker being the ideal area for their *stack it high sell it cheap* philosophy, and he wanted her to apply for it. Even the flies in the ointment were being sorted out; the creepy copper had disappeared, Matt said he was on the sick at work, and various thugs and criminals from the estate were all suddenly finding new places to live.

'Yep,' she thought, raising her warm mug to her lips and draining the remains of her cocoa in one go, *'life couldn't be better.'*

Special

Leaning across to the coffee table, she put it down on the coaster next to the lamp and felt for the switch. Matt wasn't coming round and she fancied an early night; she would sleep like a baby, a fucking knackered one. The hand that suddenly grasped hers disabused her of this notion instantly. A fraction of a scream passed her lips before another hand clamped itself roughly over her mouth and a balaclaved head came into view.

"No time to sleep, slag. We've got far too much to talk about."

All for You

"John Latimer is a good man and he didn't deserve to be messed around by a slag like you. Do you know his dad was killed when he was a small boy, murdered by one of the elder members of the Falcus family? His father, an upstanding, moral citizen, executed while trying to do his job by an axe-wielding thug, leaving him an orphan. He spent his childhood being bullied by his adoptive family and still turned out well, even giving up his free time to help out the community. Yet *you* mess him around and reject him for a drug-taking layabout. What's that?"

She was mumbling something through the gag and he thought about taking it off, but not yet. She had to hear why he did this then maybe he would let her plead her case. Mind you, they'd all tried to talk their way out of it so far, but he was definitely a hanging judge as well as jury and, in some cases, *executioner*. That last one was the most ridiculous; kept claiming he was an undercover copper, even as the nail was going into his head he kept it up. Bloody idiot; do they think he's stupid?

The bloody mugger was the same. 'I only do it because Falcus makes me.' He smiled at the thought of his reply as he'd stunned him then stuck that card on his tongue.

"Well, now I'm making you stop!"

Yes, they'd all learnt over the past few weeks and now the spectre of Falcus was removed from the estate and he'd avenged his friend. He could never tell him though; John was far too law-abiding and honest to know that he, Reg Runcorn, had gone outside of the law. John hadn't even dealt with Falcus senior when he'd been released, even though he'd wanted to. He'd gone as far as confessing to Reg that he wanted to kill him, but couldn't break the law. Reg had sympathised with him and thought nothing more of it but then...

"Mmmm... Mmmm."

The slag's eyes looked frightened and she was shaking her head.

"You don't know do you, slag, why I do this? Well, let me enlighten you before you plead your case to me. I wasn't bothered by the Falcus family, I don't even live on this estate and, as none of you ever bother to come to Residents' Committee meetings, I was certainly not bothered about helping you. When Falcus senior died though, his son – the king of this shithole – went mad and started attacking people, one of these being my wife, Rita. He broke her jaw in a rage at the amusement arcade on Shields Road where she worked. He was arrested and got community service. A slap on the wrist and he was out while my wife, who never hurt a soul in her life, suffered panic attacks and depression that got worse and worse until eventually, one day when I was out, she took her own life.

"That day I swore I would do something about that bastard and became even friendlier with John. He fed me information on the movements of Falcus's criminal gang and also got me a little toy that enables me to incapacitate anyone bigger and stronger than me. After that, it was open season on him and his boys. I even dealt with that Ghostboy character purely because John felt strongly about him robbing your house and attacking your boy.

That was done for you and still you treat him like shit. So, then... let's hear why I shouldn't kill you here and now."

Reg leaned over her, enjoying the feeling of power, even contemplating a little sexual humiliation as her eyes widened and she shook her head frantically. He smiled at the thought of her offering herself in a vain attempt to save her life... then he realised she was actually looking past him.

'Shit... the boy...'

THUMP

Such a Clever Boy

Nick had never been as scared in his life. Well, not since the park a few days ago. He could hear the nutter in the living room ranting on at his mam about the weird copper and he was shitting it.

'What'll I do? What'll I fucking do?'

He was becoming frantic in his mind, but desperately trying to keep quiet. Should he ring Matt? No – take too long. Ring the law? Pointless. There was only one thing he could do; creeping closer to the living room door, he risked a quick look in.

His mother was tied up and gagged on the settee while the headcase stood over her with his back to him. His mam saw him and her eyes widened as, through the gag, she started trying to tell him to run. Nick silently shook his head and retreated back into the kitchen, quietly rummaging through the cutlery drawer before his hand came to rest on the thing he wanted.

When he got back to the living room door the nutter was going on about that Ghostboy prick and Nick started padding towards him, his mother was panic-stricken now and wriggling about on the couch in desperation, but Nick felt calm, even slightly amused. The irony of saving his mam with the one kitchen implement she had never used was not lost on him and probably wouldn't be on her once they got out of this.

He raised the rolling pin high above his head, just as the vigilante started to realise he was there, bringing it down with as much fury and determination as he could muster. He struck him a sickening blow to the side of the head, sending him straight to the floor. Ripping the gag off his mam he then used the kitchen scissors to cut off her ties.

"Why didn't you stab him with the bread knife?" she shouted at him as soon as she was able.

"No, Mam, you're welcome," he replied. Then seeing her anxious face, "It might not have stopped him. He might be on drugs for all I know, but we did it at school... an unexpected blow to the head wobbles the brain and will usually knock out the recipient."

She smiled; he was such a clever boy. "Good lad. Ring the law."

Nick smiled back, he knew he'd done well. Then, as the prone figure moaned and started to stir, he grabbed her arm.

"Let's ring them from my mobile and get the fuck out of here."

As the two of them headed for the back door, Vicki looked back, he was already up on his knees and those eyes were blazing at her.

Being Men

Barney was out of the police car before it had properly stopped and racing across to the Hughes household. The wide-open back door and gawping neighbours were already telling their own story before he got there. Suzie was about two seconds behind him and he pointed her at the neighbours before entering the house.

There were definite signs of a struggle; furniture skewed across the room, pieces of a smashed cup on a coffee table and strangely, a discarded and bloodied rolling pin lying forlornly on the floor. Barney was taking it in when Suzie burst into the room shouting, "They took off towards the park. Matt Blake wasn't far behind them either, apparently."

Barney heaved a small sigh of relief; at least they weren't badly hurt or even worse – abducted by the nutter. With a bit of luck Runcorn might have been spooked enough to have run off or... Barney's face screwed up as the implications of another double, or even triple murder flooded his mind.

"Suzie, call back up and everyone to the park... *NOW*."

'She is mine, the boy as well. She has made the bed for both of them and they will both be lying in it for eternity now as my dear wife had to. They're up ahead, hiding in the bush behind the swings; they think I can't see them. They think they've lost me because I carried on past them pretending I couldn't see them, but I knew they were there and now I'm doubling back. Slowly eating up the ground between us. Softly, softly catchee slag.'

Vicki's panic was making her desperate to gulp in air, but her survival instinct was telling her to be as quiet as possible. They'd raced off with the headcase not far behind and stupidly headed for the park instead of banging on a neighbour's door. Now though, the danger appeared to have passed. They'd hid in the first big bush and he had blundered past them about ten seconds later as they'd hid their faces.

Nick had tried to double back as soon as he'd gone past, but Vicki had held him back, *let psycho get as far away as possible* that's what she'd whispered to him. Really, though; part of her just wanted to hug her son. Her breath was controlling itself now and she felt better. Moving into a crouch she gave Nick a nudge. They'd give it another couple of seconds and then head back up the street. A series of flashing blue lights and screeching tyres indicated they would be safe back at the house now, so she made to move. It was over and they were safe.

"You're going nowhere, slag," a cold voice whispered behind her as a knife was clamped to her throat. "On your back, boy. Or your mother dies."

Vicki felt herself being eased backwards until she was lying down next to Nick; she felt his hand take hers as he whispered, "I love you, Mam."

The tears were streaming down her face as she thought how unfair it was that their lives should end like this. She had only just discovered love and personal ambition, only just discovered life really and it was being snatched away by this madman. Her son, who had it all before him, who had never went down the path most tabloid editors would have predicted for him at birth, he too was having it all taken away just as he realised what life was about.

Her tears of self-pity turned to tears of rage; this bastard wasn't just snatching their lives without a fight. She grasped a fistful of earth and prepared to fight to the death. Squeezing Nick's hand one last time, she went for it. Throwing the earth at balaclava's face, hoping to blind him, she tried to get up and bite, scratch and punch a way out for her son at least, but he just headbutted her as she was getting up and put her straight back next to Nick. The hopelessness of the situation overwhelmed her and she started to sob.

"I was going to give you a quick death but, just for that, you can watch your son die before you, slag," he hissed and then there was a crackling sound and a tiny flash of blue light and Nick twitched once before lying motionless on the ground.

Vicki squeezed her baby's hand frantically, hoping for signs of life, while glaring up at the vigilante, "What have you done to him, you evil bastard?"

Special

He simply smiled and Vicki realised, fractionally too late that whatever it was, it was happening to her next. She felt the pain surge through her; trampling her insides and bursting her heart clean open.

Then she felt nothing.

Her eyes were still open and she could see the vigilante smiling at her and holding his knife up in her eye line. She couldn't move, or scream, or kick, or bite. She was fucked, Nick was fucked, it was all fucked. She couldn't even cry.

But she could hear.

"Firstly," he said, his black shark's eyes glinting through the mask holes, "I'm going to kill your boy there. That'll be one less teenage delinquent in the world. After that, I'm going to kill you and that'll be one less slag in the world, one less cock-teasing slut and one less parasitical drain on the taxpayer."

He moved out of her vision, presumably over to Nick, and she could do nothing. After a second he was back, smiling again, Vicki managed to squeeze out one tear for her son; a massive effort of maternal grief over technology and then prepared herself as best she could for death.

"Oh… don't cry, slag. He's not dead yet. I've just decided to add to the party, make it a ménage a trois if you will. Something I'm sure you're used to."

Then she heard his voice; Matt was calling to her, calling to Nick, he had come for them. She wanted to scream at him to be careful, tell him where they were, that the nutter had a weapon. She wanted to warn him, to give her man a fighting chance, but her body was betraying her mind and her heart.

The vigilante just smiled at her again, able to read her thoughts.

"He won't know what's hit him, but don't worry. I'll bring him back here so you can die together."

Then he was gone.

Matt looked around the deserted playground; spooky places these at night, the equipment forming weird shadows.

'Where the fuck is she?' he thought. *'And where's the nutter?'*

The copper who'd dropped him off hadn't even stopped the engine, just waited until he'd closed the door and screeched off. That meant that when Matt had clocked the open kitchen door and ran into the obviously dishevelled living room he had no one to tell. He'd considered ringing the bizzies, but the running figure all in black he'd caught a brief glimpse of heading for the park brought home the fact he didn't have enough time to wait for them clowns.

Looking back into the blackness he wished for the umpteenth time in ten minutes that he'd had the presence of mind to bring a torch. Then he heard a noise by the swings to his right and he swivelled quickly; the cunt was there, just looking at him.

"Where are they, you sick twat?"

"Why, Matthew... first things first: we have to behave like men and fight it out for the fair lady, or in her case, loose-moralled slut."

"Oh, we'll be fighting all right. I'm gonna pull your fucking head off and shit down your neck. You'd better tell me where she is just so you can stay alive, you bastard."

Matt had never known fury like he did now. Vicki had never hurt anyone in her life and if this cunt had harmed her in any way, then he was going to kill him stone dead here and now, coppers or no coppers.

The twat just smiled and held out his hand, "Let's touch gloves then, Matthew my boy, and have at it."

Matt could feel his arm extending in spite of his reservations; he would rise above this twat and extend him basic courtesies before he smashed his head in. He was better than this prick. As their fists brushed, in a parody of boxers touching gloves before a fight, something crackled and Matt felt his arm go limp and his legs wobble. What the fuck was happening?

"I've just given you the lowest charge on my stun gun, Matty boy. In a minute I'm going to give you the full works and then you can meet up with your slag and her offspring again. A nice, touching reunion just before I kill you all."

Matt was swaying; he tried to move, but his legs were taking no orders from his brain and he stumbled. The nutter moved in closer, he was fucked and he knew it, he'd let them down again. He hadn't even managed to throw a fucking punch; he really was a failure as a man.

Hoping his mouth still worked, he started to speak, maybe he could save Vicki and Nick at least.

"Listen," he said as the distance between them closed, "just kill me. They've done nothing to you. Vicki has never been a criminal in her life; she's got a good job and pays her bills. Young Nick, he's a good lad. It was my fault he was in the park, I gave him the drugs and made him go out to the park, just to get him out of the house."

He dropped to his knees and looked up at the vigilante, "I'm the bad bastard, always have been. Don't kill them, you'd be going off your policy, I'm offering myself. Kill me, spare them."

Through the mask he could make out a smile as the vigilante placed the stun gun onto his neck and he waited for death hoping he'd done enough to save his loved ones at least.

Then there was a gasp of pain as the gun, and the vigilante, were removed in one swift jerk. As Matt struggled to his feet, the moon was blotted out again by the biggest bloke he'd ever seen. This fucker worked for Falcus, that he knew. The man mountain had the vigilante's neck under one of his feet and the stun gun was on the ground ten feet away. Matt could feel his limbs returning to normal; the shakes were gone from his legs and he contemplated booting the prone crusader in the head.

As if reading his thoughts, Crowbar shook his head, "Your family's over there, son," he nodded towards the bushes. "Go and take care of them."

Then he looked up at the sky and mouthed something before looking back at Matt and saying, "And I'll take care of mine."

Matt could hear the sirens getting closer as he cradled Vicki and Nick in his arms; the tears ran down her face as the paralysing effects started to wear off and she tried to whisper something to him without success. In the end she gave up and just smiled at him.

Matt stroked her head and held her to him, "I'll never let you down babe, never," he promised. Nick stirred next to him and managed to croak out, "We know Matt, we could hear you."

Hordes of burly coppers led by the plainclothes man came steaming through the park gate and made a beeline for them in the bushes as Matt shouted where they were. The paramedics took care of Vicki and Nick as Barney took Matt to one side to ask him what happened.

"About fuckin time and—" he started to say before his attention was diverted to the right under the slide, where numerous police were milling around. There lay the unmoving and prostrate figure of the vigilante. He could tell by the odd angle of his head to his shoulders that his neck was broken and the blood trickling out of his mouth and ears meant he was probably dead.

Going back to Vicki and holding her hand, he looked back towards the scene, the little pile of calling cards that were scattered about him had started to move in the wind, almost as though they had a life of their own.

EPILOGUE

New Beginnings

Across the estate at the back of the bookies, Francis Collins was face down in the mud, a tortured expression on his face. The police physician had already declared him dead and Barney Netherstone was on the scene, getting the full facts about his death while his new full-time assistant, Detective Constable Suzie Holmes, secured the area. Once she was satisfied that no evidence could be lost, she approached the new Head of Criminology on Tyneside.

"Is this it then, Barney? Have we got another vigilante on the go?" she asked anxiously.

He smiled at her, "I'm assuming you didn't find any cards, Suzie?" he asked back and, then without waiting for an answer went on, "That's because Mr Collins died of heart failure, brought on by the over exertion of trying to get through the little window up there. So, no, I don't think we've another vigilante case beginning... and therefore, no need to work this weekend."

She looked like she was going to say something. Barney knew he had to get it out now or he'd struggle to say it at all. Holding up his right hand to silence her. He continued, "What are you like at quizzes?"

*   *   *

Vicki Hughes jerked suddenly in bed. Thinking quickly, she shook Matt awake. He'd been so tired just lately trying to get his new sandwich business off the ground that she felt a bit guilty about waking him, but this needed doing.

"Matt," she hissed. "Matt, wake up. I heard a noise downstairs."

"Wha-What?" He grunted back, bleary-eyed. He'd used the compensation money from German Wizard to set up Sandwich

Man; mobile purveyor of proper sarnies to proper blokes and the six o'clock starts were leaving him knackered.

"I heard a noise downstairs."

Matt was wide awake now, he knew he had to get up and confront whoever it was. Picking up the hammer from under the bed, he moved towards the door. Taking one look back at Vicki he thought of how his life had changed for the better. Being in love was great and whichever cheeky bastard had entered their house in the night wasn't going to spoil it for any of them. She smiled bravely back at him, her and Nick had been through so much and Matt was determined they would never be exposed to danger again. He gave her a reassuring wink and, heart pounding, he headed for the stairs. This was his job now, he was the man of the house and he would do whatever it took to keep this, his family, safe. Gulping softly, he padded silently down the stairs and explored every inch of the home he and Vicki now shared. There was no one there. He checked every window and door; all of the locks were still in place and functioning properly.

'She must still be a bit spooked by that nutter,' he thought sympathetically as he headed back up to the bedroom. Stopping at Nick's door, he listened and heard him snoring. He was all right as well, no bother there. Feeling proud of himself for having done his manly duty by his fiancé, he walked back through the bedroom door to see Vicki clutching the quilt up to her chin. His heart went out to her and he was by her side in one bound stroking her head and saying, "It's okay babe there was no one there."

She looked up at him, smiling broadly and whipped back the quilt to reveal a brand new set of sexy undies, a pair of handcuffs and a spray can of whipped cream saying, "Oh well, Mathew. You're awake now."

He looked at the gear, looked back at her pretty, laughing face and then dived straight on top of her.

He fucking loved this bird.

If you liked this then you'll love these…!

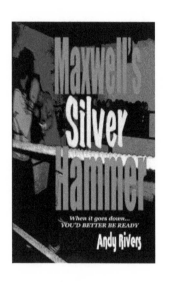

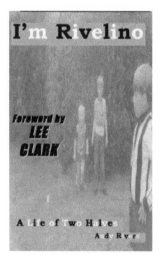

Thanks for supporting independent publishing.
Byker Books was set up to give a voice to working
class authors and, as such, we hope you enjoyed this
book and think you'd like the rest of our list as well.

They're all on the Kindle and priced for every pocket! Go on have a look.

More Burglar Diaries – Danny King
A Four-King Cracker – Danny King
Infidelity For Beginners – Danny King
'Laugh-out-loud funny' *The Sun*
'One of the few writers who can make me
laugh out loud' *David Baddiel*

Maxwell's Silver Hammer – Andy Rivers
'Fast paced and gritty edged. I implore you to buy this cracking book'
New Crime Fiction

Dumb Luck – Tom Arnold
'Fast, furious and fantastic' *Andy Rivers*

I'm Rivelino – Andy Rivers
'Funny, fanatical and thoroughly enjoyable' *Lovereading*

The Radgepacket series – Vol 1–6 – Various authors
'Packed with hit after hit' *Sheila Quigley*
'Imaginative writing' *The Crack*

Shit Happens – Eileen Wharton
'This is what kindle was made for, Finding new authors.
I would have been gutted to have missed this one!'
'Bookworm' – Amazon

Lightning Source UK Ltd.
Milton Keynes UK
UKHW010638120221
378684UK00002B/367